CITADELLE

A PETER GRANT MYSTERY-SUSPENSE NOVEL

By

Donald G. Geddes III

ISBN: 1496067223
ISBN 13: 9781496067227
Library of Congress Control Number: 2014904221
CreateSpace Independent Publishing Platform
North Charleston, South Carolina

FOR MARILYN
AND
IN LOVING MEMORY
OF
"HEMINGWAY"

The little fellow does what he can;
the big fellow does what he wants.

A Haitian Proverb

PREFACE

It was in the early 1950s when I first visited Haiti during the Magloire presidency, a relatively calm period preceding the tumultuous tyranny of Papa Doc Duvalier and his successor son Jean-Claude known as Baby Doc. This black nation, strikingly alone in a white world, held for me a fascination I have never experienced elsewhere. Herbert Gold, author of *Best Nightmare on Earth,* claims, "Haiti is one of the greatest adventurers a traveler can have." And he is right if one can stomach abject poverty and violence along with exotic beauty and mind-blowing sights.

What initially took my breath away was an immense fortress, known as The Citadelle, on a remote mountain top in Northern Haiti. It was built by a former slave who could neither read nor write, although as a general he succeeded in helping liberate his adopted country from France's yoke of slavery, served briefly as king of Haiti and, finally, as emperor of northern Haiti. His name, Henry Christophe, later to be immortalized in American theatre as Eugene O'Neill's *The Emperor Jones.* My many trips to Haiti and the Citadelle over forty years left me with a burning desire to use this impressive fortress in a novel. Not willing to trust my memory to the complexity of the fortress' interior, I sought out the architect of the UNESCO restoration after the World Heritage Committee of UNESCO declared the Citadelle a World Monument. Jacqueline Simon of New Orleans graciously supplied me Patrick Delatour's name and Patrick generously responded by sending me a full set of his architectural plans. I am indebted to them as well as to John Ed Bradley and Allison Kendrick who took their valuable time to critique my manuscript and suggest changes, and additionally to Ron and Mary Kenner and friend, Todd Frazier for their splendid editing.

Finally I would like the reader to know that some of the Haitian names I have used are in memory of personal friends, including a senator of the Haitian Government, either cruelly murdered or forced into exile by three decades of Duvalier tyranny. Otherwise this work is entirely one of fiction.

The Author

CHAPTER 1

In the diffuse and eerie light of a July dawn we ascend a trail that snakes steeply toward the fog-shrouded summit of the *Bonnet a L'Eveque* otherwise known as the Bishop's miter. Michelina proceeds me. Her spirited stride causes her bobbed raven hair to ripple like dark wavelets against her crisp white shirt collar. Pausing, she turns to me and through perceptive brown eyes, under lovely dark lashes, she regards my labored progress. Her tossed hair settles around her face as two strands arrow in on dimples which spontaneously erupt on either side of her sensual mouth.

"Peter, are you all right? "she inquires, grinning at me.

"I'm fine," I huff, trying to return her smile, though mine is more akin to a grimace.

Stepping to the side of the earthen and cobblestone trail, Michelina stops. Statuesque against a tropical curtain of pale green banana fronds under a cornice of shiny dark green mango leaves she waits for me to catch up.

"Perhaps we should have taken the horses after all," she teases.

I had declined. They were small pathetic-looking animals with sad eyes, deeply swayed backs and exposed ribs and I pitied their condition. "We'd rather walk," I had said to their disappointed handler, while Michelina eyed me with unspoken skepticism.

"It's only a short distance to the fortress," I had assured her, "no more than a kilometer." And at that early hour in the cool damp air, the sun still imprisoned behind the Chaine Bonnet Mountain range with its thick veil of morning mist, the walk up the mountain looks effortless.

As I reach Michelina's side I feel slender fingers slide up my back and slowly tighten on the back of my neck as she leans over to kiss me.

"*Tu esta' bien?*" she asks in a near whisper, her eyes boring into mine.

Her intimate Spanish and her sensuous gaze evoke arousal as my mind replays last night's feral coupling by pale moonlight in our Cape Haitian hotel's swimming pool.

"I'm all right, just winded," I reply, purposely averting my eyes from Michelina to prevent embarrassment as Gabrielle, our taxi driver and self-proclaimed tour guide, now studies us from the palmate leaves of a breadfruit tree while mopping beads of perspiration from his ebony face with a filthy rag.

"Careful," he warns, calling our attention to the sheer drop-off less than half a meter behind where we embrace. Stepping toward us he grins, his teeth broken pickets on an aging fence; his rheumy eyes burning fire opals set in gleaming anthracite. He raises a charcoal arm, extends a bony finger and points to an exotic landscape of craggy mountains and plunging valleys only now emerging beneath the gradually rising mist.

Looking over the precipice, I feel myself in the grip of a familiar fear. Acrophobia! As a twelve-year-old in Florida I had once climbed to the top of an Australian pine tree to swing about in the wind with my companions who had climbed adjoining trees. Suddenly a branch beneath my feet snapped and I fell, tumbling twenty meters through limbs and needles. Luckily, my legs hooked over the last bough. Back and forth I swung like a circus acrobat, my head scant centimeters from a concrete sidewalk.

"What's wrong, *mi amor?*" Michelina asks, intuitively sensing my fear.

"It frightens me to look down."

"Then you must only look up," she chides, reaching out with her index finger to lift up my chin. As my gaze segues up the mountainside, abruptly I gasp, "My God, look!" An enormous silvery-gray shape as tall and as wide as a battleship ominously emerges from the fog. It appears to bear down upon us as the mist swirls from its towering prow and titanic flanks like a massive bow wave.

Michelina steps behind me for protection and her arms encircle me. I feel her body tremble as she peers over my shoulder at this terrifying illusion. In open-mouthed awe we watch as the ghostly shroud of mist lifts to reveal the towering walls of an immense fortress.

"*Voila . . . La Citadelle Laferriere!*" proclaims Gabrielle.

At that moment, suddenly bathed in brilliant sunlight, streaked with wispy tendrils of rising mist, Henry Christophe's huge granite and brick bastion that straddles the mountain's summit reveals itself in all its eerie, menacing majesty.

"*Fantastico,*" Michelina marvels as I mutely stare, recalling that some historians believe a crazed dictator erected this, the largest fortress in the Western Hemisphere. However, others argue that the black dictator of Northern Haiti, though illiterate, had created a work of sheer genius. Regardless, all concur that Henry Christophe's Citadelle not only thwarted Napoleon's effort to recapture Saint Domingue but ended the French Emperor's dream for a North American Empire.

"*Attencion,*" calls Gabrielle, pointing over the precipice to an extensive architectural ruin not far from the base of the mountain. "The palace, Sans Souci, where Christophe lived, and then died, by his own hand."

"Why would he commit suicide?" asks Michelina.

"His horse had fallen on him. He was in constant agony, so he loaded a pistol with a single silver bullet."

"And shot himself?"

"*Oui madame.*"

Fearful of approaching the escarpment, I whisper an aside to Michelina before she joins Gabrielle to view the palace ruin. "It's a replica of Frederick the Great's palace at Potsdam in Germany."

"His wife, children and servants," Gabrielle rattles on, "carried the dead emperor up the mountain and once inside the fortress they threw his body into a pit of quicklime."

"But why?" asks Michelina, turning to Gabrielle whose brows are knitted in great conviction.

"To keep Christophe from his enemies, *bien sur,* else they would have turned him into a Zombie."

As Michelina stares down at San Souci, she reaches behind her back for my hand. "It must have been very grand, but now it's only just a pile of rubble with three walls standing. What happened to it?"

"Destroyed by an earthquake," says Gabrielle.

"And the octagon-shaped building with the onion dome?" asks Michelina, pointing to a neighboring structure.

"Christophe's chapel," answers Gabrielle.

I listen, but find myself distracted by Michelina's grip as she continues to lean over the four-hundred-meter precipice for an all-encompassing view of the scene below. Her daring unnerves me and I'm compelled to ask her to step back. She complies, but as she turns her face toward me I see apprehension in her eyes. It is not the fear of heights, which I know all too well, but the concern she harbors that the vast sullen fortress towering above us may not yield its secrets concerning her father.

Trying to assuage her anxiety, I pull her to me and put my arms around her. "Don't worry, we're in this together and if it's any comfort, I know how you feel. When I was five-years-old, both my parents were killed in a plane crash."

"*Lo siento,*" she murmurs. "I'm sorry. Don't worry Peter, I'm a stubborn optimist."

She didn't have to reassure me. I already felt the horror she had faced as a child.

On a moonless night in 1970, five sullen men with grim ebony faces had come to New Orleans' Fauberg-Marigny. Wearing sunglasses, dark trousers and loose white shirts that concealed weapons, these sinister carbon copies of one another gathered outside a quaint 'shotgun' double-painted pale blue with gingerbread trim as lacy and white as a finger-bowl doily. They were the dreaded Ton-ton Macoutes of Papa Doc Duvalier. Descending upon the house with the stealth of cat burglars, they gained silent entry. Once inside, their leader, wielding his machete, savagely butchered Michelina's elegant French Creole mother in her bed while the others bound and gagged her horrified artist father who vainly struggled to intervene. Then, stripping the artist's studio of every last painting, they loaded their wild-eyed prisoner and his works into a waiting van and departed. Upstairs in the house they quietly drove away from, they left behind a pretty six-year-old girl who had remained asleep.

Later that morning, when the child awoke she got out of bed and went downstairs. Walking toward her parent's room, she rubbed her eyes and called out for her mother. There was no response. When she entered her parent's bedroom she discovered the reason. Atop the bed, sprawled grotesquely in a dark crimson lake, lay her mother's headless torso while overhead twirling in lazy circles hung her mother's severed head tied to the ceiling fan blades by her long black hair.

Hearing a child's hysterical screams the neighbors rushed to her aid, then summoned the police.

I give Michelina a reassuring hug and we walk hand in hand up the mountain, drafting behind Gabrielle who reeks of rum and body odor. Our noses tell our feet to pass him, but we're unable to because of our struggle to suppress our laughter while Gabrielle rants on about the Citadelle.

"This fortress is the eighth wonder of the modern world," he says. "It took Christophe sixteen years to build it and it was barely finished before he died. Over thirty thousand peasants were employed in its construction and every granite block and every cannon brought up here took a life."

"How many died?" inquires Michelina.

"More than twenty thousand I am told," Gabrielle replies.

Michelina glances at me in disbelief.

"How many guns are there are inside the fortress?" I ask.

"One for every day of the year, mostly English and French cannon. The peasants hauled them up a trail steeper than the one we are on. Each day they had to move the guns a certain distance up the mountain. If they didn't, Christophe had the tenth man in each detachment... shot."

"That's barbaric!" Michelina fumes.

"Though effective . . . as you will see."

Gabrielle stops and points out some lichen-like objects on an immense stone block in the fortress' foundation. "On these stones is the blood of the peasants who died here."

"Another tourist myth," I whisper to Michele, as we stop to examine the stone's surface, which is spackled with patches of tiny brown lichens.

"They look convincing enough," says Michelina.

Like the proverbial child unable to resist the lure of a sign proclaiming, "*wet paint*," I reach out and touch one. It is slimy to the touch and when I examine my fingertip, it is crimson!

"You see," Gabrielle cackles with laughter.

"Over there," says Gabrielle, pointing to a town barely visible in the distance. "The people of Minot will tell you that every night Christophe's ghost walks the battlements. They say they can hear the sound made by his heavy boots. That is why no one dares remain here after dark. This is an evil place!" From a side pocket of his baggy dark blue pants, dusty and shiny from wear, Gabrielle extracts a half-empty bottle of Barbancourt Rum. Twisting off the metal cap, he takes a reassuring swig, then offers me the bottle.

"*Non, merci,*" I tell him. "It's a bit too early for a dry daiquiri."

CHAPTER 2

After solving a bizarre art theft in Venice which included the recovery of stolen Renaissance paintings and a priceless relic from the True Cross along with uncovering who had murdered a Benedictine monk and a comely artist's model, I was able to convince my estranged wife, Claire, to accompany me back to New York. Almost a murder victim herself, Claire gratefully agreed to give our shaky marriage another try, but after less than a week in our Beekman Place apartment she got cold feet and once again threatened to leave.

"I just can't cope, Peter," she says suddenly as we relax on the living room sofa over a cocktail.

"Claire, what's the matter?"

"I'm claustrophobic. I can't breathe. I can't sleep. I feel trapped."

"I don't understand?"

"I know," she says, shaking her long blonde hair. "I don't either."

"Would it help to see someone?" I ask softly, looking intently into her peridot-colored eyes, which quickly avert my gaze.

Startled, her eyes lift and segue into an angry glare as she nervously swings one shapely leg back and forth atop the other while a Chanel pump dangles precariously from her big toe. "You mean a shrink?"

"I do," I reply, putting down my glass.

"You think I'm nuts, is that it?" Her lips compress until they form a taught narrow crease and her eyes become mere slits.

"No, I didn't say nor imply that."

"You don't have to, Peter, it's written all over your face," she says forcefully banging her highball glass down on the glass coffee table.

"Claire, you're imagining things."

"I don't think so. You say you love me, but lately all you do is look at me with that same exasperated expression that speaks volumes: *she's 'round the bend, that one.'* Anyway, what good's a shrink? They're all a bunch of prescription junkies who condemn their patients to a blur of Librium and Prozac. Everyone I know agrees. I'm not going to live my life in a coma. I'm going to do what my niece, Melody, suggests . . . go to India . . . study yoga."

"Come on Claire, you're not a college kid anymore. This is absurd."

"Not any more absurd than you screwing my Venetian real estate agent, Cinzia Aliverti."

"So that's what this rant is all about?"

"Yes, and I dare you to deny it," she says, glaring at me.

"I don't deny it," I respond, returning her gaze. "We had a fling and as a result you and I are still alive."

"That's bullshit and you know it is."

"Damn it, Claire, if you're going to argue with me at least stick to the facts. Cinzia saved both our lives and whatever happened between Cinzia and me was all over in twenty-four hours. Afterward she was sick with remorse, but that hardly compares to you running off with that air-head lesbian who stole your family silver."

Suddenly, Claire's leg swings up. Her pump flies off her big toe, sails past my face and clatters to the parquet floor. "That's the problem with you Peter," she shouts. You think you have all the answers yet you don't even know me nor do you even give a damn."

"Wrong," I respond in a calm resolute voice. "All I want is a loving wife, but all I have experienced is a trouble maker with a capital T. Your excuse when you left me in Venice was you had to find yourself and that is so very childish for someone your age. What is it you really want?"

"In a word, . . . fulfillment! I need peace and contentment. Studying yoga in India like my niece Melody did would be perfect for me."

"So you can follow in her footsteps, pleasuring men in the Tantric arts of Yoga."

"Shit! That does it, Peter. I can never communicate with you. You're so . . . so cruel, so insensitive. You don't need a wife, Peter. You need something that won't talk back . . . like a dog. Yes, that's it, man's best friend, a little creature that will obey and follow you around like your shadow. Before I leave town I'll get you one . . . . Consider it a going away present."

"Fine!" I reply, standing up. "As long as it's not some weird creature like, Franco, that black widow spider you adopted as a pet in Venice," I shout, stalking into my library where dejectedly I flop into my desk chair, turn on my computer and go for a spin on the information highway. Better for me to scope out the countryside like some leaf inspector than to succumb to road rage and blow a gasket.

Claire makes good on her threat. She moves into our guestroom and before leaving me and flying off to India she presents me with a five-month-old Yorkshire Terrier, which I really don't want. The carpets don't want him, either, nor do the kick-pleats on the sofa nor the leg of an antique drop leaf table in the foyer. What I really need is my wife, not an animal I have to feed, bathe and housebreak. It annoys me that I'm suddenly responsible for a four-legged creature's welfare even though a plaintive look from his soft brown eyes can melt steel. At least Claire was considerate enough to provide instructions from the breeder, but they appall me. In order to housebreak my dog I have to walk him four times a day . . . . Good grief.

One morning a neighbor who shares the elevator with me looks at the dog cradled in my arms and tells me I'm brave. "Yorkies are the pits to housebreak, trust me," she says. "I had to replace all my carpets, then he proceeded to destroy the new ones. Finally, I had it up to here," she gesticulates, waving her hand a foot over her head. "I threw in the towel and gave him up for adoption."

Vaguely I recall her dog. I believe Spike was his name, a feisty little bugger, silver and tan, with a face like a ferret, a long snout and little beady viper-like eyes. He was a yapper, a growler, a snapper, and he hated strangers, especially men! Is this to be my fate? Just thinking about it makes me break out in a cold sweat.

"Are you all right?" the woman asks me, looking alarmed. Reaching for my pocket-handkerchief I mumble, "A bit stuffy in here is all." As the elevator doors open onto the lobby she steps out and leaves me to continue mopping my forehead while hyperventilating.

My doorman, whom I can't abide, gives me what I once called in college a shit-eating grin as he admonishes me to pick up after my dog. Tearing off a half page of classifieds from the *New York Daily News* that he'd been reading, he stuffs it into my hand. "Thanks," I mumble, and take my leave, anxious not to let him see the redness rising up from my shirt collar as my self-image of aloof respectability is about to evaporate in a single squat. *Scooping up dog poop in public — what if someone I know sees me?* Mopping more beads of perspiration from my brow and upper lip, I affix the leash to my Yorkie's harness and set off with him. Almost immediately he slams on the brakes by a fire hydrant, takes a sniff and hoists his leg. I nearly succumb to a panic attack thinking of all the fire hydrants there must be in New York City.

Halfway up Beekman Place at the corner of Fiftieth Street my dog squats, spins in strange circles and does his duty. Bending over I struggle to pick up his deposit with the half page of classifieds, while praising him as instructed, "Good boy, that's a good fellow." Trapping his feces in the fold of newspaper I straighten up to find myself face to face with a stunning redhead who is in the process of bending over to pet my dog.

"What a cute puppy," she says, giving me a dazzling smile.

I feel my face turn crimson as I gape at her lovely face framed by dark auburn hair. She resembles an actress whose name I'm too flustered to recall. This movie star clone wears a form-fitting emerald green linen shift which matches her eye color and reveals an enticingly curvaceous figure.

"What's your Yorkie's name?" she asks.

"Oh . . . ah . . . Hemingway!" I blurt out.

"As in Ernest?" she grins, her eyes flirting with me.

"My favorite author," I reply.

Hemingway stares up at her; it seems he, too, is an admirer of good figures, but he's closer to the ground and gets to gaze up her skirt.

"Are you a resident of the neighborhood?" she asks.

"I live at Two Beekman."

"You're so fortunate. This is such a lovely area."

"And you," I ask, as Hemingway meanders over to sniff at a shapely ankle. Lucky dog! "Where do you live?"

"Hey, that tickles," she laughs. Bending down, she scoops him up and cuddles him to her ample bosom. Hemingway yawns with contentment and licks his chops, while I stare at him with envy. "Do you mind?" she asks, scratching his ears with beautifully manicured fingernails.

"Of course not." Awkwardly I hold Hemingway's slack leash and packet of dog crap.

"I'm staying with a friend of mine at Twenty-four Beekman."

"You don't live here?"

"No. I'm from Los Angeles."

"Has anyone ever told you–"

"Often," she interrupts, "which is probably the reason I don't get very much work."

"Then you're an actress?"

"Yes. Mainly I do soaps and sitcoms. Thus far, I've not had much success breaking into film."

"I'm Peter Grant. I'd offer my right hand, but as you can see. . . ." I blush.

She laughs, eyeing the wadded up newspaper. Her laugh is wonderful, clear as a bell, with a hint of mischief. "I'm Dawn Harriman," she says.

"I'm delighted to meet you, as is Hemingway."

"He's such an enchanting little fellow," she replies, stroking his head. Hemingway closes his eyes. "Your papa's nice too," she coos, examining Hemingway's contented face.

"Thanks. Ah . . .perhaps you have time for a cup of coffee?"

"I'm afraid I can't," she says, glancing at her watch. "I'm about to be late for an audition. "Here," she holds out Hemingway.

I take him from her and venture, "Perhaps tomorrow morning?"

"Under any other circumstances, Peter, I'd love to," she says, laying a hand on my arm, "but I'm staying with my boyfriend. We'll run into one another again."

"Well, break a leg as they say."

Flashing me a lovely smile, she draws her hand away. "Thanks. I need a bit of luck. Bye Hemingway . . . . Bye Peter."

"Ciao, Dawn." Without thinking, I wave the newspaper at her and as she walks away dog feces spill out onto the sidewalk.

Glancing over her shoulder, she grins in amusement as I struggle to reclaim Hemingway's business. Then with a toss of her auburn hair she hurries along Fiftieth Street, crosses First Avenue and is promptly swallowed up in the insane morning rush of humanity.

"Well, Hemingway, It looks like you have a name and I have a chick magnet."

As I speak, Hemingway's alert brown eyes look up at me, one ear straight up, the other flopped half over. This dog has the appeal of a homeless street urchin. Irresistible! As are pretty woman to me and I know why. My mother was strikingly beautiful. Although I barely remember her I can admire her lovely portrait every day in my living room and thus I'm compelled to seek out enchanting women.

On his noon outing Hemingway trolls up a comely brunette with large almond eyes, pouty red lips and sensational legs; clearly of Eurasian descent. She makes a fuss over Hemingway, but I notice she sports a diamond engagement ring the size of a Rolls-Royce headlight which loudly proclaims . . . off limits!

Then on his six o'clock constitutional Hemingway enchants two lovely blondes. The one with streaked hair and huge round tortoise shell-rimmed sunglasses perched on her forehead turns out to be a buyer for Bergdorf. Engaging me in wide-eyed conversation about how adorable Hemingway is, she breathlessly produces her business card and hands it to me. "Drop in and see me sometime," she says, steering her girlfriend into the doorway of the corner florist.

I hate to admit this, Hemingway, but it looks like you're a keeper.

That night, the famous author's namesake jumps up and takes over Claire's side of the bed. Despite my anguish over her abrupt departure from my life, she has provided me with a companion who is much livelier than my stuffed Teddy Bear, *"Arrigo,"* named for the owner of Harry's Bar in Venice. Falling asleep I dwell fitfully on Claire's impending baptism in the Ganges, wondering all night if she's remembered to get her typhoid shots.

On a late spring morning under a threatening sky with the air oppressive with humidity, I take Hemingway out for his morning stroll. As we amble past the brick façade of Mitchell Place toward the corner of Forty-ninth Street and First Avenue where he encounters his favorite fire hydrant, I hear someone call out my name. Looking around I see a dignified old friend, Selwyn Podmore, waving to me. He hurries across the intersection, his unbuttoned raincoat flapping in his wake like a collapsed sailboat spinnaker.

"Selwyn, what a pleasant surprise," I say, gripping his leathery outstretched hand. "I thought you were a permanent fixture of the Republic of Haiti."

"I was, dear boy," he pants, "but things there have spun out of control. Sheer anarchy ever since Baby Doc fled the country. I don't feel safe there anymore."

"That's a telling admission, Selwyn. You're as much a fixture of Port au Prince's landscape as is the ginger bread Grand Hotel Oloffson."

"Not right now, I'm afraid." His brow furrows into a look of pained distress. "Who's that little chap on the end of the leash?"

"Hemingway. He's a going away present from Claire."

Selwyn's tangle of eyebrows arch and a puzzled expression washes over his face. "Going away present?"

"We've separated."

"Sorry. Truly I am. Smashing looking woman, Claire. Surely a keeper I'd have thought."

"God knows I tried," I emote, raising the back of my hand to my forehead in mock Shakespearean martyrdom. Straining at his leash, Hemingway barks furiously. I turn to see a regal-looking Afghan that's got him worked up. As the dog prances toward us like a dressage horse, its impeccably groomed and layered reddish coat stylishly flounces up and down.

"I say, that lanky lady with the Afghan looks rather familiar."

"The wife of a former Secretary of State."

"Ah, of course, I recall her now from the tabloids. Be careful, Peter that beast propelling her toward us may mistake Hemingway for a canapé."

Over a flurry of furious barking, I loudly reply, "I rather doubt it. Yorkies think they're lions."

"Trained him to go for the jugular have you?"

"Yes, but he's only able to reach the Achilles."

"Good one, Peter," Selwyn chuckles. "At least your wit hasn't vanished along with your wife. As for you, Hemingway, you can calm down now, the "social X-ray" has beat a hasty retreat with your nemesis."

Selwyn, indeed a rare breed of Englishmen, had been a journalist by training and then a spy, British Intelligence's MI-5, during the Cold War years of Stalin. A confirmed bachelor, he was Edwardian in manners and dress, tweeds, even in summer, always with a vest and bow tie. I found him intricate, intrusive, and intractable. Due to his height and bearing I always thought he would have made an excellent diplomat, but after his retirement from British intelligence he joined Cockburn's, a very old and respected London art gallery. Concerned about the possibility of acquiring art that had belonged to holocaust victims, they hired Selwyn to vet the provenance of prospective acquisitions before committing to purchases. Selwyn had an instinctive feel for art and a good eye, which occasionally involved him in controversy. On the occasion I first met him I had been invited to participate in a lively discussion about the authenticity of a certain tapestry in the Victoria and Albert Museum. Though it had hung there for nearly two decades Selwyn and I both felt it was bogus. We both agreed the tapestry was the work of a Romanian forger by the name of Theodor Tuduc, and so after much public ado it turned out we had been correct all along. Rejoicing over an excellent call, we became fast friends.

In the late nineteen-fifties Selwyn jetted off to Haiti on holiday. For whatever reason, he fell madly in love with the place at precisely the time another of his countrymen excoriated The Black Republic in a well-known novel with a bizarre title that barely masked the book's edgy sinister satire.

Selwyn left Cockburn's and settled down in Haiti's capitol city of Port au Prince where he soon became infamous as the country's resident art expert. In my library I have three of his many books and hands down he's the leading authority when it comes to Haitian primitive art. "How long has it been since we last set eyes on one another, Selwyn?"

"Oh, three years I dare say, when I was last here visiting my publisher."

"My how *tempus fugits.*"

"Yes, especially when you're having such a jolly time," grimaced Selwyn, glancing anxiously at his watch.

"Selwin, are you all right?" I can sense his nervousness, like a man only a step ahead of his creditors. "Is anything wrong?" Hemingway sits beside my shoe and paws at my sock, annoyed by the interruption of his daily routine.

"There's a matter I'd like to discuss with you . . . a bit dicey, but terribly important. Could we meet for a drink this afternoon?"

"How about my flat at Two Beekman?"

"Splendid."

"Five-thirty good for you?"

"Perfect. Good seeing you Peter, you, too, Hemingway," he says, glancing down. "My, you certainly are a cute well-behaved little bugger and an excellent *bird* dog, I'll wager."

"And how," I laugh, amused at Selwyn's avian terminology for a striking British girl. "He recently flushed a ravishing redhead and a brace of enchanting blondes."

Chuckling aloud, Selwyn's eyes sparkle as he takes his leave and makes his way uptown along First Avenue.

I consider crossing First Avenue to walk Hemingway past the alluring Sycamore trees of Turtle Bay, but then demur. The building rush hour traffic along with ominous rain clouds cause me to reconsider. Instead we trace Selwyn's path, albeit lagging a fair distance behind due to Hemingway's interest in food particles on the sidewalk. He's also a scarfer.

I'm distracted by an ear-splitting roar as a black BMW motorcycle careens around the corner from Forty-ninth Street. Hemingway darts across the sidewalk to cower against the side of The Beekman Towers Hotel, but he runs out of leash and hunkers down instead on the pavement. Swearing under my breath, I watch as the bike and two helmeted riders roar recklessly up First Avenue between a line of cars and the curb. At the intersection of Fiftieth Street, the motorcycle slows and a sinister-looking black object emerges in the extended hand of the motorcycle's passenger. I freeze in horror. "Pop, pop, pop . . . pop, pop, pop, pop," echoes down the street. Glass from the corner florist's window shatters and cascades onto the sidewalk. A figure in a khaki-colored raincoat slowly topples over and falls in a heap among the glass shards.

Jesus Christ! "Selwyn!" I shout. Scooping up Hemingway I dash to his side. Moaning, he lies on his back, his eyes fixed on mine in a desperate plea for help. Blood spurts from a terrible wound in his neck as I kneel beside him with Hemingway struggling in my arms. Instinctively, I know he's dying in front of my eyes.

"Take this," he gasps, pressing a hotel key into my hand. "Briefcase," he sighs deeply, then bloody froth bubbles from between his lips. His eyes blink rapidly and roll back in his head. Emitting a great sigh, he dies.

"Call 911," I scream at a faceless assemblage. Spectators fall back as I stand up beside Selwyn's body. Jerking my cell phone from my jacket pocket, I plow through several onlookers. In shock I lean against the side of the flower shop and telephone 911 myself. The moment I press "End" I realize I must get to Selwyn's hotel before either the police or his assassins show up.

Carrying Hemingway, I rapidly walk east on Fiftieth Street, away from the crime scene, turn the corner at Beekman Place and trot toward my apartment building. Glancing at the key Selwyn gave me, I see it's from the Pickwick Arms, a small hotel on East Fifty-second Street, dependably English, inexpensive rooms, no frills, bathrooms in the hallways. Undoubtedly he was headed back to his hotel when he was gunned down. For an instant, I find myself wondering where Selwyn had been at such an early hour before he chanced to run into me. His path had not been from his hotel, but from the direction of the United Nations building on First Avenue, but even that might not be a valid supposition.

After putting Hemingway inside my apartment, I swiftly walk the few blocks to the Pickwick Arms, take their cozy elevator to the third floor and locate Selwyn's room. Opening the door with his key, I stand to one side as I push open the door, to make certain no surprises await inside before I enter. The room is small, dimly lit by a single window with half-closed Venetian blinds and cheap, flowered side curtains that are partially drawn. The view outside is the brick façade of the adjacent building. As I flip on a light switch a naked ceiling bulb illuminates the room. Along one wall stands a single bed that barely allows the door sufficient clearance to open and close. A simple desk of blond wood with a matching chair stands at the foot of the bed. A lamp, a cheap porcelain imitation of Chinese export, sits atop the desk. Opposite the bed is a wash basin with a few towels that dangle from a wall rack. To the right of the sink, perched on a metal stand, is a Zenith color TV so old it predates remote controls. Selwyn's shaving kit sits atop it. To the left side of the wash stand, partially hidden behind the entry door, is a closet with a mirrored door. Seeing my own reflection makes the depressingly small room appear overcrowded and I wonder how Selwyn was able to cope in such cramped quarters with hardly enough room to change his mind much less his clothes. Then, I recall his parsimony, which explains his tolerance for small spaces, one which I don't share since I'm also prone to claustrophobia.

Taking a deep breath, I open the closet door. Inside hang two suits, a sports jacket, trousers and several shirts all suspended from those insulting theft-proof metal coat hangers. Sitting upright on the floor beside a pair of shoes is Selwyn's briefcase. It's one of those aluminum jobs plastered with travel stickers and so battered that it looks as if it was once a gorilla's playtoy. Pulling down Selwyn's garment bag from the closet shelf I search the pockets, but find only dirty socks, underwear and handkerchiefs. Shoving the bag back onto the shelf, I grab the aluminum case by its handles, wipe my fingerprints from all doorknobs with my handkerchief and exit the room.

Emerging from the elevator, I sidle up to the front desk behind a group of jabbering Japanese tourists who compete with one another for counter space to fill out registration cards. Deftly I reach among them, slide Selwyn's room key across the marble countertop and walk briskly across the lobby to a glass door that opens into a wine bar. Entering it, I find myself inside a French café with small tables that spill out onto the street. As I leave the café, I make certain I'm not being followed.

At my apartment Hemingway, happy to see me, jumps all over me, greeting me as if I'd been away for a month. If Claire had ever wiggled her rear end at me like Hemingway, I'd have pursued her across the Pacific.

Inside Selwyn's aluminum case, which I force open with a screwdriver is a manuscript he's recently finished. Since all the other things inside are personal items, unanswered letters, address book, unpaid bills, checkbook and the like, I surmise what he wanted to talk about must be somewhere in the pages of the manuscript.

Ringing up my faithful secretary, Catherine, I ask her to cancel my appointments for the day. I also advise her that my personal life has taken another dramatic turn. "Oh goodness!" she exclaims, followed by "I'm so sorry, Peter," but I detect in her voice she's really not at all sorry that Claire has finally terminated our marriage. I've been aware for years that Catherine's had a crush on me, but she conceals it behind a facade of matronly clothing, prim hair, unbecoming eyeglasses and well-intentioned fussing over my welfare. There've been times I've been sorely tempted to pay for her to have a makeover at Elizabeth Arden along with a chic outfit from Saks . . . but on second thought a good loyal secretary is hard to come by.

From his sitting position on the carpet Hemingway lifts his head, both ears erect and stares at me as I stretch out on the living room sofa with Selwyn's manuscript. Jumping up beside me, my tiny shadow curls up in a ball and snores.

Opening the manuscript I begin to read:

THE LIFE AND ART
OF ROBERT ROI"

"Introduction"

"Amid the desperate squalor of Haiti, the poorest nation on earth, there arises from the limestone and chalk a tree of unparalleled beauty. It is called the Flamboyant. Its luscious flowers form a bright vermilion canopy that elevates one's gaze from all the surrounding wretchedness and, for a breathtaking instant, enriches one's soul. Such is the manner in which one beholds the work of the esteemed artist Robert Roi. His vibrant colors and his stark symbolism, which protest his country's tyranny, cause the viewer to gasp in awe and admiration. But where is Robert Roi's work today? Unfortunately his admirers do not know. Even I cannot tell you."

"Robert Roi's work has not been seen since 1970 when the artist was kidnapped in the City of New Orleans, most believe, by Tonton Macoutes on orders from Dr. Francois Duvalier, then President of Haiti. During the kidnapping, Robert Roi's wife was brutally murdered, his artworks looted and his young daughter orphaned. To this day it remains unknown whether Robert Roi remains alive."

"In the fall of 1969 I visited Robert Roi in New Orleans and at his request photographed nearly all his work. The reason for this biography is to tell this courageous artist's story and to honor his compelling work with a photographic retrospective long overdue."

Selwyn Podmore

All at once it becomes clear why my friend, Selwyn Podmore, has been murdered on the streets of New York. The manuscript I hold in my hands is a telling indictment. Whoever shot him or, most likely,

ordered him assassinated, does not want Robert Roi's biography published. More powerful than Selwin's words are the photographs of
Robert Roi's paintings that accompany his text. They are a dramatic
and compelling indictment of Haitian corruption under the Duvaliers.
The photograph for the cover of the book is a painting entitled, *The
Harvest*. It is unlike anything I have ever seen by any Haitian artist.
Absent are the ubiquitous bucolic scenes of natives engaged in care-
free daily life under pastel skies replete with billowy clouds, tranquil
palm-lined beaches and aqua seas teeming with quaint fishing boats.
Also omitted are the fanciful colored wooden shacks with their corrugated tin and thatch roofs that tilt haphazardly on the sides of rolling
green hills or peek out from outlandishly lush tropical foliage long
since fallen victim to the blade of a machete. Missing also are the
charming serpentine paths alive with picturesque natives and donkeys
both laden with baskets of produce and burlap sacks of dusky charcoal.
Nowhere are there gaily-tattooed pickup trucks and "tap-tap" buses,
roadside goats, chickens, and little children frolicking in the dirt. Nor
is there any attempt at Christian or Voodoo abstractionism or symbolism so prevalent in Haitian artwork. I find no subtlety in Robert Roi's
work, only starkly vivid truth, as cruel, blatant and grotesque as human
and animal figures in the works of Breugel, all of which portrays the
feral desperation of life under tyranny.

The Harvest provides the most powerful evidence of how the Haitian
dictatorship has obtained its vast wealth. In the painting's foreground
emaciated laborers harvest a crop in fading twilight in the mountains
of northern Haiti. Among them stand heavily armed soldiers, some
engaging in vicious beatings, others performing acts of rape and murder judging from the number of corpses that litter a nearby denuded
hillside. In the background other laborers load ominous looking
trucks with the harvest; and beyond the vehicles, on a distant mountain top silhouetted by the setting sun, stands the Citadelle, a brooding
monument to past oppression. But the one thing that's so damning
about this brutal scene is the harvest itself. Familiar looking fronds
with slender serrated leaves identify the harvest as *cannabis sativa* and
the other crop as *erytwoxylum coca*. And lastly, between two mountains is

the gleam of reflected sunlight that glints off the wings of a two-engine cargo plane, a DC3, workhorse of the marijuana and cocaine trade.

No wonder the Duvaliers had wanted Robert Roi's work suppressed. His graphic paintings threatened to expose their darkest secret, the illicit source of their vast wealth: drugs!

I recall that Papa Doc Duvalier died in 1971. His son, Baby Doc, who succeeded him, later fled to Paris in 1986. Last I heard he was living in Monaco with his bored, self-indulgent wife, the two of them fearing for their lives while constantly surrounded by bodyguards. Essentially the Duvaliers are history, but what of their successors?

Who is it that ordered Selwyn murdered and wants his book suppressed? Is it an official in a powerful post in the government of Haiti who fears the past? Is it the Tonton Macoutes leader responsible for Robert Roi's kidnapping? Or is it the heir to the Duvalier's drug trafficking? As I ponder these questions a feeling of dread suddenly washes over me. Suppose Selwyn's killers noticed me talking with him on the corner of Forty-ninth Street and First Avenue. If they want Selwyn's manuscript and they haven't yet found it, they will soon be looking for me. I've got to get this manuscript in the hands of Arthur Melrose, Selwyn's publisher without exposing myself. Of course, I'll scan the entire document into my computer, compress it then e-mail it to him. After that I'd better clear out of Dodge and attempt to track down Robert Roi's daughter. Selwyn hints in his manuscript that Robert Roi may still be alive, unlikely I think, but in any event Selwyn suggests Robert Roi has left his daughter a hidden legacy.

CHAPTER 3

Secure in his obscenely expensive black and tan Louis Vuitton traveling case beneath the seat in front of me, Hemingway peers intently at me through brass grillwork as we feel the plane's wheels make contact with the tarmac. A telltale puff of smoke erupts from beneath the left wing as tires grip concrete, permitting the craft to settle onto the runway with a jarring metallic shudder. Out the window I see flaps extend toward the ground like a wet cormorant trying to dry its wings. A roar follows as the engines reverse as the plane jerks to a slow roll. Brakes! Coasting for a bit, the plane suddenly pivots hard right and taxis with the rattle of a scrap yard toward the passenger terminal.

"Well here we are in New Orleans," I say to Hemingway, who simply yawns and looks at me inquisitively, one ear up the other half drooped over. Selwyn's manuscript is more persuasive than Selwyn himself, though I expect he would relish convincing me of the necessity of finding out what's happened to Robert Roi. And no doubt I would have agreed to help him anyway as a sign of loyal friendship. But now after his violent death I feel obligated . . . compelled, actually, to get to the bottom of things, to find Robert Roi, if he's still alive, unearth the mysterious legacy he left and hopefully bring Selwyn's killers to justice. Clearly Selwyn counted on my commitment to help him, since prior to our chance encounter he had already made arrangements with his publisher to pay my expenses out of his advance royalty from the sale of his biography of Robert Roi.

Immediately after receiving the e-mailed manuscript text and photographs of Robert Roi's paintings, Arthur Melrose had telephoned me. He informed me of Selwyn's arrangements and told me twenty thousand dollars was available to me to go to New Orleans, locate Robert Roi's daughter, try to find her long missing father and locate the mysterious legacy. Immediately I knew Selwyn's advance would hardly cover such an undertaking. Nevertheless owing to our long friendship, my traumatic parting with Claire and a compelling fear urging me to get out of New York for awhile, I told Melrose I would accept the stipend and take up the cause. What I fail to envision is the danger that would soon envelop my furry companion and me.

During the first few days in New Orleans Hemingway and I take up residence at The Soniat House, an enchanting inn in the lower French Quarter. Comprised of two historic French Creole style houses dating from 1829 and 1840, the inn nestles anonymously behind a shaded façade of well-aged brick with tall wooden doors and shutters painted an unusual hue of dark green. The Inn's portal, actually an old carriage way, leads to a brick patio laid out in a herringbone pattern lush with palms, magnolia, banana, hibiscus, ginger, lilies and other tropical plantings. An inescapable aroma of sweet olive permeates the sultry air, and from the bottom tier of a wedding cake shaped cast iron fountain the water splashes onto lily pads floating in a round pool made of old brick. Lavish ferns in wire baskets hang from the eaves that shelter the upper story galleries of the main building and slave quarters. The underside of the eaves are painted a pale blue, which disturbs me since the color clashes with the rich terra-cotta walls of the buildings that enclose the patio. Later I learn the blue ceiling discourages mud daubers and wasps from building nests under the eaves. The color fools insects into believing the eaves are sky, and so they nest elsewhere.

Inside the inn I find tall ceilings, whirling fans, wide board cypress floors with the patina of newly waxed shoes, decorative plaster cornices, triple-hung windows, antique period furniture, and painted wood balconies with lacey iron balustrades cast more than a hundred and fifty years ago. Painted wooden stairs bear the concave wear of decades of use; walls cant, chimneys tilt, and roofs sag like old plow horses under a mantle of heavy slate. And most confounding of all, these exquisite structures are erected on posts driven into soil the consistency of gumbo. Surprisingly they remain intact, withstanding hoards of ravenous termites and nature's whimsy with the willfulness of a Venetian palazzo.

Living in a noisy city like New York, I'm accustomed to tuning out the cacophony of noises. But whenever I travel elsewhere I become acutely aware of strange sounds. It's the same experience for Hemingway. In New York he's usually very quiet and only barks at other dogs or at a person approaching our apartment door. Hearing unfamiliar sounds such as the melodious tooting of the calliope from the riverboat Natchez, the clang of the riverfront trolleys, the warning blast from ships plying the Mississippi and the tolling of Saint Louis Cathedral's bells, all elicits a low growl. And the "clip-pity-clop" of the mule-drawn buggies in the street below evokes fierce aggression. Up on his hind legs with his snout protruding through the ironwork, Hemingway lets the carriage driver and his passengers know by his high pitched yapping that he's ready to do battle with the mule. They laugh at the absurdity, unaware that Yorkshire Terriers really do believe they are lions.

I hope to locate Robert Roi's daughter within a few days of our arrival; but alas, no such luck. There's only one listing in the phone directory under, "Roi." I phone and it's not the person I'm seeking. Also, he denies having any female relative about age thirty-seven.

After hanging up I realize I face a daunting task. I decide to sublet a Vieux Carré apartment for the next two months. Leasing one is not particularly complicated as many of the locals flee the summer oppression in favor of the cooler climes of Colorado, North Carolina, or Europe. In the classifieds of a local weekly newspaper, *Gambit,* I find an advertisement for an artist's studio on Governor Nichols Street just around the corner from the Soniat House. The lessor turns out to be a man whose party I had attended one summer in Venice, Italy, while working on the theft of Renaissance art from an Austrian Archduke. Duped by a former mentor I had become the prime suspect in the murder of a voluptuous figure model and a Benedictine monk who had been robbed of Christendom's holiest artifact, a nail from Christ's crucifixion. Antonio Verdi, a well-known French Quarter artist and musician, is delighted to have me as his tenant. Though his furnishings are sparse and eclectic, the ambience — old brick walls festooned with original art works, high ceilings, exposed beams, whirling ceiling fans and good north light — appeals to me. And to satisfy Hemingway's curiosity a narrow balcony overlooking the street allows him to monitor the passage of both man and beast. The day after signing the lease, Hemingway and I vacate the Soniat House and move to our new lodgings. Antonio is already gone, on his way to Venice for the summer.

It's readily apparent to me from Selwyn's manuscript that he has purposely protected the identity of Robert Roi's daughter. He never once discloses her name. All I am certain about is her approximate age and that her roots are in New Orleans, a fact Selwyn's publisher has also confirmed. My task is to uncover her name, then try to locate her. Count on a devious mind like Selwyn's to challenge mine. Mind games had been typical of our long friendship. In the old days we taunted one another with riddles, mysteries and puzzles. Selwyn usually prevailed. He fancied himself an intellectual, a clone of John LeCarré's George Smiley. I was not equally flattered. Selwyn compared me to the hapless vacuum cleaner salesman mistakenly recruited as a British spy in Graham Greene's *Our Man in Havana.*

In this endeavor I am hardly alone. I am convinced Selwyn is peering over my shoulder from his lofty perch. I can sense his presence, those piercing, relentless blue eyes, that ribald smirk arcing across his weathered face and that keen mind which second-guesses my every move. Overcoming an adversary with strategy and style intrigued Selwyn more than simply winning contests. "It's how the game's played that counts, old chum," he'd say. I envision him gleefully rubbing his hands together as I attempt to unravel his final bequest, undoubtedly an enigma obscured within a puzzle.

In his manuscript Selwyn states that Robert Roi had lived in an area known as the Fauberg-Marigny. I discover it is in fact nearby, only two blocks north of my flat on the other side of Esplanade Avenue, a wide divided boulevard lined with stately brick and stucco homes and

Greek revival mansions that separates the French Quarter from the Marigny, as the area is familiarly known.

"Hemingway!"

Dashing into the room, he alertly stares at me, both ears rigid with expectation.

"Later this afternoon you and I are going for a walk."

The word, "walk," evokes an immediate response. Hemingway is on his hind legs, pawing at the air in expectation.

"We have to find Robert Roi's house."

Hemingway cocks his head and I realize he's looking for his leash to materialize. When it's not forthcoming, he gives me a bored look and lies down. Suddenly, from the street an alien noise echoes between buildings. I recognize the sharp staccato sound of a child with bottle caps imbedded in the toes of his shoes tap-dancing on the sidewalk. Hemingway leaps up and scampers onto the balcony to lodge his protest. Returning to my thoughts about how to find Robert Roi's house, it occurs to me that perhaps I should check the property records at City Hall.

The black and white United Cab pulls up to the front of a bleak gray building shaped like a huge cereal box lying on its side. Its façade, a stark monotony of cluttered casement windows is so drab and out of place it reminds me of the typical postwar apartment buildings of East Berlin under the Russians.

"Is this City Hall?" I am certain my cab driver has delivered me to the wrong address.

"That's what the sign says, mah man," he drawls, poking his arm out the cab window to waggle a thick stubby finger at the top of the building. I lean across the back seat and look up. Sure enough, across the face of the edifice in red block lettering: "CITY HALL."

The interior of the building is even seedier than the outside, a dismal way to promote a city renowned for its hospitality. Inside there is an aura of cold indifference as I seek assistance locating the tax assessor's office. I feel more an interloper than a city guest.

Were it not for a jovial and high-spirited Patty LaBelle-like lady who helps me in my search, I probably would have abandoned my effort earlier. After nearly an hour of careful searching she cannot find any record of a property in the Fauberg-Marigny that once belonged to one Robert Roi. Kindly, she suggests I try The Williams Research Center on Chartres Street in the French Quarter. "If you follow your nose *down* Chartres Street from Conti you'll find it. It's right before you reach Chef Paul Prudome's Cajun/Creole restaurant," she beams, then emits a hearty laugh that accompanies me all the way down the long hallway back to the elevators.

Initially, I mistake the handsome granite structure of the Williams Research Center for a bank and walk right past it. It's only when I've joined a line of eager diners basking in savory aromas that waft from the restaurant that I realize my error. Retracing my steps back to a tall set of polychrome wood doors encased in granite, I enter the building. Its immaculate and spacious interior houses a vast library and a valuable collection of historical documents that date from the French occupation of New Orleans, 1699 to 1762, and the shorter Spanish occupation of 1763 to 1803. Also on the premises are a treasure trove of property records, private papers, art and memorabilia, all documenting the lifestyle of New Orleans before and after the Louisiana Purchase.

"I'm trying to find some information concerning a Haitian artist who lived and painted in the Fauberg-Marigny during the Nineteensixties," I tell a tall slender woman seated behind the second floor reception desk.

"The name?" she asks, turning to her computer's keyboard.

"Robert Roi, last name spelled R-O-I."

She types in the name on her keyboard and waits a few seconds. "I'm sorry. We have no references for any individual with that name."

"He was kidnapped from his home in the Fauberg-Marigny in 1970, his wife murdered and all his paintings stolen."

"Have you tried the newspaper archives at the New Orleans Public Library? They have all the newspapers on microfiche."

"Thank you, I'll go there tomorrow morning."

"I think that's your best bet."

Disappointed, I leave and walk back to the apartment. The sun is relentless and the humidity so oppressive it's difficult to breathe. Heat waves shimmer from the hoods and roofs of cars parked along the street. The slates in the sidewalk are so hot the heat penetrates the soles of my shoes and off in the hazy distance, like a mirage, I see the spire of St. Louis Cathedral, which appears to waver unsteadily in the heat.

Changing into khaki shorts and a short-sleeved polo shirt, I attach Hemingway to his lead and like 'mad dogs and Englishmen' we amble 'out into the noon-day sun.'

The Marigny turns out to be a warren of streets within the confines of a large triangle. Some streets are bisected, end and resume elsewhere. It's all terribly confusing, a bit like Venice except there are no canals to cross. We view an impossible number of houses, many restored to their original charm while others appear to be dilapidated rentals no doubt owned by slum landlords. Largely it is an area of Creole and Victorian cottages, shotgun singles, doubles and camelbacks some raised other built on slab. Through the middle of the triangle along Frenchman Street are bars, restaurants, and jazz joints and the people appear more bohemian than in the French Quarter. After an hour and a half of wandering about in shirt-clinging heat and overwhelming humidity it's time to head home. Hemingway is panting, his pink tongue dangling from his mouth. Completely enervated we shamble back to the apartment and collapse. No wonder New Orleans natives flee the city for the summer.

On the way to the public library to hopefully turn up information from old newspapers I stop for morning coffee at Croissant D'Or, a storefront café on Ursuline Street which is frequented by locals resilient enough to endure a sweltering summer. They gather to share local news and gossip while drinking a laundry list of various brews and munching on a much too tempting assortment of freshly baked French croissants and pastries.

Carrying my *New York Times,* obtained from a newspaper dispenser outside, an apple croissant and an iced cappuccino, I find an empty table against the back wall and slide into an ice cream parlor chair. As I drink my coffee and peruse the second page of the *Times,* I am distracted by high-pitched greetings exchanged between two ladies who judging by their shrillness apparently have not seen one another in some time. Looking over the top of my paper, I see a matronly woman introduce a stunningly beautiful young woman to another rotund matron with bleached blond hair seated at a nearby table. Hovering over her café latte and slab of apple strudel like a raptor atop its kill, the seated woman smiles benignly and extends a pudgy hand.

"Magda, my neice, Michelina Coidavid."

"Of course, Why it's been ages, won't y'all join me," she drawls.

My disbelieving eyes do a double take and my heart takes off racing as I scramble to locate my pen while repeating over and over so I won't forget, *Michelina Coidavid, Michelina Coidavid, Michelina Coidavid.*

"*Con mucho gus–,*" says the younger woman, suddenly stopping. "Sorry, I mean, "with pleasure."

Her aunt, emitting a nervous laugh, explains, "Michelina's just left Madrid after six years doing modeling for Versace."

Hastily, I scribble her name on my newspaper, which I fail to notice is now draped across my croissant.

"How nice," comments Magda, her tone of voice belying envy over the younger woman's perfect figure.

Looking up, I find I have been observed. Michelina Coidavid stares at me through alert brown eyes, one eyebrow arched over her questioning smile.

Heat rises up my shirt collar. I can feel my face color as I return her gaze with an awkward smile and a feeble attempt to take refuge behind my newspaper. However, as I lift up the *Times* I am confronted by a large translucent grease spot, which is then followed by an audible giggle.

Lowering the paper, I meet my tormentor's eyes, which sparkle with mirth as she tries to suppress her laughter by covering her mouth with her hand.

Willingly, I acknowledge my hapless state with a shrug and a grin. Suddenly the aunt turns toward me and gives me a wilting Monopoly glare that says, "do not pass go, do not collect $200, go directly to jail!"

Abandoning my croissant and eye contact with the woman's niece, I fold up my soiled newspaper with its vital information, leave my table and head for the exit. My path takes me directly behind Michelina Coidavid's chair and as I pass, she quickly glances up at me and gives me her own radiant Monopoly smile, which I interpret as "a get out jail free pass and let's resume play."

All the way to the library my mind spins with image and recollection. Before I leave New Orleans, I vow to meet this gorgeous woman.

At the New Orleans Public Library I stare at the microfilm screen while scrolling through month after month of *The Times-Picayune* for 1970. I have trouble concentrating for my thoughts keep wandering back to my encounter with Michelina Coidavid. Then just as I'm about to take a coffee break from the monotony of staring at moving reels of film, I hit pay dirt.

"Gruesome Murder in the Marigny

New Orleans, May 17,

> *Shortly after dawn yesterday morning New Orleans Police, responding to a call from neighbors, found the nude decapitated body of thirty eight-year old Marie Louise Roi, wife of Haitian artist, Robert Roi in the bedroom of their shotgun double in the Fauberg-Marigny. Police report that Mr. Roi is missing along with more than fifty of his paintings which were slated for an exhibit next month at the New Orleans Center for Creative Art.*
> *Police found the couple's daughter, Michelina, age six, in the care of neighbors. Suffering shock, she was taken to Charity Hospital for observation.* Police are at a loss to explain the murder and they are asking anyone with any information about the crime or the whereabouts of Robert Roi to contact them immediately. *Mr. Roi is described as a Haitian mulatto immigrant, age 42, approximately 6 feet tall, 175 pounds with dark brown eyes, long black hair tied at the back, and a full beard. A tattoo of a serpent is imprinted on his upper left fore arm."*

Having learned the first name of Robert Roi's daughter, Michelina, I'm also excited by the possibility that the woman I saw at Croissant D'Or is the same one I'm looking for. Surely it can't be the same woman; it's too much of a coincidence, besides she had an entirely different last name. Anyway Michelina is a fairly common French name and there must be hundreds of New Orleans women of French origin with a similar first name.

Though I have details about the crime I still haven't found any information that can lead me to Robert Roi's daughter so I continue my search in the hope of finding a follow up article. My effort soon pays off. There is a second article dated May 19, 1970. It states that the police are looking for a gray or tan Volkswagon van with Florida license plates last seen by a neighbor leaving the Roi murder scene at approximately four A.M. the morning of May 16th. "Three men sitting in the van's front seat all wore dark glasses and as it was pitch dark, I remember thinking they looked suspicious," said an unidentified witness. A spokesman for the NOPD speculated that the murder might have occurred in the course of Mr. Roi's abduction by Haitian political extremists. The spokesman went on to describe Roi's artistic work as highly critical of the Haitian Government under the Duvalier regime. Dramatic paintings by Diego Rivera of suffering peasants and of Pablo Picasso's massacre victims of *Guernica* flash through my mind.

Next, I comb through the obituaries, seeking information about Mrs. Roi's funeral arrangements. I locate the notice and name immediately jumps out at me. Mrs. Roi's sister's name is Marie Teresa Coidavid!

Collecting my notes, I rush to the library's information desk and ask for a telephone directory.

CHAPTER 4

I t's the following morning, another hazy, hot and humid day in the Big Easy whose monotony is broken only by a sudden rain shower. Temporarily it brings a modicum of relief then just as quickly the atmosphere turns into a sauna. Hemingway and I walk back into the Marigny looking for 2220 Royal Street which turns out to be a Victorian shotgun double painted yellow with light green shutters, yellow gingerbread trim and two polished mahogany doors. The charmingly maintained house looks as though it's been airlifted from the Caribbean and relocated in New Orleans. The house reminds me of an article I had once read in a travel magazine, which said the "shotgun" originated in Haiti and was so named because it was long and slender like the barrel of a shotgun. There is a popular misconception it went on to add that the name originated from the act of firing a shotgun through the front door where the pellets would traverse the length of the house and exit the back door without hitting anything. Knowing how shotgun pellets disperse I'd rather not be in the way should anyone try to test that theory.

I ring the doorbell and in a moment lace curtains part on the other side of the glass set into the front door. Surprised dark brown eyes under arched brows stare back at me. Then the fabric swings closed like the shutters of a camera and the door opens. Michelina Coidavid greets me with an amused smile of recognition. I'm sure she thinks I've tracked her down to ask her out. "Can I help you?" she says, tossing her head to free several strands of black hair that have strayed onto freshly applied lip-gloss.

"I'm Peter Grant, Ms. Coidavid. I've come from New York City to New Orleans to show you a manuscript that a friend of mine wrote. It's a biography of an artist named Robert Roi. Is he your father?"

As I proffer the envelope containing the manuscript, she turns as white as an oyster cracker and recoils from the manuscript, putting both hands out as if to prevent it from coming closer. "There must be some mistake," she says, starting to close the door, but a sudden movement at her feet catches her attention. She looks down to see Hemingway sniffing her bare feet.

"Aye, *perrito!*" she exclaims, letting go of the door, which once more swings open.

Pulling pull back on Hemingway's leash, I force him to sit on his haunches. He glares at me, annoyed that I've jerked him backward by his harness.

"Goodness, I nearly closed the door on him!" Abruptly she squats down to Hemingway's level and he bounds to his feet, his tail wagging furiously. She slowly extends her hand to Hemingway, palm up and lets him sniff her fingers before she pets him. Obviously she's been around small dogs and knows how easily intimidated they can be. "What an adorable little Yorkie. What's his name?" she asks, looking up at me with that same lovely smile that caught my attention at the café.

"Hemingway," I tell her, my heart racing. *God, she is really beautiful.*

Rising effortlessly she says, "I'm sorry. Your mention of Robert Roi as my father caught me by surprise. I didn't mean to be rude. Actually I thought you were here to ask me out."

"Since you mentioned it, would you consider having dinner with me?"

"I might. Look, why don't you come inside and we'll talk about it."

"Sure." Picking up Hemingway, I step into a foyer with highly polished wide board cypress flooring that is brightly illuminated by sun streaming through a large oval window halfway up a staircase to a second floor.

As Michelina closes the door behind me she says, "Anyone with such a wonderful little dog must be a nice person."

"Thank you, I resemble that remark."

She laughs. "I like a confident man. Follow me, won't you? We'll have a chat on the back patio. Would you care for a glass of iced tea?"

"Only if you're having one."

"I am. How about some water for Hemingway?"

"He only drinks Evian."

Michelina gives her head a toss and laughs again. "Me too, though my aunt swears by New Orleans tap water."

"Doesn't it come out of the Mississippi?" I'm suddenly conscious of a sweet musky aroma emanating from star-gazer lilies in a Chinese celadon vase atop an antique drop leaf table by the staircase.

"Yes, there are chemical plants and refineries from here all the way to Baton Rouge which is why I won't drink tap water," she explains, leading me through an arched doorway into a huge parlor the entire width of the ten meter foot shotgun and about thirteen meters long. Fans twirl from the four-meter tall ceiling. An eclectic mix of antique and Caribbean furniture occupies the floor space, tastefully arranged around a large free standing brick fireplace in the center of the room. Sculpted wooden statues, mostly Haitian heads and a few Cuban akana wood nudes stand on tables and on the walls hang numerous colorful Haitian folk art paintings along with two metallic sculptures over the fireplace. The latter are most likely the work of Haitian artist George Liautaud who cut out fanciful silhouettes from the tops and sides of used fifty-five gallon oil drums. On the mantelpiece below the Liautaud's a squat porcine Voodoo sculpture catches my attention.

"That's Zobop, the hairless pig," comments Michelina, who notices my interest. "Haitian peasants believe Zobop will devour them if they stray from their houses after dark."

I examine it up close while Michelina patiently waits for me to follow her.

"Sorry," I blush, "my curiosity got the better of me."

"That's the second time I've made you blush," she teases. "Look around all you like. I'll be in the kitchen."

"Later maybe. It's an art gallery in here."

"The room's a bit too cluttered for my taste," she observes, gracefully stepping through another archway that leads into a dining room. Once inside I pause again to examine a large oil painting in the center of the room. The painting is on board and bears the signature of Andre Pierre. It is a portrait of the sinister Baron Samedi, Voodoo caretaker of the dead. He stands in the foreground and behind him is a luridly lush green jungle teeming with birds, snakes and monkeys. His attire is that of an undertaker in a black cutaway with gray striped pants. And on his head is his signature black stovepipe hat with a grinning human skull painted on its crown. The grin on the Baron's face reminds me of a hyena.

"That's quite a startling picture."

"Not exactly what I'd prefer in my dining room," groans Michelina. "Which is why I like eating in the kitchen." I follow her into the pantry where she removes two glasses from the cupboard.

"You seem to know a good bit about Haitian art," she says, walking toward the refrigerator.

"My friend, Selwyn Podmore, who wrote your father's biography was for many years the leading authority on Haitian art."

Opening the refrigerator and taking out a pitcher of iced tea she replies, "I believe I've heard auntie mention his name. I think we may have one of his art books in the study."

As Michelina pours two glasses of tea I look around the modern kitchen with its cozy breakfast area beside French doors set into the rear wall. They lead out onto an outdoor patio with a magnificent magnolia tree with huge dark green leaves so shiny they look as though they have been recently polished.

Slicing a lemon, Michelina asks, "Sugar?"

"Yes, please." Beyond the broad trunk of the magnolia I notice a two-story structure on the other side of the patio. Partially obscured by tall blooming red ginger, large fronds of banana and blooming white oleander it appears deserted; its shutters are closed and its peeling clapboards overgrown with cats claw vines.

"That's papa's studio." She follows my gaze. "It was once a slave quarters that he converted into a studio." She hands me an ice tea.

Then reaching into a cabinet she removes a bowl into which she pours Evian water and sets it on the floor. "Papa painted there before he was abducted."

"I see." I now realize the house is the same one Michelina had lived as a child and where her mother had been brutally murdered and her father abducted. It makes me wonder how she can bear living here with the memory of those terrible events, but before I'm able to ask her about it I'm distracted by Hemingway's loud and eager lapping.

"He's really thirsty," says Michelina.

"He's not used to this heat and humidity, nor am I."

"After all the cold gray days I spent as a runway model in Milan and Paris, I don't really mind the heat. Shall we go out on the patio?" she says, holding a French door ajar for Hemingway and me to step outside.

Hemingway makes a beeline for the magnolia as we walk across very old bricks laid in a herringbone pattern to a set of black metal chairs decorated in an oak leaf and acorn pattern that surround a matching round glass top table. As I set my ice tea and manuscript atop the table, it cants slightly and I realize what appears to be heavy cast iron is instead something much lighter.

"I'm afraid the bricks are uneven," says Michelina, adjusting the table to prevent it from wobbling.

"What are the table and chairs made of?" I ask.

"Cast aluminum."

"Nice furniture."

"Very practical, it never needs repainting."

"My kind of furniture. I could use some for my apartment terrace in New York."

"Do you enjoy living in such a large city?" she asks.

"I do. I'm never at a loss for things to do." A sweet aroma wafts through the air and appears to emanate from small white blossoms on a vine clinging to a wooden fence enclosing one side of the property. "What is that scent?"

"Confederate jasmine."

"Lovely," I reply, turning my gaze to the magnificent magnolia tree which I can see is about fifteen meters high, its branches covered with large waxy white blossoms that have bloomed and are now beginning to wane and discolor.

"You should have seen that tree about a month ago," she says. "The flowers were magnificent."

Hemingway explores the tree's gnarled roots that protrude from the ground and lead off in several directions, under the patio, beneath the house and the property's brick boundary wall, cracked in places where it has been heaved up by the tree's roots. On the other side of the wall is the rear of a pale yellow two-story camelback, so-called because the two-story addition to the one-story house looks like a camel's hump. "Do you ever get used to living right on top of your neighbors on these narrow lots?"

"It can't be any worse than living in a New York apartment."

"*Touché*, I deserved that. At least you have trees and a garden. Cheers," I add, picking up my glass of iced tea and taking a sip.

"*Votre santé*," she responds, drinking from her glass. "It was the French surveyors who designed lots this way, very long and narrow. It was supposed to be practical, but it caused most of the French Quarter to burn twice; too many wooden structures too close together. But I'm sure you didn't come all the way from New York just to inquire about New Orleans architecture. Why is it you're so anxious for me to see this manuscript, Mr. Grant?"

"Peter, if you please."

"Fine, so long as you call me, Michelina."

"Certainly. Well, to begin, I'm an international art expert. Usually my clients hire me to authenticate and appraise paintings and other art forms, but sometimes I'm engaged to attempt to recover lost or stolen art works." Reaching into my shirt pocket, I extract a business card and hand it to her. While she examines it, I continue, "Two weeks ago a longtime friend of mine, Selwyn Podmore, the author of Robert Roi's biography, was gunned down by unknown killers on First Avenue in New York. I was by his side when he died of his wounds, which happened only minutes after we chanced to run into one another.

Just before he died Selwyn pressed his hotel key into my hand and implored me to recover his briefcase. It contained the manuscript you have in front of you."

"I'm so sorry." Michelina lays her hand on my arm in a sympathetic gesture.

"Thanks." Swallowing hard, I continue. "The biography is illustrated and contains photographs of all the works Robert Roi painted before he was abducted. He's your father, right?"

Lowering her gaze, Michelina stares at the bricks in the patio and nibbles on her lower lip, then abruptly looks up. "What makes you think I'm Robert Roi's daughter?"

"Well, for openers, you resemble him. You're your father's daughter, anyone can see that." Pulling the manuscript out of the envelope I show her a photograph of a handsome young Robert Roi slated to adorn the book's jacket cover.

She stares at the photograph and instinctively raises her hand to her face. Her eyes blink rapidly, her lower lip trembles and tears well up in her eyes. Averting her head, she chokes back her emotions. "Sorry," she murmurs.

"It's okay, I understand."

Sensing something is wrong Hemingway stands up on his hind legs, places his forepaws on Michelina's leg and looks at her anxiously.

"Hemingway?"

"He's upset because he sees you're upset."

Reaching down, she picks him up and cuddles him. "*Perro precioso,*" she says in Spanish, 'precious dog.'

"Is Robert Roi your father or not?"

"He is . . . or was. I don't know if he's alive or dead."

"I came here to find you because Selwyn thought there's a chance your father may still be alive, possibly he's still being held as a political prisoner."

"By whom?"

"The Government of Haiti, I presume."

"Will you help me find out?"

"Yes, I owe that much to Selwyn. He wanted to talk with me about Robert Roi's disappearance and a certain mysterious legacy. He was apprehensive about his safety and I know he wanted my assistance."

"I've prayed that one day I'd see my father again. If you could make that happen, I'd be forever grateful." Beginning to lose her composure again, Michelina abruptly excuses herself and goes inside the house.

Reaching down, I pick up Hemingway. "It's all right," I reassure him. Seeing someone grow upset makes Hemingway nervous. He reacts by trembling and insists I hold him until he stops. When he calms down I set him down on the patio, pick up my iced tea, and sip at it until Michelina returns.

Perfectly composed, she smiles and sits down beside me. Crossing her lovely long legs she gives me a brave smile. "I'm sorry, I couldn't help getting teary eyed. Papa's photograph got to me."

"No apologies necessary." Standing on his hind legs, Hemingway paws at Michelina. She glances down, picks him up and pets him while he settles contentedly into her lap. "What a sweet dog you are," she says to a contented canine.

I'm envious, but manage to ask, "is this your father's house?"

"No. It's always belonged to my Aunt Teresa. When we came here from Port au Prince auntie insisted we make it our home."

"You all lived together?"

"No, just us; auntie lived nearby in another house she owned.

"Why do you use Coidavid as your surname instead of Roi?"

"It was my mother's maiden name. After her death I went to live with Aunt Teresa. She insisted I use Coidavid because she was worried that the people who killed my mother and abducted my father might come back looking for me."

"That makes sense. When did you and your aunt move into this house?"

"About two years after Papa's disappearance. No one wanted to rent or buy this house because my mother had been murdered here."

"That's usually the case everywhere, unless it's a New York City rent controlled apartment."

"Why, because they're in such great demand?"

"I'll say they are. Most people would kill to have one, because all rents were frozen at pre World War II levels and they haven't changed since."

"My goodness, I never heard about that when I lived in New York."

"It's New York's best kept secret."

"Well anyway, after auntie unsuccessfully tried to sell this house she finally gave up and completely renovated it with the money she got from selling her own home."

"Weren't you upset, having to live with all the terrible memories associated with the house?"

"I was at first, but my aunt convinced me to confront my demons and overcome them. You'll probably laugh at this, but before we moved in she hired a voodoo priestess and we watched as she exorcized the bad spirits from the house. For the first few months I remember having nightmares and at other times I imagined hearing strange noises that frightened me. Eventually, though, I developed a kind of spiritual bond with my dead mother and the house itself, after which living here didn't bother me anymore."

"I think you were exceptionally brave."

"I don't know about that. My problem was not being able to vent my grief. I suppose the shock of seeing my mother's dismembered body kept me from releasing it, but once that event began to fade in my memory I was finally able to weep and relieve my pain."

"Michelina, what can you tell me about your family genealogy?"

"Quite a lot actually. My mother's family came from Cape Haitian. We were descendent from African slaves that were set free and second generation French Colonials born in Haiti, known as Creoles."

"Your family were Mulattos?"

"Correct, light skinned members of the Haitian minority that are commonly referred to as *High Yellow* or *The Elite,* so called because of their education and wealth. Most of my family were highly educated professionals who over time became comfortably wealthy, and until Papa Doc came to power Mulattos had been Haiti's de-facto government. The president, usually a black descendent of slaves, was a figurehead."

"Like President Paul Magloire?"

"Exactly, The Senate and House which were controlled by Mulattos officially ran the country. A number of Senators and their elegant wives were close friends of our family."

"Selwyn often regaled me with descriptions of Haitian Mulatto women. He spoke glowingly of their great beauty, describing them as unusually tall, incredibly elegant and aloof, and certainly among the most sensual women anywhere in the world."

"I agree with Selwyn. My mother was as he described, tall, slender and strikingly beautiful. Aunt Teresa was also a beauty when she was a young woman; though she was much shorter, and prone to putting on weight as she aged."

"Did your Aunt Teresa ever marry?"

"No. For many years she had a live-in boyfriend, a Haitian businessman who traveled back and forth from Haiti. They were together until I was a teenager. He was my surrogate father. I called him Uncle August. He was fairly well off, got auntie started in the catering business and helped her expand it into a very successful bakery enterprise. Then one day he packed his bags, returned to Haiti and never came back. I suspected all along that he probably had a wife there."

"When was that?"

"In the fall of 1979."

"Tell me about him."

"He was an extremely good-looking black man, very disciplined but with a highly enigmatic personality. At times he could be outgoing and fun. He was always quite considerate and generous, but on some occasions he could be introverted, stern, and unapproachable. He was by nature competitive and very impatient. Oh, yes, and he was a fanatic about neatness and his personal appearance."

"In what way?"

"He wore very expensive clothes that had been impeccably tailored to fit him. He was like a peacock or a soldier in his military dress. Along with his obsession for clothes he had this bizarre habit, wearing gold-rimmed sunglasses with dark lenses both day and night."

"Why?"

"I don't think he wanted anyone to look him in the eyes. With all his pompousness, I think he felt insecure, and by hiding behind dark glasses he couldn't be intimidated. In spite of his eccentricities he was always kind to me. He read me stories, took me to the movies, bought me presents and clothing, and he was very generous to me on my birthdays and on holidays."

"What was his last name?"

"Funny you should ask me that. I don't remember if I ever knew it. Auntie would know, of course, assuming you could make her to talk about him, though I doubt she will. After he left her, auntie acted as though he'd never existed, but, frankly, I think he broke her heart."

"That's too bad. You mentioned your aunt had a catering business?"

"Yes, Crescent City Caterers. It's auntie's whole life. Though she lives very modestly, she's made a fortune from it. The company has over two hundred employees, a fleet of delivery vans, three food service kitchens and a large bakery."

"Really, do you have an interest in the business?"

"Auntie won't let me near the place. She told me my face and figure were my fortune."

"I won't argue with that assessment," I grin.

"All body and no brains is that what you think?" she says, her eyebrow arching over a wilting glare.

"No, that's not what I think." I'm hoping to extricate myself from a most awkward moment. "I happen to think that you are a highly intelligent woman who is blessed with extraordinary beauty."

"Really?" She breaks into a lovely smile.

"Yes . . . and . . . I'd be willing to wager you've got an advanced degree of some kind."

"An MBA from Columbia University."

"Ah-ha, so that's why you were living in New York."

"Yes, college and modeling; it was my life for six years. I hope to go back to graduate school one day and get my doctorate in Human Resource Management."

"I'm impressed."

"It's simple really, after a few years one gets a bit long in the tooth for modeling and I'd like to have a meaningful career in corporate life."

"I'm sure you will. Now, tell me what happened to your family when Papa Doc became president of Haiti?"

"Fine, but first you need to know a little background on Duvalier. He was from a wretchedly poor peasant family, black descendants of impoverished African slaves. He overcame a desperate struggle to become a medical doctor, but was so embittered by class distinction and the wealth and privileges of the Mulatto *Elite* that he turned to politics instead. His avowed purpose, so he maintained, was to improve the lot of the peasants who constitute ninety percent of the nation's population. They supported him at the ballot box and once elected he wrested control of the legislature from the Mulatto *Elite* by sheer terror. This task fell to the notorious Ton-ton Macoutes, whom Papa Doc organized and dispatched to terrorize influential mulattos and their families. Those who weren't killed or imprisoned were driven into exile. After they were no longer a threat, he created a virtual dictatorship. However, the killing never stopped. Papa Doc was paranoid about his personal safety and he eliminated anyone whom he even vaguely perceived as a threat to himself or his regime."

"I take it you father became a target?"

"Eventually. You must remember, my father was also a poor black man of the peasant class. As a struggling artist he was overlooked although he knew Duvalier for what he really was, a betrayer of his own people and a cruel and blood thirsty tyrant. Then one day a Ton-ton Macoutes leader saw some of papa's work in a Port au Prince art gallery and told Duvalier that papa's paintings were not art but political statements critical of the regime. That was when we were forced to flee from Haiti."

"When was that?"

"1967, I was three years old. I can still remember watching our house going up in flames. Papa set fire to it to keep his work from falling into the hands of Duvalier's henchmen. We fled to St. Marc where papa paid a fisherman nearly all our money to take us to Florida aboard his boat."

"I learned a great deal about your father from Selwyn's manuscript. When you read it, I'd appreciate knowing if there's anything in it you think needs editing?"

"Sure, but —" Michelina pauses to pick up her glass and take a drink of iced tea, "Remember, I was only six years old when he was kidnapped."

"I understand, just do your best. Do you think I might have a look at your father's studio."

"I'm sorry but my Aunt has it locked up and she won't allow anyone inside."

"Were you ever . . .?"

"Once when I was a teenager. I remember it was totally vacant except for a few boxes containing papa's brushes and art supplies and an old easel, nothing more. Do you really think there's a chance my papa could still be alive?"

"Anything's possible, but look here, I need you to read this manuscript so we can discuss whether it's worth the effort to go to Haiti and try to find him. Bear in mind it's going to be dangerous and there's a strong possibility we might fail. And there's one more consideration, trying to uncover the mysterious legacy your father left you."

"I'll read the manuscript tonight, I promise."

"Great. Now, Hemingway and I best be running along," and with that I rise from my chair.

"Hemingway is precious, how long have you had him?"

"About two months now."

"And what convinced you take on the care of a dog in a busy city like New York?"

"My wife gave him to me—"

"I didn't realize you were married."

"Neither did I."

"Oh dear, I hope I haven't broached anything unpleasant."

"Actually you haven't. Claire left me, but before she left for India she gave me Hemingway as a going away present."

"So you're separated?"

"Permanently, I dare say and it's for the best. We had a dreadful love-hate relationship," I admit and bend over to attach Hemingway's leash to his harness.

"Come, let me walk you to the front door."

"*Avec plasir, mademoiselle.*"

"With pleasure, is fifty dollars extra," laughs Michelina. "Please phone me in the morning?" she asks, opening the front door."

"Certainly and would you like to have dinner with me?"

"Why not," she says, smiling. "you're fair game and I've already fallen in love with your dog."

CHAPTER 5

On the way back to our French Quarter flat I pick up a copy of the *New York Times* from a dispensing machine. The front page is a litany of world unrest including an article on sanctions imposed on Haiti as the result of an incident involving the downing of a U.S. Army helicopter and the death of its crewmen by a surface to air missile. "Looks like we need to read this," I tell Hemingway who looks up at me and wags his tail.

While Hemingway trots toward his water bowl, I sink into the sofa and begin reading. The *Times* reports that the United States Ambassador to Haiti has been recalled for consultations while President Bush has imposed trade sanctions on Haiti for what he terms an act of bold aggression and murder. A U. S. Army "Huey" helicopter has been shot down by a shoulder fired surface to air missile near the Haitian border with the Dominican Republic with the tragic loss of all three of its crewmen. Haitian President Jean Claude Baptiste claims the helicopter was unmarked and had violated Haitian airspace. Quoting his Commanding General, Clement Augustine, the president says, "We believed the unmarked aircraft to be yet another cross-border provocation by the armed forces of the Dominican Republic. Their intent was to scout out campsites of Haitian migrant workers whom they intended to abduct and force into slave labor inside the Dominican Republic. Under such circumstance I felt entirely justified ordering my soldiers to fire upon the aircraft. While it is regrettable that three North Americans were killed in this incident we still do not know their names, their official status and the reason they violated our airspace in an *unmarked* helicopter."

"This is going to make travel to Haiti a bit dicey," I say out loud to Hemingway whose ears perk up immediately. "Hmmm, best I phone my old friend Douglas Christie and get a briefing."

Douglas and I had met on a Long Island beach fifteen years earlier at the Club at Point of Woods on Fire Island. At the time he purported to be employed by The International Rescue Committee, an international organization that provides medical assistance to citizens of foreign countries who are casualties of war, famine or other catastrophic events. Returning from one of his excursions to Pakistan, ostensibly to provide medical care for wounded Afghan Freedom Fighters, he had invited Claire and I to accompany him to a dinner with certain Mujahedeen leaders in a lower west-side New York apartment building. From the second we walked into the building basement Claire was uncomfortable. "Good God, Douglas, who are these bearded men standing around in turbans with automatic weapons and hand grenades?"

"The tribal chieftain's body guards," he told her. "Don't worry they're all friends."

Turning to me, Claire whispered, "You told me Douglas arranged medical assistance to wounded Afghan civilians."

"That's what he told me," I whispered back.

"He lied to you. I don't like this; these people are suspicious of us. I can feel their hostility."

"Relax Claire, Douglas is cool, you can bet your undies on that."

"I never wear undies," she snarled. "You know how I feel about panty lines. Please get me out of here, now," she implored.

Claire feigned a sudden illness and we left. In the taxi on the way back uptown Claire adamantly announced to me, "Your pal Douglas may work for The International Rescue Committee, but I'll bet he's a spook for the CIA."

I was later able to confirm that fact when I visited Douglas in a New York Hospital where he was supposedly recovering from an automobile accident. I could tell by the nature of his wounds that they had most likely come from shrapnel so I confronted him. As expected, he refused to admit he was CIA, but he did allow that a Russian helicopter gun-ship had blown his jeep out from under him and his Afghani driver as they raced toward the safety of the Pakistan border. The mere fact he had been ambushed inside Afghanistan was sufficient evidence to convince me of his CIA credentials.

"Douglas Christy here."

"Douglas, Peter Grant calling."

"How are you my friend?"

"Hanging in as they say."

"Everything all right?"

"Not really. Claire and I have split again, but this time it's permanent."

"I'm sorry, Anita will be also."

"Yes, well Claire's off to India, to study tantric yoga or some such nonsense."

"I see. I trust she's not being duped by one of those charlatan gurus or whatever those chaps call themselves."

"Me too. Anyway . . . Douglas, I'm phoning you from New Orleans."

"Ahhh, the Big Easy."

"Right and I'm thinking about taking a trip to Haiti."

"Are you indeed?"

I could hear concern in Douglas's voice. "I take it you're not too keen on the idea?"

"Well you know how it is with these third world nations, all kinds of problems, economic, political, and right on down the list."

"But is it safe?"

"That depends."

"On what?"

"On the purpose of your visit."

"I need to find a missing person."

"A business trip then."

"Of course. I need to know what to expect from the top down."

"As you may know the chief honcho is Jean-Claude Bertrand, quasi educator and lawyer, black as an eight-ball, a tall, gaunt chap who wears horned-rimmed glasses with lenses as thick as a champagne bottle. He speaks in a high pitched, erratic voice. He's the epitome of a nervous intellectual. He spent years in exile in New York and Washington D.C. where he wormed his way into the good graces of the Chairman of the Senate Foreign Relations Committee."

"Thairgood Russell."

"The very same. The Senator is sympathetic and can't seem to provide enough foreign aid for President Bertrand in spite of his inept and corrupt administration and a suspected link to drug trafficking.

"Sounds ominous."

"Wait until you hear about who's really the power behind the throne."

"And who might that be?"

"General Clement Augustine. He's the true boss man in Haiti. Baptiste is merely his puppet. The general trusts no one and he keeps Baptiste in line with iron-fisted control over the army, his own hand-picked elite palace guard, and intimidation by a murderous group of former Ton-ton Macoutes who are blindly loyal to the general. I'm told the general guarantees Baptist's cooperation by holding his older half-brother a hostage. It was the General who hand-picked the exiled Baptiste to campaign for the presidency because the United States Government had thrown its political and financial support behind the scholarly-looking lawyer whom the long-suffering peasants came to revere as a national icon. Baptiste's idealism, his fiery oratory and his assurances of better times ahead for the world's poorest nation rallied the nation around him. But for all his rhetoric, Baptiste is simply an idealist and an ineffectual dreamer."

"So the General engineered Baptiste's return to Haiti with the promise of the presidency and full support of the military."

"Correct."

"Anything else?"

"Well there are a number of rough fellows who surround General Augustine. You need to avoid them.

"Can you name names?"

"Probably not but one does come to mind, watch out for Hector Baguidy, he's the general's hatchet man and meaner than a wolverine."

"And there's the usual State Department's traveler's advisory which suggests you vacation elsewhere in the Caribbean."

"I've got urgent business there."

"And so you have."

"Forewarned?"

"Well, as best I can, Peter."

"Right, and now what can you tell me about the helicopter incident?"

"Nyet, nada, nothing."

"Classified?"

"Right."

"Is the DEA in on it?"

"No comment."

"Fair enough, I won't pursue it further."

"Best you don't."

"Thanks, Douglas I appreciate your help.

"No problem. If you need additional assistance with the landscape I could recommend someone for you to talk with. Of course I'll need to identify who you are and secure her okay, but that shouldn't present any problem.

"I could use a briefing on a fortress known as the Citadelle near Cape Haitain. It seems to be the focal point of my quest."

"That's right up her alley. I'll be back to you, Peter.

"Ring me on my cell phone, okay?"

"Roger that, Bye, Peter."

CHAPTER 6

Michelina agrees to look after Hemingway, while I fly to New York. Striding into the offices of The United Nations Educational, Scientific and Cultural Organization (UNESCO), I stop before the desk of a pudgy brown-haired receptionist who wears far too much perfume and enough pancake makeup to cover a ski slope. Smiling, I ask politely to see Douglas's contact, London Bridges.

"Do you have an appointment?" she asks.

"No, but tell her Peter Grant is here." She picks up the telephone receiver and carefully punches buttons on the phone to avoid chipping her nails which are painted an iridescent-green imbedded with tiny silver stars.

"Ms. Bridges, I have a gentleman here to see you, a Mr. Peter . . . ."

"Grant," I interject.

"Grant," she repeats . . . "Yes, I'll send him in. Down the hall, third office on the left, sir."

London Bridges, a soft, curvy blonde of medium height with an oval face and large liquid blue eyes, leans casually against the doorframe to her office. She smiles as I walk toward her.

"I'm pleased to meet you," she says in a British accent and extends her hand in greeting.

"Me too," I reply, shaking her hand.

"Douglas, sings your praises; he finds you quite fascinating."

I smile politely and follow her inside her office all the while noticing her casual use of Douglas' first name and wondering how intimately acquainted they may be. "You and Douglas old friends?" I inquire, as she directs me toward a chair in front of her desk and takes the other chair facing me.

"Lovers . . . before Anita of course," she smiles and crosses her shapely tanned legs.

"Of course," I mutter, fascinated not only by her frankness, but her heavy breasts that threaten to burst through her crimson silk blouse.

"Douglas told me you'd like a briefing on Henry Christophe's nineteenth century fortress in Haiti?"

"Yes."

"It's curious because you're only the second inquiry I've ever had, both this month."

"The other chap, was he by chance an older fellow, bit frayed around the collar, white-haired, also a Brit?"

"He was, indeed. You know him then?"

"He's an old friend of mine, Selwyn Podmore."

"I gathered some information for him but he never rang me back."

"Unfortunately, he died very suddenly."

"I'm so sorry."

"Me too, we were good friends for many years. Do you mind my asking what it was he requested?"

"Architectural drawings of the fortress, the ones that were prepared for UNESCO and the World Heritage Committee.

"Ahh, so the Citadelle is a world monument.

"Yes," she answers, re-crossing her legs. "As you probably already know, the Citadelle is the second largest fortress in the world."

"After the Tower of London!"

"Right you are," she smiles. "The Citadelle covers about 10,000 square meters, with walls up to 40 meters high and 4 meters thick. It stands at an elevation of about 900 meters atop a mountain peak called Bonnet-a-l'Eveque or the Bishops Miter, which overlooks the town of Milot about 50 kilometers inland from Cape Haitian. Its builder, Henry Christophe, was illiterate so it's believed he hired French architects to design the fortress. The construction, mostly by forced labor, took sixteen years, from 1804 to 1820 and is said to have involved upwards of thirty thousand men with an immense loss of human life."

"On my," I groan, looking suitably appalled.

"Grim I know, but the terrain on which it sits is quite foreboding, sheer cliffs on three sides of the fortress and presently the only egress is a four kilometer steeply winding, cobbled and dirt trail. The fortress has 365 cannons and mortars."

"One for every day of the year," I muse. "Are all those cannons still inside the Citadelle?"

"Your friend asked the same question. I told him that with the exception of one abandoned cannon near the base of the fort and some field mortars that lie between the fort's rear wall and the powder magazine everything else is within the walls. Frankly, I can't fathom anyone trying to make off with any of the armament as those cannons weigh anywhere from one to three tons apiece."

"Makes sense. I've heard the fortress' construction is somewhat unique."

"Yes, because the peak of the mountain is its actual foundation. Stone masons laid down hewed blocks of stone that they cemented to the natural rock with mortar made of limestone, molasses and of all things, cow's blood!"

"Good heavens!" I exclaim. "Can you imagine what an appalling number of livestock must have been slaughtered?"

"I'd rather not, thank you very much," she responds with a visible shudder. "I suppose that's one reason I chose to be a vegetarian."

"Also do you know how many soldiers were sequestered inside the Citadelle?"

"Approximately five-thousand."

"And did anyone ever attack the fortress?"

"The French considered it, but they demurred. As the story goes, they sent a general up to the fortress under a flag of truce to assess the garrison's strength. Christophe had his five thousand soldiers march in review before the French general and as they disappeared from view they quickly changed uniforms and reappeared twice. After estimating Christophe had fifteen thousand soldiers in the fortress the French general advised his superiors that the Citadelle was impregnable."

"Since the Citadelle was never involved in a major battle why did the United Nations decide to designate it a World Monument?"

"For a number of reasons." First, it's the largest fortress in North America, often referred to as the eighth wonder of the modern world. Second, it's a stunning architectural achievement undertaken by an illiterate black despot. And lastly, it's an enduring symbol of the resolve of the Haitian people to forever rid themselves of the yoke of slavery."

"You're a virtual encyclopedia, Ms. Bridges. Is there anything else you'd care to share with me?"

"Well," she hesitates. "Christophe supposedly hid a vast treasure inside the fortress. A number of large iron-strapped strong boxes were found empty inside a vault in the fortress, but no treasure has ever been found. I imagine it's probably just a myth. Oh yes, and there's an important historical footnote I should tell you. When the slave revolt of 1791 finally succeeded in driving the French out of Saint Domingue in 1802, Napoleon was forced not only to abandon the richest island in the Caribbean, but it brought an end to his dream of North American conquest. The loss of Haiti was the reason he agreed to sell the Louisiana Territory to the United States."

"And quite a real estate bargain that turned out to be."

"I daresay," she replies, with a toss of her head and a hearty laugh, "four cents an acre!"

"Ms. Bridges can I borrow the set of plans to the fortress that you were going to provide to Selwyn?

"As I never heard from Mr. Podmore I recently loaned them to an architect from the International Monument Foundation who has already left for Haiti to see what additional restoration work is needed at the Citadelle."

"When is he due back?"

"Not for several months, I'm afraid."

"And there are no duplicate copies available?"

"Unfortunately our only other copy is now in Geneva under review."

"Can you give me the fellow's name from the IMF?"

"Certainly, Juan Martinez Guilarte."

"Spanish?"

"Actually he's an Isleno from Louisiana.

"Isleno?"

"It's a Spanish term for immigrant descendents of Canary Islanders.

"Can you describe him? I'll try to look him up when I'm in Haiti."

"He's rather a young Elvis look-a-like; find a hoard of drooling females and he'll be in their midst."

"That handsome?"

"So gorgeous, I daresay, it's unfair to the opposite sex."

I break out laughing. "Age?"

"About thirty-five. The day he picked up the plans he invited me to lunch. I can't remember the name of the restaurant much less what I ordered. I was totally smitten by him, terrible thing to admit, I know."

"I venture to say his companion was equally as attractive," I say with conviction.

"Very kind of you," she blushes. "Oh my, the time, I must be off. I've a briefing in three minutes . . . how to stem the looting of sacred temples in Malaysia."

"Thanks for your time, Ms. Bridges."

"Bye and good luck, Mr. Grant."

CHAPTER 7

After arriving back in New Orleans, I shower, change clothes then telephone Michelina who invites me to walk over to her house. When I arrive, she ushers me inside and unexpectedly busses me on the cheek. Once more I see she's barefoot, dressed now in jeans and a short bright orange tee shirt that leaves her midriff bare and reveals a small sexy gold ring suspended from her navel. Hemingway stands behind her looking up at me, his tail wagging happily. As I bend down to pet him he leaps into my arms. "Miss me?" I ask, but he squirms out of my grasp and runs to Michelina. "You see, he belongs to me now," she laughs.

I notice the usual sparkle is gone from her eyes and she looks tired. "Don't tell me . . . you and Hemingway partied all night."

"No, I just didn't sleep very well. Yesterday, while I was out walking Hemingway, Auntie found Selwyn's manuscript."

"And she read it?"

"Scanned it and last night over dinner she gave me a lot of grief about it."

"What did she say?"

"She doesn't think the manuscript should be published. She says it will only cause trouble for us." Michelina reaches for my hand and leads me into the library where she playfully pushes me onto the sofa then perches on the arm with her bare feet on my knees.

"Michelina," I say looking up at her, "neither you nor your aunt's name are mentioned anywhere in the manuscript."

Hemingway who has followed us, jumps up on the opposite end of the sofa and curls up.

"I know Peter, but she's convinced bad people will come after us and they'll find us just the way you did."

"What do you think?"

"I've got mixed feelings, Peter. On the one hand I'd love to see this book in print because it's an exquisite tribute to my father. On the other hand, I'm also a bit apprehensive."

"How do you feel about the prospect of looking for your father?"

"Frightened, but it's something we must do. As long as there's any hope he's alive, I have to try to find him."

"I thought you'd feel that way. Now look, regarding the book, maybe I can get publication delayed until we get back from Haiti."

"That's another matter. Auntie is adamant that I not go to Haiti. She thinks if I go I'll never come back alive."

"Why?"

"She's convinced the Ton-ton Macoutes killed my father after they destroyed all his work. She thinks that all I will do is arouse suspicion among those still living who might be culpable and I'll end up just like my father."

"But no one knows for certain whether your father is dead or alive."

"That's what I told auntie and I said I have to find out one way or the other."

"And she doesn't understand?"

"More like she refuses to understand."

"Would you like me to talk to her."

"Sure, if you want. I'll ask her, but she may refuse. "She's at work, I assume. When does she get home?"

"She said she'd be late, which means around seven. She said she had to stop by *Gris-Gris* on the way home. It's a store she owns in the Quarter that sells occult paraphernalia imported from Haiti. Auntie's involved in a number of business ventures, but, as I told you, she doesn't discuss that with me."

"Well that's her prerogative."

"Peter, there's something in Selwyn's manuscript I don't understand."

"What's that?"

"Well, toward the end of the text, he makes a strange statement and I want to know what you think it means?"

"Whoever finds 'Romulo' will uncover the true genius of Robert Roi."

After studying the words I comment, "I don't know. All I can tell you it's probably Selwyn's cryptic way of providing us with a clue to something your father wants us to find, his whereabouts or his legacy to you, perhaps. Bear in mind that Selwyn was once MI-5 branch of British Intelligence and for years he and I played mind games with each other. I suspect that was the reason he was so keen for me to have his manuscript."

"So he's saying that somewhere in Haiti there is a person named Romulo?"

"Not necessarily a person, it could be an object of some kind, for example the name of a boat. Judging from what Selwyn tells us about your father's obsession for painting the Citadelle in so many of his works he indicates we should focus on the fortress."

"I understand. I can't help thinking the name reminds me of the twins Romulus and Remus, the founders of Rome, who supposedly abandoned by their parents and then discovered and raised by a female wolf."

"Romulo may very well be of Latin origin, though in this case I just don't know except I never underestimate Selwyn. That clever devil is probably looking down on us this very moment and having a jolly good chuckle over our dilemma."

Michelina laughs and sticks a foot in my ribs. "Selwyn's a big tease, like me, she says, wiggling her toes."

"Hey, that tickles." Laughing, I squirm away from her foot.

Michelina stands. "You and Hemingway have to go now. I've got to do something with my hair before this evening."

"Going out?" I ask standing up beside her.

"Yes," she answers leaning in close to me, her eyes locked on mine. "Where?"

"Your place." she answers, her lips approaching me like a butterfly looking for a place to land. Then suddenly she flits away, does a charming pirouette and announces, "I've decided to take you up on your dinner invitation."

"Have you?"

"Yes, I'll be at your place at seven-thirty."

"Lovely."

"Now you two run along so I can look ravishing tonight."

"Let's go Hemingway." Pulling his leash from my trouser pocket, I clip it onto his harness.

It's early evening. I relax on my balcony with a glass of wine and gaze toward the west where I see clouds billow into massive thunderheads that threaten to blot out the setting sun. A breeze blows from the southwest and as it begins to stiffen it brings with it welcome relief from the intense heat of the day. I sip on my sauvignon-blanc and enjoy the refreshing breeze as I wait for Michelina's arrival.

Interrupting my reverie, Hemingway spots Michelina rounding the corner from Chartres Street and he barks, letting her know she's under observation. Looking up at him she breaks into a grin and waves. Putting my glass down, I stand up and wave back, dwelling on how pretty she looks in a flowered frock that appears to have a life of its own as it swirls about her body in the breeze. Holding a shopping bag in front of her, she prevents the dress from flying up around her waist.

I walk over to the cast iron railing to find her standing below me in the middle of the street. Expectantly she looks up at me. Leaning out, I drop her the gate key nestled inside an old woolen sock and as it falls, swooping and fluttering like a wounded pigeon, she nimbly adjusts her feet like a baseball player awaiting a fly ball and snatches it out of the air.

"Bravo!" I shout.

Giving me a smug glance that says, "*I'll bet you thought I wouldn't catch it,*" *she* steps spryly between two parked cars and disappears.

Scampering indoors, Hemingway dashes to the stairway and panting with excitement stands at the top looking down. Expectant, we listen to the sound of her footsteps as she ascends the three flights of stairs to my flat. Ears cocked, Hemingway peers intently down the stairs, his head swiveling first one way and then the other as Michelina turns corners. Then, as she rounds the last turn and comes into view, he charges down the stairway to greet her. Putting down the shopping bag, she catches him as he leaps into her arms.

"Hey, remember me," I protest.

Carrying Hemingway and her shopping bag to the top of the stairs, she sets them both on the floor, then straightens up to give me a kiss on the cheek.

"I think I vaguely remember you," she chides, handing me the shopping bag, "A present."

"That's not really necessary, but thank you." Taking Michelina by the arm I escort her into the apartment. "Are you ready for a glass of wine?"

"Stop," she cries. Reaching into the shopping bag she pulls out an icy bottle of champagne. "Surprise!"

"Cristal! It's my favorite; how did you know?"

"Hemingway told me. Just kidding," she says, wiping her lip print from my cheek with her forefinger. "I made an educated guess."

"Well done. I suppose we'll have to drink it."

"Lovely idea."

"What else have you got in this bag?"

"Your house key," she says smugly, "the manuscript and another bottle of champagne."

"My goodness what are we celebrating?"

"Whatever we like."

With Hemingway at her heels Michelina looks around the studio while I pop the cork on the first bottle of champagne. Pouring two glasses, I carry them into the bedroom where Hemingway stands atop the bed watching Michelina as she walks around the room gazing at Antonio Verdi's oils paintings and sketches which hang floor to ceiling. Some are pictures of Venice's imposing statuary, ornate church facades, graceful bridges, and decorative water wells and others are water scenes of gondolas and stately *palazzi* along the Grand Canal as well as commercial watercraft lining the Zattere. Dispersed among the scenic artwork are several oil portraits of nude women.

"Do you like his work?" I ask, handing her a glass of champagne.

"I do. I've attended several of his exhibits and I think he's quite gifted. *Salud.* She smiles, touching her glass to mine.

"Cheers."

"That's certainly beguiling nude hanging above the head of your bed."

"She reminds me a little of you."

"Peter." Her jaw drops. "How can you say that? you've never seen *me* naked."

"Hope springs eternal," I reply.

"I'll ignore that. And for your information I happen to know her," she says, inclining her head toward the painting. "We attended Ursuline Academy together. She was the prettiest girl in school and very popular with the boys. Already twice married and divorced and to think I envied her."

"Why? I think you're far more beautiful."

"Thanks, but back then you wouldn't. I was a late bloomer. Anyway, no one ever offered to paint me, nude or otherwise."

"As a model haven't you ever posed for a photographer?"

"Not in the buff. I mean I'm not a prude about my body, but I don't take my clothes off for money. That's not to say I haven't been photographed in some pretty risqué designer clothes and along with other women I've had to change in front of men, most of whom are gay and couldn't care less, but that's all part of the job."

"What would you say if I offered to sketch you? I'm pretty adept at figure drawing."

"Maybe after I've had enough bubbly," she taunts, then drains her glass. "May I have a refill?"

"Of course."

In the kitchen, I refill Michelina's glass, top off mine and return to find her sitting cross-legged on the bed with Hemingway across her lap. Her pumps lie on the floor where she's kicked them off. "I'm sure you made plans for us to go somewhere for dinner," she says taking her glass from me, "but would you object if we just hung out here and ordered something in."

"Not at all, besides it looks to me like we're going to get rain."

"Thanks, I like being casual, drinking champagne, listening to some music and providing I get to keep my clothes on, maybe I'll let you draw me."

"Sure, come on into the studio. For starters suppose I sketch your face in profile."

"Okay," she agrees. She gets off the bed with her champagne in hand and follows me. I find a pad and a stick of charcoal and have her sit on a stool under a battery of track lights. "How's this," she says, arching her back to sit tall.

"Good, now raise your chin a bit and don't move. If you get tired just let me know."

After about twenty minutes, Michelina calls for time. She eases down from the stool and walks behind me. Resting her hands on my shoulders, she gazes at my sketchpad. "Peter, you really *can* draw." She hugs me around the neck. With her cheek pressed against mine, she asks, "Am I really that glamorous?"

"Better actually."

"I'm impressed. Where did you learn to draw like this?"

"When I was a prep school senior I was allowed to take courses at the Whitney School of Art in New Haven. One of my teachers was John Whitticomb the portrait artist and illustrator. Before photography took over magazine covers he illustrated fashion magazines with the faces of very beautiful women with wonderful sparkling eyes. It became his trademark and I learned his technique."

"I'm not familiar with him; I guess he was a bit before my time."

"Do me a favor, hop up on the stool, five more minutes and I'm done. Then the picture's yours to keep."

"Thank you, I love it," she says, planting a soft kiss on my cheek.

On the balcony we kill off the first bottle of champagne while listening to the rich Baroque strains of Vivaldi's *Four Seasons* and Corelli sonatas that usher forth from the stereo. The wind abates and we sit in sultry darkness visible to one another only by the glow of candlelight and an occasional flash of distant heat lightning. Hemingway, at the far end of the balcony, peers into the street below and all at once begins barking.

"Why is he carrying on?" asks Michelina, noticing his agitation.

"I don't know." Getting up, I walk to where Hemingway has his head between the struts of the cast iron railing and below on the opposite side of the street I see a man half concealed in a doorway lighting a cigar with a lighter. The flame briefly illuminates a thin black face partially obscured beneath a shabby Panama hat.

For some reason the flame from the man's lighter has upset Hemingway, but when it goes out he stops barking and walks away grumbling. Turning around to speak to Michelina, I'm startled to find her standing behind me staring over my shoulder at the shadowy figure in the doorway who is only visible by the glow from his cigar when he draws on it. I hear her breath catch and I intuitively feel she's alarmed.

"What's wrong?"

"Peter, I know this is a strange thing to ask, but would you mind if I stayed with you tonight. Auntie went to Biloxi on business and I don't want to be home by myself."

"Of course I don't mind, but what's troubling you?"

"Maybe it's my imagination, but on the way over here this evening I believe that black man in the Panama hat down there is the same man who followed me here."

"Why would he do that?"

"I don't know, but I'm afraid of him." She takes me by the arm, turns me around, and suddenly she's in my arms, her head snuggled against my chest. "Thank you," she murmurs.

"No problem, now how about we order something to eat before we get totally wasted?" Putting an arm protectively around her shoulder I walk her back to the table.

"I'd love a Caesar salad and a pepperoni pizza . . . and more champagne?" she asks, giving me a lopsided grin.

"Okay, I'll phone in an order if you'll open the other bottle of champagne."

"Yes, and I'll set the table too."

"Let's go Hemingway. We're going inside."

Just as I finish ordering, I hear a loud pop, a gush of liquid and a string of invectives in Spanish or Italian, I'm not sure which. Hanging up the receiver, I shout, "What's wrong?"

Michelina stands in the kitchen doorway, a look of surprise washing across her face. The front of her dress is soaking wet, nearly translucent as it clings to her breasts and stomach. Her expression turns forlorn and I can't help laugh as I declaim in Italian, "*Accidente!*"

"It's not funny, damn it, the champagne exploded and this is a really expensive hand printed dress."

"I'm sorry . . . I apologize. In the bathroom on the back of the door you'll find my paisley bathrobe. Take off your dress off and put on my robe."

On the balcony, sitting across from me in my silk robe, Michelina shakes hot pepper flakes on a slice of pizza, which she then ravenously attacks. "I adore pizza," she gushes, "but I hardly ever eat it."

"With all those hot pepper flakes your stomach must feel like you swallowed Mount Etna."

"The spicier the better," she laughs, reaching for her champagne glass, which causes the robe to separate and reveal some splendid topography.

Catching my gaze, she looks down. Her free hand reaches down and quickly pulls the robe together. "Sorry, that was unintentional."

"And just as I was beginning to enjoy the view," I tease.

Michelina turns scarlet.

"Now who's blushing?"

"Me," she smiles. I'm sorry I lost my cool when the champagne got all over my dress. I bet I looked pretty pathetic."

"Like a half-drowned orphan," I chuckle. "Anyway, let's change the subject. Would you mind telling me something about your mother and your Aunt Teresa."

"Of course not, but first I have to tell you Auntie Teresa doesn't want to meet with you."

"Oh, . . . and did she give a reason?"

"She wouldn't say."

"That's disappointing."

Michelina reaches across the table and takes my hand. "Don't let it bother you; I told you my aunt's difficult at best. Ready for a little family history?"

"Sure."

"Aunt Teresa was born in Cape Haitian in 1932. A year later my mother was born. They lived there until after the end of World War II, after which Aunt Teresa and my mother were sent to Paris to live with relatives. They attended school and university there until 1955 when Grandfather Coidavid was appointed Minister of Culture in President Magloire's cabinet. Instead of returning to Cape Haitian they went to their parent's new home in Petionville, a fashionable suburb overlooking Port au Prince. "Mmmmm," Michelina coos, "this pizza is fabulous, especially with champagne."

"I'm feeling pretty happy myself."

Startling Hemingway and me, Michelina suddenly jumps up from her chair, throws her hands in the air and does a fast shuffle with her feet. "eeeeeEEYOW! I feel good," she sings, aping a guttural rock voice, "da, da, da-da, da, da, dum . . . like I knew I would."

Hemingway begins barking and I crack up laughing. "Godfather of Soul!" I exclaim as Michelina sits down in her chair, her face an expressionless dead-pan.

"You are full of surprises," I laugh.

"It's just the champagne; sometimes it makes me a little wild." Now, where were we?" she says, with an impish grin.

"Petionville."

"Right, . . . well, when mother and Aunt Teresa returned from France my grandfather arranged jobs for them at the National Gallery. That's where my mother met my father. He was a struggling young artist and my grandparents weren't very pleased about their relationship, but my mother had a mind of her own and she refused to give him up. They quietly got married in 1956 and—"

"Sorry to interrupt, but when did Papa Doc become president?"

"1957. Shortly thereafter both my mother and Aunt Teresa lost their jobs to Duvalier supporters then two years later the Ton-ton-Macoutes expropriated our home and imprisoned my grandparents in Fort Demanche as enemies of the state. After that no one ever saw them again."

"I'm sorry," I say, as Michelina bites her lower lip and bows her head for a moment before she looks at me again. 'And when did your Aunt Teresa come to New Orleans?"

"The same year I was born, 1965."

"Do you know why she left Haiti?"

"She said Papa Doc had begun another round up of mulattos, stripping them of their wealth for no apparent reason other than his paranoia. So Aunt Teresa abruptly left Haiti and flew to Miami."

"She arrived here destitute?"

"No, she told me she had arranged to sell a property that my grandparents had secretly owned through a foreign corporation. The transfer of title took place in Miami and Auntie never went back to Haiti. Supposedly she received nearly a half-million dollars from a French developer who later built a posh resort on the property known as Habitation LeClerc."

"I know it. It was a highly touted exotic jet-set resort in the southeast suburbs of Port au Prince. A walled in collection of private cottages each with its own swimming pool and a main house, which was said to have once been owned by Pauline Bonaparte who, while her husband General Le Clerk was fighting the slave uprising, was purportedly engaging in all kinds of sexually deviant behavior."

"You've stayed there?" asks Michelina, wide-eyed.

"For a week with a former girl-friend. It was a gorgeous place, a lot of rich and handsome European guests with their stunning mistresses and girl-friends, plenty of nudity and lots of mischief. I was a bit too square for that crowd."

"If you say so," she says with a modicum of skepticism evinced by an arched eyebrow.

"Was your aunt seeing anyone during this time?"

"Uncle August. He went to Miami with her and later they moved to New Orleans."

"You never thought it odd that Duvalier allowed your Aunt and her boy friend to leave Haiti?"

"No. Papa Doc was anxious to expel the mulatto *Elite,* so he encouraged them to leave. She and Uncle August were part of the exodus."

"Then not long after that you and your parents had to flee."

"In 1969. On Christmas day we waded ashore in North Miami with nothing but a few dollars and the clothes on our backs."

"How much of that do you remember as a child?"

"I'll never forget the boat ride to Miami; I was so seasick I was afraid I wasn't going to die." Picking up the champagne bottle, she refills our glasses. "Anyway, here I am," she says as we touch glasses together. "*Salud!*"

"*Salud, y amor y pesetas . . . y tiempo para . . . sacarlo,*" I offer.

Michelina's eyes get big and she nearly gags on her champagne as she bursts into gales of laughter.

"What did I say?"

"That's hilarious," she comments, laying her forehead on the table, her entire body shaking with laughter.

"Tell me."

Looking up at me, she fights to keep a straight face. "You said . . . health, love and wealth and . . . and time to take it out!"

"What?"

"You mixed up your verbs. You said, "*sacarlo* instead of gustarlo!"

"Oh my God."

With her chin in her hands, elbows on the table she keeps laughing until tears run down her cheeks.

Her laugh is so infectious that even though I'm horribly embarrassed, I can't help laughing myself.

Michelina gets up. Lurching around the table, she plops down in my lap, throws her arms around my neck and hugs me. I can feel the tears on her cheek as she giggles, "Peter, you're priceless."

"And for everything else there's MasterCard!"

"Stop!" she cries, nearly hysterical. "I can't laugh any more or I'll be sick. Tossing her head back, she looks into my eyes and suddenly our lips come together. Rain begins to pelt down. Hemingway barks. We're kissing. Everything is happening at once.

"Hey, it's raining!" I mutter, still in lip contact.

"I don't care," she mutters back. Holding my face in her hands she looks lovingly into my eyes. "From now on I'm only speaking Spanish with you," she says. Grinning, she leans over and kisses me long and hard while the rain continues to drench us.

Finally we separate and scurry inside the studio where Hemingway anxiously awaits.

Soaking wet, Michelina grins at me. Reaching out she takes me by the hand and leads me into the bedroom.

"But you said—."

"A woman's prerogative," she interrupts me. Turning to face me, she strips off the wet robe and alluringly naked she begins unbuttoning my shirt. "*Tu* quiero, *Pedro*," she murmurs.

I understand her perfectly.

Within seconds we lie naked on the bed, rolling around, hands and feet splayed every which way, touching, caressing, playing, kissing, licking, nipping. Then suddenly she's astride me. Inserting me inside her, she rides me wildly, my face a willing prisoner between firm breasts whose taut nipples seek pleasure between my lips and teeth.

Michelina lies next to me; her head rests on my shoulder. "I like making love with you, she murmurs.

"*Yo tambien,*" I answer back, glancing at my digital clock radio on the nightstand. A red digital readout stares back at me, 11:46 P.M. "You know it's nearly midnight?"

"Which reminds me if we were in Madrid, we'd have just finished dinner and we'd be going dancing."

"Really."

"Uh-huh, but I think I enjoyed this more," she teases.

"What motivated your sudden urge?" I ask.

"The champagne . . . no that's not altogether true. You're fun to be with and God do you make me laugh. I guess I'm pretty attracted to you."

"*Egualmente!*"

Michelina shifts to her side and props her head up with her arm and stares at me. "You're Spanish keeps improving by the minute."

"I'm trying to impress you."

"You just did, *amor*, nearly through the mattress after *you* rolled over on top of *me*," she grins. I think you like making love to me."

"Correction, I *love* making love with you and I must confess that ever since that day I first laid eyes on you in Croissant D'Or I wanted you. I love your sensual figure with your silky olive skin, your dark intelligent eyes and your voluptuous mouth and your charming dimples. Then there are some small delights like the beauty marks on your chin and your right ankle and that sexy navel with its tiny gold ring and—.

"Peter, never would I have guessed you'd be such an observant lover."

"Quiet, you're interrupting my train of thought. Besides having absolutely fabulous legs, gorgeous breasts and a fantastic derriere, you're smart, well spoken, worldly, fascinating and delightful to be with . . . and as I'm just now finding out, you're somewhat impulsive, and occasionally unpredictable."

"But am I good in bed?" she laughs, gently raking my stomach with her long fingernails.

"Exquisite."

"Maybe it's my mulatto blood."

"That's a turn on."

"I'm curious. You don't have to answer if you don't want to Peter, but have you ever made love to a black woman before?"

"Yes, an elegant African-American woman I dated in Paris. After dinner one evening at Tallievant she invited me up to her apartment where we got pretty drunk on brandy and decided to play "strip" backgammon, you know for items of each other's clothing instead of for money."

"To see who gets naked first?" she giggles.

"Right, I lost big time and then one thing led to another—"

"And you ended up in her bed," she interrupts. "Did you enjoy her?"

"I guess I must have, but to be honest I was pretty blitzed and I really don't remember a lot about that night."

"So, you had a one night stand," she says, running her fingernails in lazy circles across my chest.

"I guess you could call it that, but we continue to be good friends. When I'm in Paris we often have lunch or dinner together."

"So you're not the least bit embarrassed to be seen out in the company of a black woman."

"No."

"I know this sounds silly, Peter, but I sometimes get sensitive about my mulatto heritage."

"Michelina?"

"Yes?" she looks inquisitively into my eyes.

"I form attachments with the big head not the little one, besides I already knew from Selwyn's manuscript that you were a mulatto."

"I'm glad you said that," she says, kissing me very gently. "It's nice to know that I'm appreciated for more than just a nice body."

"Peter, tell me something. When I caused you to blush that morning in Croissant D'Or what was it you were doing?"

"Writing your name down on my *New York Times.*"

"I thought so and you know I got goose bumps wondering if you'd actually try to find me."

"I was determined."

"I'm glad you were persistent.

"Me too."

"I'm sleepy. Roll over and hold me?"

"*Por cierto si, senorita.*"

CHAPTER 8

I awake to screams and barking. Leaping out of bed, I dash through the studio into the hallway and collide with Michelina who has her hands to her face, screaming hysterically at a bloody animal carcass that dangles from a rope affixed to the top of my entry door frame. Its throat and belly have been slit open and blood and entrails spill out onto the floor. Trailing his leash Hemingway stands at the top of the staircase. He lunges and barks at an unknown intruder whose escaping footsteps I can hear echo up the staircase. Guiding Michelina back into the studio, I sit her down on a sofa and run back out the door to prevent Hemingway from following the perpetrator. Snatching him up in my arms, I start back inside the apartment. At my feet are ritual symbols drawn in chalk on the hallway's wooden floor. Carefully stepping over them I enter the apartment and close the front door. On the sofa Michelina trembles uncontrollably and looks up at me with wide-eyed fear. "It's all right, Michelina," I assure her. "Whoever it is has left. Did you get a look at him?"

Ye . . . ye . . . Yes," she stutters, "that same black man . . . the one who followed me. How could someone do such a horrible thing?"

"I don't know, but I have to call the police. What were you doing in the entryway?"

"I was taking Hemingway for a walk so you could sleep. I opened the door and . . . *Madre de Dios,* that dead animal was right in my face, blood and intestines everywhere and the man was in the stairwell, grinning at me through the balustrade."

"He left a drawing on the floor, voodoo symbols I think. I have to take a picture of them.

"I'll call the police," says Michelina. "You get your camera."

"You sure?"

"Yes." Taking Hemingway from me she goes to the phone, while I retrieve my digital camera and go into the hallway to take images of the symbols scrawled across the floorboards. As I'm finishing I hear in the distance the strident wail of approaching sirens.

I'm at the street door holding open the gate when two blue and whites from New Orleans Police Department's 8th District screech to a halt. Leaving their car lights flashing, officers bail out of their cars and run toward me. The lead officer, a handsome, burly man in his mid-thirties with black wavy hair signals me to move aside as he and his backup officer reach the open gate. "Where's the assailant?" asks the lead cop, a weapon in one hand, a radio in the other.

"Got away," I tell him. "Tall skinny black guy with a Panama hat on his head."

"And your name, sir?"

"Peter Grant, I'm the tenant."

"Anyone injured?" asks the second officer.

"No, but my girlfriend's a basket case."

"Any other details on the perp?"

"He's about six feet tall, maybe a hundred fifty pounds, age I'd guess maybe forty to forty-five, dark pants and shirt, that's it."

"Officers Micheu and Burns requesting backup on a code 63," says the burly officer into his radio. "Request a lower French Quarter canvas for a tall, thin black male on foot, about six feet tall, hundred fifty pounds, dark clothing wearing a Panama hat, ten-four."

"I'm officer Micheu," says the burly cop sticking out his hand. And this is Officer Burns," he nods toward the other officer.

"How you doin'?" says officer Burns, a slender, serious looking man with close-cropped hair also in his mid-thirties.

"I'm all right."

"What floor you live on?" asks Micheu.

"Third."

"We'll lead the way, you follow us," Micheu says to me, his hand resting atop his gun which he's returned to its holster.

"Okay."

I follow them up three flights. As Micheu turns the corner at the top of the stairs, he sees the bloody carcass hanging from the doorframe, the entrails, blood and symbols on the floor. "Jesus, what the fuck is this?"

"Looks like some kind of weird ritual, Santeria shit.... Oh, pardon me ma'am, says Officer Burns, ashen faced as he notices Michelina approaching the door from the hallway with Hemingway struggling in her arms, growling at the policemen.

"Does he bite?" asks Officer Burns, looking anxious.

"No, he's just protective."

"It's those feisty little ones that sneak up from behind and take a chunk out of you when you least expect it. Me, I prefer Dobermans and German Shepherds, there's no guesswork about what they're all about, you know what I'm—"

"Exactly what happened here?" asks officer Micheu interrupting his fellow officer.

"Officers, this is Michelina Coidavid.

"Hello," she mutters.

"Officer Micheu, ma'am, and this is Officer Burns. "What happened here?"

"I was taking Peter's dog for a walk. When I opened the door I saw this grotesque sight and there was a black man wearing a Panama hat grinning at me through the balustrade. Then he ran down the stairs."

"Okay, but why you two?"

"I don't know," I tell them, "Ms Coidavid thinks the man may have followed her here last evening."

"I'll need details," Officer Micheu explains.

"Meanwhile, I'm calling the crime lab unit to come to look for evidence and the SPCA to remove that carcass."

It's early afternoon before the SPCA and the NOPD's Crime Laboratory Unit leave. As soon as they're gone, I mop up the hallway to remove the bloodstains and the chalk impressions. I have the impression the police lab thinks the matter is nothing more than a cruel practical joke. Since no one has been injured and there's little in the way of property damage I expect they will relegate the matter to the back burner unless they get lucky and pick up the perpetrator on the street.

Michelina remains edgy and with good reason. I'm convinced that the man we saw from the balcony is the same one who performed this sadistic ritual after he was certain Michelina was spending the night. It's undoubtedly a warning of some kind meant to frighten both of us. I resolve to find out what the Voodoo symbolism means.

Later that afternoon, I leave Michelina asleep in my bed with Hemingway curled up beside her. I walk over to Dauphine Street between Royal and Bourbon where I had noticed a sign advertising The New Orleans Voodoo Museum. It appears to not only to draw curious tourists, but serious devotees of the occult, same as those who visit Vampire author, Anne Rice's home, or search ancient walled- in cemeteries for renowned Voodoo Queen, Marie Laveau'a vault.

Entering the dimly lit Voodoo museum which reeks of incense, I speak to an employee a heavy black woman with long dreadlocks rearranging objects on what she tells me is an African Petwo altar. Despite the eerie surroundings the woman has a kind face. Judging by her earth-colored African robes, a leather pouch hanging from around her neck and a stack of silver snake bracelets on her arms she appears to be well versed in Voodoo practices. When I ask her about Voodoo rituals, she attempts to sell me tickets to an upcoming street ceremony, which I decline. Producing my digital camera I ask her to view the screen and see if she can identify any of the images.

"Ahhhh," she sighs, with a solemn nod of her large head as she squints at the tiny illuminated screen, "A veve."

"What's that?"

"A ritual drawing usually created on bare earth using ground cornmeal. It's done to invoke a loa or spirit."

"Do you know which spirit this is?"

"Of course," she says abruptly. Turning to face me, her eyes narrow to slits and she says in a low gruff voice, "This is not meant for you, only for a woman."

"This was just left on my doorstep for a lady friend of mine."

"Tell her to be careful." she takes my arm in a vice-like grip.

"Why?"

"Because this is the veve of Gran Brigit," she remarks, her eyes narrowing, her forehead sprouting furrows like a newly ploughed field.

"What does it mean?"

"That your friend is in grave danger. Gran Brigit is the female symbol of death. She's the counterpart of Baron Samedi, the undertaker!"

"And there's more." I flip to a picture of the disembowcled goat.

The woman stares at the new image, her eyes as big as butter plates. Releasing her grip on my arm, she gasps, "Enough!" Backing away from me, she nimbly turns and steps behind a thick black curtain.

Recovering from her surprise exit, I try following her through the curtain and a doorway that leads into a long narrow dimly lighted corridor. But there is no sign of her. She's vanished.

Stunned, I walk out of the museum into blinding sunlight. My eyes smart as they adjust; a weekly sensation I recall as a youngster when I emerged from the ritual Saturday afternoon movie matinee.

Still unnerved by the black woman's comments I walk into the apartment where Hemingway greets me with his usual enthusiasm, dancing around on his hind legs. Turning he scampers into the bedroom where I join him on the edge of the bed beside Michelina. When I lean over and kiss her on the forehead her eyes flutter open and she gives me a lazy smile. Then she stretches, arching her back and throwing her arms over her head.

"Did you have a nice nap?"

"Un-huh."

"Can I get you anything?"

"No thanks. Where have you been?"

"The Voodoo Museum."

"And?"

"That ugly business with the goat and the symbols. It's a warning . . . directed at you."

"What kind of warning?"

"The woman I spoke to at the museum said it was a death threat. Who besides your aunt knows about Selwyn's manuscript?"

"No one I know of."

"Then your aunt must have told someone about it."

"But who?" Michelina sits up in bed, enticingly bare to the waist, which provokes a familiar stirring within me as I watch her thrust out her chest and yawn. "Excuse me," she smiles, aware that I'm ogling her lovely breasts.

I can hardly keep my hands off her, but restrain myself. "By my count only five people knew about the manuscript, you, me, my secretary, Selwyn's publisher and your aunt."

"I doubt my aunt would tell anyone. Don't you remember she told me how concerned she was about our safety if the manuscript got published."

"I do."

"Perhaps the publisher told someone."

"It's possible. I've never met him personally and I haven't a clue as to how he might go about promoting a book that he's about to publish."

"Why don't you phone him and find out before we start accusing my aunt of something she may not have done."

"Fair enough. I'll phone him." Leaving the bedroom, I go into the studio, pick up my cell phone and call New York information. After obtaining his number, I phone his office.

"Hello, may I speak with Arthur Melrose, please."

"Whom shall I say is calling?"

"Peter Grant, calling from New Orleans."

"I'm Betty Koch, Mr. Grant, Mr. Melrose's assistant. We've spoken before."

"Of course, how are you?"

"Not very well, I'm afraid."

Suddenly I get a sinking feeling in the pit of my stomach.

"I'm sorry to tell you this Mr. Grant, but Mr. Melrose passed away very suddenly."

"I'm dreadfully sorry."

"Terrible news, I know. Day before yesterday he had an apparent heart attack during a breakfast meeting at the St. Regis. After the police notified his family they phoned me. As you can imagine everyone in the office is in shock."

"Yes I expect they are. Again, I'm sorry Ms. Koch. What's going to happen now?"

"You mean about funeral arrangements?"

"Yes, that and the plans for Selwyn's book?"

"I haven't heard from Mr. Melrose's family about the arrangements, but when I do I'll be happy to phone you if you'll leave me your number. As for the book, everything is on hold. We are a small press as you know and it will be up to Mr. Melrose's family and their attorney to decide our future course."

"Pardon my asking this question, but is Mr. Podmore's manuscript in your possession?"

"Why yes. It's locked up in our safe."

"Good. Please tell Mr. Melrose's family I'm sorry for their loss."

"That's kind of you, Mr. Grant." Her voice trails off to a whimper, which probably means she's crying.

"Why the serious face?" asks Michelina, now dressed in her flowered frock, as I terminate the call by closing my cell phone's cover.

"You won't believe this, Selwyn's publisher had a heart attack and died."

Michelina's face suddenly drains of color as she realizes her aunt is the one who has betrayed her trust.

"You still want to go and check out the Citadelle?" I ask.

"Now more than ever," she responds, the fingers of her hands clenched as fists.

CHAPTER 9

As the sun casts its last golden hues over Haiti's vast Plain Du Nord and darkness descends swiftly in the mountains of Hispaniola we begin our descent into Cape Haitian. Distant mountains to the east turn a somber purple and barely visible atop a dusky crag is a stark silhouette framed against the indigo sky. It is an alien object, which for a few transitory moments reflects the ebbing twilight in a curious hue of silvery burnt umber. Its shape resembles an ark bereft of both mast and sail, but it is not the famed biblical vessel of Noah, nor is it perched atop the legendary Mount Ararat of ancient millennia. This monolithic-looking structure never designed nor built to traverse oceans is instead a solitary sentinel to both tyranny and freedom. By the time the plane's tires grip the runway the distant angular silhouette is black against the night sky, a desolate and foreboding arsenal of fear that strikes terror into those either brave enough or foolish enough to approach it. For contained within its massive stone walls lie dark secrets, accounts of suffering and brutality, tales of horror, and stories of restless spirits that roam its battlements. And from within its damp recesses emanate eerie noises that reverberate among neighboring mountain summits, settle into fog shrouded valleys and unnerve an already superstitious populace.

As we taxi toward the terminal I muse about how Haitians believe the ghost of Henry Christophe nightly stalks it's battlements as he futilely seeks atonement for his despicable deeds. Legends abound how he had his architect murdered, thrown from atop the fortress to prevent him from revealing the whereabouts of the hidden treasure room and the secret staircase that insured escape in the event of mutiny. Another grim tale involves Christophe ordering a platoon of his Royal Dahomets to march off the parapet. Beside him a stood a French general who watched in horror as the hapless victims tumbled to their deaths, 1500 meters to the rocks below. It was a cruel display of loyalty and discipline meant to dissuade any attack on the Citadelle. Other stories involve countless slave laborers who were murdered on Christophe's orders for failing to complete their tasks in the erection of the fortress. So it is not only Christophe's restless ghost that Haitians fear in the stygian darkness of the crumbling bastion above, but it is the near certainty of encountering other supernatural rulers of the underworld, loas, vampires and zombies.

By day, the fortress is benign. It is simply a tourist attraction of imposing magnitude, hard to reach, difficult to comprehend in its reclusive setting, and confusing. An enigmatic jumble of sun drenched courtyards and buildings, musty gun galleries and ammunition rooms, vast barracks and battlements, empty cisterns and storerooms, vacant royal chambers and hollow ballrooms, rubble strewn stairwells, secret vaults and dank dungeons. Inside this daunting stronghold we will begin our search for evidence that we believe will unlock the mystery of Robert Roi's disappearance.

The long trip from Miami to Port au Prince, through immigration and customs, thence on to Le Cap as Cape Haitian is commonly called, takes its toll on us. Michelina, Hemingway and I arrive exhausted at the Hotel Mount Joli, where we promptly tumble into bed and fall asleep.

The following morning after waking and realizing we will most likely have bright sunshine all day we decide to spend our first day at the beach. After breakfast we change into swimming suits and take the hotel shuttle van to Cormier Plage, a picturesque expanse of white sand beach at the tip of the north coast of Cape Haitian. As it is off-season there are only a few tourists, mostly Canadians judging by their airline bags, white imprinted with telltale red maple leafs. Close to the site where we stake our claim in the sand is a stunningly beautiful black woman wearing sunglasses and little else save a miniscule gold thong.

She sits cross-legged on a beach towel beside a khaki nap sack and beach bag while intently fixing her gaze at the ocean. Clearly she lacks any inhibitions, brazenly flaunting her sleekly sensuous body.

"Wow," exclaims Michelina, "Look Peter, . . . see the black woman at one o'clock."

"I know. Already I have sun-burned eyeballs."

"Her name's Danielle," whisper's Michelina, "she's General Agustin's mistress."

"How do you know that?" I ask, astonished by Michelina's information.

"Gabrielle told me."

"Who?"

"Our cab driver from the airport. Surely you remember him?"

"Oh yeah, the tall skinny guy with the bad breath who wants to be our new best friend and drive us everywhere."

"Right. Well, while you were busy shaving I went outside the hotel to walk Hemingway and Gabrielle was there with his taxi. He walked over to me to find out if we needed him. I told him maybe tomorrow as we were only going to Cormier Plage in the hotel van. As we were talking that woman, escorted by an army major, came out the front entrance with a beach bag. They got into a black Mercedes sedan and drove off. I asked Gabrielle who she was. He told me her name was Danielle and she was the general's whore."

"He certainly didn't pull any punches."

Michelina laughs, "I don't think he likes her or the general either. Anyway, he told me the general keeps a suite in our hotel. I wonder what she's doing here all by herself."

"Maybe she's not alone, but I suspect we'll find out soon enough. Would you like to hit the water?"

"I'll do just about anything to keep you from staring at her," she says with a smirk.

"Jealous?"

"Who wouldn't be, she's drop dead gorgeous."

"All right," I say, getting to my feet. "Last one in the water is a rotten egg."

Michelina leaps to her feet, laughing and fumbling with her bikini bra. Unhooking the front, she removes it and pitches it on her towel. "When in Rome," she cries and takes off running with me in hot pursuit.

Galloping through shallow water we simultaneously dive into a breaking wave. Emerging on the other side I find Michelina beside me. Two quick strokes and her arms encircle my neck, her legs lock around my calves and she presses cool breasts against my chest. "I won," she announces.

"Would you believe a tie?"

"No way," she replies, her hand suddenly darting down the front of my bathing suit.

"Hey, no fair."

"Admit I beat you or I squeeze the family jewels . . . hard."

"Okay, you beat me."

"That's more like it," Toying with my partial erection she plants her salty lips against mine. "Mmmmmmm," she sighs, "I can't wait to fool around with you again."

"If you don't stop that, you may have to wait."

"I see." Laughing, she removes her hand from my trunks. "I have a rule Peter. I never do quickies in public." Then, looking past my head, she says, "Ah-ha, developments ashore."

I pivot around as Michelina releases my legs. With one arm draped around my neck she turns with me. "Look, Danielle has trolled up a guy."

"Sure enough, but what's he doing?"

"He's kneeling behind her, rubbing lotion on her back."

"And now he's slipped his hand around her left boob and they're laughing."

"That was fast work. Was he on the beach when we got here?"

"He was by himself in the ocean and was just getting out of the water when we ran by him."

"He's quite handsome from what I can tell."

"Considering what he's doing with his hands I don't think we'll see him on his feet any time soon." Just at that moment I get a mental flash; could that fellow possibly be Juan Guilarte? Probably not, that's too much of a coincidence.

"All this touchy-feely business is making me horny. Want to go back to the hotel and make love?"

"My dear, I thought you'd never ask."

CHAPTER 10

Gabrielle shuffles over to the towering eastern wall of the Citadelle and wearily leans back against its stones. Mopping sweat from his face with a filthy rag he's pulled from his pants pocket, he announces with a sigh, "*Nous sommes arrivés.*"

"That's obvious," I reply. "Now, tell us how we get inside?"

Pulling the rum bottle from his back pocket, Gabrielle takes a swig, wipes his mouth with the back of his hand and fixes his rheumy eyes on me. "No good for me inside, but you go around this corner, walk along the back wall and when you come to a door in the tower at the far end you enter. Up the stairs is the inner courtyard where you can look around. I will find shade and wait for you out here."

Taking Michelina's hand, I lead her around the corner along the back of the fortress. "I can't help feeling sorry for Gabrielle. Poor chap's got nothing better to do than prop himself against one of the most remarkable engineering feats in the world and get drunk."

"He's frightened by the place," she says.

"Hard for me to imagine. Doesn't he realize this fortress is nearly as important as the pyramids at Giza?"

"I think he's only concerned about existing one day at a time."

"You're right of course, but it seems a shame he doesn't realize what an awesome legacy Christophe left."

"Tell me about Christophe."

"Supposedly he was born on the island of Saint Kitts, the son of a brick mason. At about age ten he went to sea as a cabin boy on a French warship carrying troops to the American colonies to fight the

British. He later came to San Domingue as Haiti was known under French rule and settled in Cap Francais."

"Now called Cape Haitian?"

"Right. The French called Cap Francois the Paris of the Caribbean. Though Christophe couldn't read or write, he was able to find a job working for the proprietor of a small hotel where he later had a confrontation with a French officer and was forced to flee the city."

"Is that when he joined the slave rebellion?"

"Yes. he first served under Toussant L'Overature and later alongside Dessalines during the liberation of Cap Français from Rochambeau in 1801 after which Dessalines appointed him general of all Northern Haiti."

"When did Napoleon send his brother in law, General Leclerc to Haiti?"

"In 1802, along with twenty-two thousand men. After Leclerc landed he demanded Christophe's surrender, but Christophe replied by putting Cap Français to the torch, first setting fire to his own house."

"Is that really true?"

"Supposedly."

"With such a formidable army why were the French so easily defeated?" asks Michelina.

"It wasn't because of battles so much as it was Yellow Fever that depleted the French forces. General Leclerc himself died from the disease in the fall of 1802."

"And what became of his wife Pauline?"

"She escaped to the Isle de la Tortue from Port au Prince which was captured by the British who were also at war with France. The British had a powerful naval presence in the Caribbean. After capturing Port au Prince and Haiti's southern peninsula, they blockaded Cap Français. With Christophe's help they landed troops and drove the French out. Following General Rochambeau's defeat Napoleon was forced to give Saint Domingue its independence in 1804 and Dessalines became Haiti's first emperor.

"But I thought Christophe was the emperor?"

"He was, but not until 1806 when mulattos under Alexander Petion deposed Dessalines then killed him. Christophe was named to succeed him, but he served only briefly due to his own mistrust of Petion and the mulattos. Failing to defeat them in an uprising for control of Port au Prince he withdrew to northern Haiti, seceded from the Republic and in 1807 established his own empire in northern Haiti."

"Fascinating," says Michelina, her gaze now directed toward stacks of rusting cannon balls and several large bronze siege mortars lying beside a thick low stone wall enclosing a one-story building without windows. "What is that building?"

"I expect it's the fort's powder magazine. Christophe had it built outside the fort to safeguard against an accidental explosion."

Michelina's eyes scan upward toward a hill behind the powder magazine where a small square building stands. "And what's that?"

"It looks to me like an outpost where a sentry kept watch to prevent an enemy attack on the fortress from the rear. See the stone aprons and vee-shaped channels that run downhill from the sentry post?"

"Are they foot paths?"

"No. The aprons catch rainwater and the channels transport it into the Citadelle's cisterns."

"So our *Emperor Jones* thought of everything."

"With a little help from his engineers. Did you know the play, *Emperor Jones,* was about Henry Christophe?"

"You're not the only one who went to college and I excelled in my theatre course, thank you very much."

"*Mea culpa*"

"Thank you," she says with an aloof toss of her head.

I stop suddenly and reach out and place the palm of my hand against a warm block of stone in the Citadelle's wall.

"What on earth are you doing?" asks Michelina, giving me a quizzical look.

"Trying to sense the fortress's vibes," I explain. "If only these stones could talk."

"What do you suppose they'd tell us?"

"Perhaps why the natives, like Gabrielle, are so frightened of this place," I say, resuming our walk. "You saw his reaction. He's scared to death to set foot inside the fortress."

Seconds later we come upon a doorway that is built into the abutting wall of a rectangular shaped tower forming the southwest corner of the fortress." Its doorframe is without a door and we step into a dirt-floored lobby permeated by a mustiness that seems to emanate from a number of small cubicles that were probably once storerooms.

"Phew," says Michelina, what's that awful smell?"

"Mold or mildew I guess. Let's take those stairs and try to find the way to the courtyard."

We ascend to a second floor landing then take another staircase which leads to the Citadelle's main courtyard, which is bathed in sunlight so brilliant it makes us squint and sends me into a sneezing fit.

"*Salud*," Michelina keeps repeating.

"*Gracias*," I keep answering.

"My God, Peter, I had no idea this place was so big. How are we ever going to explore all of it? It'll take us a week to go through this place and where do we begin to look for *Romulo?*" Chewing on her lower lip, Michelina looks at me with utter despair.

"Look, this is not impossible. The fortress is built roughly in the shape of a triangle and we can examine it in an orderly fashion. First let's go back inside the tower we just left and we'll go floor by floor to try to get a sense of the fortress's structure from bottom to top. Then we'll take the east wall to the ship's prow and return back here along the fortress's west wall.

"Okay, let's just do it," she says with determination that sounds like a slogan for Nike shoes.

When once again we return to the courtyard, we have a pretty good understanding of the fortress above the level of the interior courtyard. The turret we entered, nearly rectangular, comprises the southwest corner of the fortifications. The ground or first floor where we entered is a storage area as we had surmised. The second floor is barracks with ready access to the inner courtyard and also connects to cannon galleries that stretch along both the back or south wall and part of the west wall. On the third floor is another cannon gallery that protects the southwest corner and connects with other cannon galleries along both the south and west walls. On the fourth and final floor is yet again another cannon gallery. It protects only the southwest corner and the south wall.

During our examination on the third floor gun gallery, Michelina notices something that may help us uncover the mysterious clue that Selwyn had provided. Some of the large cannons, besides having decorated barrel reinforcement, have names etched into their breach rings. We shall have to examine each gun most of which are English, French or Spanish. Good thing I remembered to bring my flashlight; we're going to need it to be able to read the markings. The cannon seem to be our only source of writing save the graffiti scrawled on many of the fortress walls.

"See, Michelina, that didn't take long."

She looks at her wristwatch. "You're right, only an hour. Shall we try the east wall?" She is seemingly encouraged.

"Sure. Maybe we'll get lucky and find our mysterious, *Romulo*."

Grabbing my hand, she breaks into a jog and leads me diagonally across the courtyard where she had spotted a stairwell. The weathered stone steps takes us down into a gallery dimly lit and very long with a vaulted ceiling and rows of foreboding cannons in decaying wooden carriages. As we begin to walk toward the southeastern end of the gallery I hear a sound that's so familiar to me in New York City I usually tune it out.

"Is that noise what I think it is?" asks Michelina.

"A helicopter." I walk over to the nearest gun port. Looking out I see in the distance an olive-drab military chopper, a Huey, swooping upward towards us. "It's the military. They're headed our way. You stay put while I go back up the stairs and see what this is all about."

Emerging into the sunlit courtyard, I watch the craft swoop up the eastern battlements like a dragon fly and go into a hover over the ship's prow. Backing up into the shade of a wall, ropes spill out both sides of the chopper and descend toward the "ship's prow." Then five soldiers dressed in black battle dress and armed with automatic weapons, quickly slide down the ropes and disappear from view. After the ropes are dropped, the pilot gives a thumbs up signal presumably to the men below. Throwing the collective forward, he sends the craft into a steep bank that carries him over the western wall and down into a wide valley which descends all the way to the Plain du Nord. As the Huey disappears from view I race back down the stairs to tell Michelina.

She waits at the bottom of the stairs, wide-eyed with anticipation.

"That chopper just dropped off five heavily armed commandos and as near as I can tell they are somewhere on the ship's prow."

"What does that mean?"

"I don't know, but I venture to say they look all business and not terribly friendly."

"What do we do now?"

I'm about to answer her when suddenly I'm startled to see a figure emerge from the gloom at the far end of the cannon gallery.

Michelina, aware of my reaction, quickly turns her head and sees a man with dark hair, dressed in a dark blue polo shirt, jeans, cowboy boots. He wear a backpack and carries a tube like object in his hand as he walks towards us.

"Americans?" he asks.

"Yes," answers Michelina.

As he advances into the light from the stairwell I hear Michelina's breath catch, an involuntarily reaction when she thinks he seems familiar.

"Hi," he says, "I'm Juan Guilarte with the International Monument Federation."

"I'm Peter Grant and this is Michelina Coidavid. I believe you're the chap we've been looking for." I shake his outstretched hand as he acknowledges Michelina with a broad smile and a nod of his head.

"Really!"

"London Bridges at UNESCO told me you were here and I assume those are the floor plans to the fortress that you're carrying.

"I'm conducting a survey,"

"Then you're familiar with the fortress?" I ask.

"Yes, but mostly on paper."

"Good, Juan, because we have company. A military helicopter just dropped off five well armed commandos on the ship's prow. We've got to make ourselves scarce until we know what they're up to."

"I heard the chopper. I'll bet they're looking for me. I had a fling with a woman who turned out to be the live-in of some big-wig general."

Michelina, eyes dancing, glances over at me, then back to Juan. "Oh my God, then that was you on the beach at Cormier Plage with a nearly naked black woman."

"Guilty as charged," admits Juan, his face turning a shade of pink. I probably used bad judge. . .

"Juan, with those soldiers here we need to see those plans," I interrupt him.

"Sure." Unrolling pages, Juan comes to the area where we stand. "Would you mind?" He says, handing me one end while he opens out the entire page. "We're here," he says, his index finger stabbing the paper, "the third floor gun gallery along the east wall."

"Gosh Peter," says Michelina, "this place is a lot bigger and more complicated than we thought."

"Are you looking for a certain area?" asks Juan, his eyes checking out Michelina like a bar scanner in a grocery store.

"Actually we're trying to find a particular object," offers Michelina.

"So you're not tourists?"

"No, not exactly," I tell him. "Ostensibly we came here as tourists, but we're looking for a mysterious object."

Michelina glances at me again, then says to Juan, "Does the name *Romulo* mean anything to you?"

"Not off hand it doesn't." He hesitates. "Hold on, I saw some names carved into the sides of cannon carriages. One was, *Bravo!* Look over there." He points to an immense cannon in a wooden carriage that has partially collapsed due to the decaying wood and the cannon's immense weight.

Letting go the edge of the plans, I take out my flashlight and shine it across the gallery. Carved into the wooden side of the carriage is the name, *Scipion.*

"That's it!" Michelina declares, sinking her fingernails into my flesh of my arm. "We just have to find the right one." Taking the flashlight from me she runs along the gallery. "They're all named!" she shouts. Breaking into a trot, Juan and I follow.

"Michelina come back . . . the soldiers."

"Look Peter it's here, it's here," she cries out, jumping up and down, her face flushed with excitement. Facing a huge bronze cannon, its muzzle partially protruding out the gun port, she shines the flashlight on its carriage. The flashlight beam illuminates letters that look as though they might have been burned with a branding iron into the grayish colored wood of the carriage. It reads:

R-O-M-U-L-O

Michelina carefully examines the gun carriage and cannon with my flashlight, as she looks for whatever Selwyn alludes to in his manuscript. "I can't see anything that makes any sense," she says, looking more despondent than ever.

"Maybe we're not looking in the right place," offers Juan, setting his backpack and plans beside the carriage.

"I'm open to suggestions?" says Michelina.

Juan climbs atop the gun carriage, "there's a broad arrow mark and a coat of arms of George III which means this is an English naval cannon. Judging from the size and the weight mark on the first reinforce, over 6700 pounds, this baby is a twenty four pounder."

"What's that mean?" I ask.

"That it shoots a twenty-four pound cannon ball, the mother of all cannon balls. This gun would have been on the deck of one of the British navy's largest warships, a first rater as they were called."

"How do you know all this stuff?" asks Michelina.

"I'm a scuba diver," grins Juan, climbing atop the cannon. "I know a lot about these guns from diving on old shipwrecks."

"How do you suppose it got here?" Michelina asks.

"I don't have a clue, but I'll bet it was one hell of a job hauling this big monster up the mountain."

"Okay," Michelina responds, "what do these initials on this *thingy* mean?"

Juan chuckles. "That *thingy* is called a trunion. It's what supports the cannon in the gun carriage and the initials on the end of it belong to the fellow who forged this gun."

"Fascinating, but I don't know how any of this helps us," I comment.

"Well, the only other thing I can think of while I'm up here is to have a look up the bore."

"Great idea," says Michelina, grinning up at Juan.

"This isn't going to be easy, he says. One slip and I'm out the gun port . . . splat! Road pizza for vultures!"

Michelina grimaces. "That's a horrible thought, you be careful up there."

"Juan you better make this quick before we have unwanted company. What if I hook my belt around your ankle and hold onto you while you slide down the barrel and look inside?"

"Good idea."

Taking off my belt, I loop it around Juan's cowboy boot just above his ankle and pull it tight. "Is that okay?"

"As long as I don't slip out of my boot," he grins, scooting down the barrel like someone astride a horse. Leaning forward, he lies atop the barrel on his stomach and inches his way it to the gun's muzzle. "A mite hairy up here," he remarks, leaning his head over the muzzle.

Michelina turns away. "I can't watch this."

I climb atop the side of the gun carriage, wrap my belt around my fist, and holding tightly to Juan's right ankle, I brace myself, ready to haul him backward should he slip.

"See anything? I ask. "Yeah a skinny black dude, reeling down the trail. Looks like he's either drunk or crazy.

Michelina looks up at me.

"Gabrielle," we say in unison.

"Who?" asks Juan.

"Our taxi driver guide," I tell him. "He must have seen the helicopter and the soldiers and decided to take off."

Juan shines the flashlight inside the bore. "I see something inside! He exclaims.

"Can you reach it," questions Michelina, still too nervous to watch.

"I'll try," he replies. Passing the flashlight back to me he carefully inserts one arm inside the bore, while hugging the muzzle with his other arm.

I realize if he slips he'll tumble out the gun port if I'm unable to hold unto him. Breaking out in a cold sweat I hang onto him for dear life.

"Got it!" He slowly withdraws his arm. Inching backward along the gun barrel with me pulling on his foot he's finally able to turn his body diagonally across the barrel and drop down to the floor. At that moment a loud metallic clatter echoes from the end of the cannon gallery.

"Oh no," cries Michelina. "They're here."

"Follow me," Juan speaks in a hushed voice. "Walk softly and no talking." Thrusting the object in Michelina's hand he snatches up his back pack and the plans and heads for the stairs.

"It's a rock," announces Michelina.

"Quiet, put it in your pocket; we'll look at it later," I whisper as we catch up to Juan at the stairs.

As we step into the courtyard now bathed in blinding mid-day sunlight and completely devoid of any shade, Juan points to a majestic two story building with a rotunda at the north end of the courtyard. "That's the Governor General's residence, we'll hide out there." Juan begins to jog towards it as Michelina and I, hand in hand, follow behind. Dashing up the outside steps and through the main doorway we stop under the center rotunda where Juan gets his bearing then leads us down a corridor in the eastern wing to an upstairs staircase. On the second floor we enter into a large room overlooking the courtyard. "Peter, you watch the courtyard," says Juan. Make sure you're not spotted.

"Where are we?" asks Michelina.

This is supposed to be Christophe's bedroom when he stayed in the fortress. We can watch the soldiers from here and if they come our way there's a rear staircase that descends into the basement where we'll find another set of stairs that will take us deep inside the fortress."

"Juan, I see the troops entering the courtyard."

"How many are there?"

"Three, all with automatic weapons. They're moving toward the southwest corner . . . where we entered. You're right, Juan, they're checking all around. They look like they're prepared to shoot first and ask questions later."

"Then as soon as they disappear inside the tower we better get out of here. No one make a sound."

"They're entering the tower."

"Okay, let's go," commands Juan.

I motion for Michelina to follow Juan while I bring up the rear. If we're to have any chance of getting out of the fortress alive, I realize we have to put our lives in Juan's hands.

Moving quickly down the corridor to the end of the building, we take the staircase which leads down to the basement. Juan seems to know exactly where he's going and grins at us as we file through a narrow doorway and find ourselves at the far end of the same cannon gallery where we had first seen him.

"Listen up," he whispers. "Peter, I need your flashlight. We have three more flights of stairs and somewhere down there are two more soldiers. You need to be very quiet and watch your step. The stairs are steep and slippery. Also there's debris on them. I'll go first. If I hear any strange noises I'll turn off the flashlight. Stop and don't move. Any questions?"

"Are there places to hide if we run into trouble?" I ask him.

"Yes, but you have to stay close behind me. On the level below us are barracks, below that another barracks where I entered the fortress. We could go out that way, but it's on the east side and totally exposed. There's another choice. According to the plans there's a ground floor exit on the western side of the 'ship's prow'."

"And where is that?" asks Michelina.

"Three floors down, beneath the barracks floors. Storerooms and cisterns are located there."

Pulling on my shirt sleeve, Michelina says, Could we pause for a minute and have a look at the rock."

"Why not?" Juan replies, shining the flashlight on Michelina as she withdraws a smooth black stone from her jeans.

"Peter, it's been incised."

"What's it say?"

Trouve Claude Fabius Jacmel - R.R.

"R.R., Robert Roi, papa's initials," Michelina gasps. "Find Claude Fabius, but what's Jacmel?"

"An old town on the south coast of Haiti."

"Then we have to go there," Michelina asserts.

"Perhaps we best get out of here first," I suggest as Juan turns and shines the flashlight on the staircase in front of him.

"Good point." Michelina stuffs the rock back in her jean's pocket. "I'm ready."

On the floor below we descend into a large foyer. Corridors stretch out in several directions and at regular intervals there are door frames with foreboding looking dark empty rooms, the barracks. Suddenly the distant sound of laughter and voices echoes down the stairway.

"They're coming down the stairs," Juan cautions. "Hurry!"

Rushing down another flight of stone steps, we come to the lower barracks lobby where Juan herds through the first doorway on the right side of the lobby. Flattening ourselves against a dank wall in the pitch darkness of a barracks room, we join hands and wait for the commandos to file past us, but when they reach the lobby one of them breaks away from the others. Uttering something that makes his comrades laugh, he steps through the doorway where we're hiding. We hear him unzip his trousers and staring into stygian darkness he urinates.

Nearly crushing my fingers, which are interlaced with hers, Michelina draws in her breath and holds it. Against the back of my hand I feel her pulse throbbing at an alarming rate. Then, after what seems an eternity, the soldier zips up his pants and turns around to rejoin his companions who have now denied our escape through the east door by chaining and padlocking the doors to the outside. Exchanging ribald comments, the commandos joke with one another as they descend to the storage area below.

Beside me Michelina exhales as Juan steps to the doorway and scans the lobby. As the soldiers' voices fade away Michelina and I hear Juan cursing.

"What's wrong?" I whisper.

"The son of a bitch peed on my boots."

Michelina, though shaken, is unable to suppress her laughter.

"What do we do now, Juan?"

"Well, we could go back upstairs to the courtyard and risk being caught out in the open, but my gut tells me we ought to stay put until it gets dark. Maybe those Haitian soldiers will clear out."

"You sure they're Haitians?" I ask, as he turns on the flashlight.

"I was concerned they might be rebels from the Dominican Republic, but they were speaking French patois."

"If they were from the Dominican Republic they'd be speaking Spanish," adds Michelina as she reaches for the water bottle attached to Juan's backpack. Taking a drink she passes it to me. "You really think those guys are only after *you Juan?*"

"Damn straight they're after me," Juan answers. "I'm not supposed to be here. My organization requested permission to send me here, but a high-ranking general intervened and said he couldn't guarantee my safety because rebel soldiers from the Dominican Republic had been infiltrating Haiti's borders. I said to hell with it and came anyway . . . on a tourist visa."

"How did the army find out you were in the Citadelle?

"Danielle," replies Juan, the black chick I met at Cormier Plage. She must have ratted me out with the general when he got back from hunting rebels along the border."

Michelina puts her hand to her mouth and utters a nervous laugh. "Is that the story she told you so you'd think she was fair game?"

"Yeah."

"Juan, I think you're naive," scolds Michelina. "It was no accident you picked up a voluptuous Haitian general's mistress and slept with her."

"She actually picked me up. I found her sitting on my beach towel when I came out of the ocean."

"There you are, case closed."

"So Danielle knew you were coming here?" I ask.

"I guess I must have told her." Juan gives both of us a sheepish look.

"I hope your tryst was worth it, Juan, because your indiscretion may cost us our lives."

"I'm sorry. I was infatuated and got carried away. I guess I wasn't very discreet."

"Understatement of the year!" Michelina shrugs.

Juan runs his fingers through his dark curly hair and stares at the floor, obviously embarrassed. Suddenly he looks up and grins. "Look, I promise I'll get us out of here."

"Promises, promises." Michelina's, voice is tinged with sarcasm. "If those commandos were sent here to find you I'm convinced it has nothing to do with you screwing their commanding officer's mistress."

"Why do you say that?" I ask her.

"Peter," she answers, irritably, "no general would ever admit something that demeaning to his subordinates."

"Then why are they here?"

"I sure as hell don't know," interjects Juan.

"Did it occur to either of you that this general may be protecting a dark secret, something he doesn't want anyone to know about?" questions Michelina.

"No," mutters Juan, as I remain silent.

"What's so important about this place the general allows tourists limited access, but doesn't want people like Juan or us here?"

"The logical answer is that he's got something going on here that he doesn't want anyone to know about," I reply.

"Exactly, but what?" "Maybe he's storing weapons for a military coup," Juan offers.

"How about drugs?" says Michelina.

"Bingo!" I exclaim, "I think Michelina's hit on it. The general is using this place as a warehouse for drug trafficking. He's moving stuff in and out at night when he knows no Haitian will ever come near this place. He's not concerned about tourists, because they're only here in daylight and escorted by guides who for safety reasons discourage tourists from prowling around by themselves. As for someone like Juan, who has a valid reason to come here, the general puts him off by citing his government's inability to assure anyone's safety."

"Michelina," Juan says, "you're probably right but whatever it is we're in deep shit."

"And clearly expendable," Michelina adds. "If the general's men kill us the rebels will get the blame. So what's our program now, Juan?"

"I agree with Juan," I interject. "We stay put until after dark. We can't risk being caught out in the open in daylight which rules out trying to cross the courtyard to the southwest tower. Hopefully, the soldiers will leave and we can get the hell out of here."

"Which means were trapped here for hours," Michelina grouses, her face tense with frustration. "And what about Hemingway, Peter?"

"Who is Hemingway?"

"Peter's Yorkshire Terrier, he's shut up in our hotel room back in Cape Haitian."

"Don't worry, Michelina, I paid the concierge a bundle to look after him; he'll be fine until we get back."

"*If* we get back," she snaps.

"Listen," says Juan, "I'll get us out of here. Even if they leave a couple of soldiers behind, we'll handle them."

"We don't have any weapons," Michelina reminds us, "except for the rock in my pocket."

"Wrong! This place is full of iron cannon balls and we've got something they don't."

"What's that?" asks Michelina.

"A secret weapon," Juan announces, leering at Michelina. "You!"

CHAPTER 11

"Okay here's what I propose," whispers Juan, huddling with Michelina and me inside a room off the lobby. "I've got a mosquito netting inside my backpack. I'd like Michelina to strip off her clothes, drape the netting over herself and stand close to the top step of the staircase. I'll silhouette her by back lighting her with the flashlight."

"Oh no you're not. I'm not going to get shot by one of those soldiers."

"Look," says Juan, "you're our only hope of getting out of here. I'm counting on the fact that whoever's left down there is going to be so curious about the beautiful apparition he sees that he's going to want to take a closer look. So as he up climbs the stairs, you slowly back up until you've lured him to the next to last step where Peter and I will be flush against the wall on either side of the stairwell. Each of us will have a cannon ball and when the soldier reaches the next to last step, one of us will bash him over the head and the other will grab for his gun. What do you say?"

"I don't like it," says Michelina. "If he thinks I'm some voodoo spirit, he might shoot me. These people are very superstitious."

"Then give me an alternative," demands Juan.

"Instead of looking like some Haitian apparition, why don't I just stand here starkers. I don't much like getting naked, but if it's going to get us out of here alive, I'll do it."

Juan and I glance at each other in amazement and break out laughing.

"What's so funny," Michelina wants to know. "I'm the one taking all the risk here. What if the guy is gay?"

Juan and I cover our mouths with our hands to stifle our laughter. "You two better stop that," she warns. "They'll hear you."

Pulling Michelina to me, I kiss her gently on the lips. "You're a real trooper, sweetheart."

"Anything to get us out of this mess," she says, unbuttoning her shirt. "You two go look for some cannon balls while I undress."

As I stand guard at the top of the stairwell, Juan wanders off with the flashlight to locate cannon balls. From below I hear the voice of the squad leader taking charge of his men and barking orders in French. Since my French is mostly non-existent, I get Michelina to join me. Wearing only panties and her unbuttoned shirt she stands beside me and listens. I feel her shivering and wrap my arms around her to keep her warm. "What's he saying?" I whisper in her ear.

"Shhh." She strains to listen, then turns her face to me. "He's telling the two soldiers staying behind that the other men are about to leave. He wants one man stationed in the lobby and the other to guard the outside entrance."

We hear the shuffle of boots as men exit the lobby and soon all sounds fade away.

"We better give them about a twenty minute head-start before we act," whispers Juan as he come up behind us cradling three rusty iron cannon balls, all about the size of softballs. He hands me one. It's heavy, about five kilos. Michelina interrupts my musing over being walloped over the head by a cannon ball. She turns around, hugs me briefly then goes into the barracks room to get naked.

When she returns she insists I set the flashlight on the floor so that it will illuminate her from the front. The effect is quite erotic and I can hear Juan's breath catch as his gaze takes in her perfect body. Sheepishly, he looks over at me where I'm flattened against the opposite wall, then he bends over and sends one of his cannon-balls rolling down the stone steps. Impacting each step with a loud thump, it gathers speed as it rolls down the staircase and across the lobby floor. Boots impact against the stone floor as a soldier rushes toward the staircase. Shouting an obscenity, he issues what sounds like a challenge. I glance at Michelina and she forces a smile, now obviously in eye contact with the soldier at the bottom of the staircase. Slowly raising her right hand, like the siren that enticed Odysseus, she wiggles her index finger and beckons the soldier to come to her. His boots scuff against the stairs as he warily ascends while Michelina ever so carefully edges backward. Then he calls out something in French and Michelina responds with a lustful smile while provocatively caressing her breasts with both hands.

Watching this splendid performance I'm driven almost to applause, which could prove fatal. I turn my attention to Juan, who is raising his right arm, the cannon ball protruding from his fist. The muzzle of the soldier's weapon suddenly appears and then the bill of his cap. Lunging sideways Juan brings the cannon ball crashing down upon the man's skull with a sickening thud. I drop my cannon ball and, grabbing the gun barrel, wrench the weapon from the soldier's hands. But as it comes away in my hand it discharges.

Screaming, Michelina dives to the floor.

The single bullet misses her and splatters harmlessly against a back wall. Feeling heat from the smoking gun barrel, I quickly transfer my grip to the gun's stock and point the weapon at the soldier who leans back against the stairwell wall. Slowly, he pitches over backward and slides head-first down the stairs.

Stay down!" I shout at Michelina, who huddles on the floor in semi-darkness after knocking over the flashlight.

"Give me the gun," demands Juan, as we hear the pounding of boots on the stone floor below. "It's the other guard." Snatching the weapon from me he rushes down the staircase, spraying bullets into the lobby below.

The noise from the automatic weapon creates a series of flashes and a thunderous echo. Michelina screams again as I scramble to retrieve the flashlight.

A sudden silence is broken by loud cursing, the clatter of a weapon hitting the floor and then quickly receding footsteps.

"Juan, are you all right?" I shout.

"Yes, but I'm out of ammo and I need the flashlight."

"I've got it," I reply, swinging it toward Michelina at my feet who stares up at me terror-stricken.

"Come and get it. I need to tend to Michelina."

Leaving the flashlight on the floor, I pick Michelina up in my arms and head for the storeroom where she had disrobed.

"I only wounded that other soldier," says Juan, retrieving the flashlight. "I need to go after him."

"What about the first soldier?"

"Dead. Is Michelina okay?" Juan asks, seeing Michelina cradled in my arms.

"How about freaked out?" Michelina laments, lifting her head off my shoulder.

Juan and I exchange smiles. "You be careful," I urge him, as he descends the stairs. I hear him ram a new clip of bullets into his gun and once again we're plunged into darkness as he goes after his prey.

"I'm going to put you down now, we need to find your clothes." Taking her by the hand I lead her to the barracks room where her clothes, barely visible by a white shirt, lie in a pile. As she dresses she asks, "How did I do?"

"Fabulous acting. I wanted to applaud."

"Really?"

"Definitely a stellar performance. Perhaps you should consider an acting career."

"Why not? I can't be a model forever. Look Peter, a light. Juan must be back."

"Where are you guys?" Juan shouts as he rushes up the stairs.

"In our star's dressing room," quips Michelina.

"Did you find him?" I ask Juan as he crosses the lobby toward us.

"He got away, but he left a trail of blood leading down the path beside the fortress. No way I'll stalk him in the dark. We need to split before he gets the word out."

"Mind if I finish getting dressed first?" Michelina chirps.

"I think you look pretty terrific in your birthday suit. That was a mighty convincing performance you put on. It saved our butts."

"I guess I don't even have enough time to blush?"

"Nope, we gotta' make tracks," answers Juan.

Inside the Christophe Chapel, beside the ruins of San Souci, Michelina lies next to me on a wooden bench, her head in my lap, sleeping. I'm still running on adrenalin and unable to sleep. I watch Juan load fresh ammunition clips in the two AK-47 submachine guns he took from the fortress. He's tired also but much too wired to sleep. Both of us worry about getting off the mountain. Juan paces the floor. At intervals he peers out the entry door to check for either the arrival of soldiers or dawn.

"Heads up!" he cries, peering through the doorway. "I see headlights. A vehicle is coming up the road. We better get the hell out of here."

"Wait, let's not panic. Maybe it's a local farmer's car. If so, we might be able to bribe him to take us to Cape Haitian."

"Okay, but one of us needs to go out there and check out that vehicle."

"I'll go, you stay here with Michelina."

"You want a gun?"

"No thanks, I'd probably shoot myself in the foot."

Ducking out the doorway, I run toward the ruins of the palace. The damp chilly air has created a ground fog that reaches to my knees and I have to carefully pick my way around piles of rubble from palace walls that had collapsed during an earthquake. Edging along the palace's back wall I reach a giant mahogany tree at the juncture of the western end of the palace. Hidden behind its massive trunk, I have an unobstructed view of the parking lot. I watch the vehicle labor up the steep road and as it comes into view I can tell that it's a car. Exhaling with relief, I wait for it to rumble over the rough terrain and come to a halt. Finally the engine sputters and quits, the headlights go out and a tall thin man emerges from a door that makes a dreadful scraping noise as metal tortures metal. The sound is all too familiar. Walking around the tree's trunk I see the driver lean against the body of the car. He looks up at the emerging daylight and tips a bottle to his lips.

"Gabrielle," I shout. Before I realize it, I'm running toward him, waving frantically. He turns his head and that dark face of his flashes a gap-toothed grin like a jack-o-lantern at Halloween.

"You see, I come back for you," he says. Lurching forward, he sticks out a slender, bony hand in greeting.

"Man, am I glad to see you," I say, nearly shaking his arm off.

"What became of *mademoiselle?* You let a zombie take her?" Gabrielle's eyelids, heavy with rum, blink slowly like automated garage doors.

"No. She's waiting inside the chapel."

"Praying?"

"Yes, that you'd come back," I laugh.

"I know, I overheard her. That's why I return, but now it's nighttime you must pay me overtime."

"No problem. We'll settle up when we reach the hotel. Here they come now," I tell him, seeing Michelina and Juan trot toward us.

"You are three now? . . . with guns?" Gabrielle asks, squinting across the parking area at the approaching silhouettes.

"Right."

"That's not a zombie with the lady?"

"No, a friend, an American."

"With two guns, like a cowboy I see in the cinema," Gabrielle says, proffering me the rum bottle.

"*No, merci.* Actually he's a tourist who lost his way."

"Good, another fare, but no guns."

"Look who's here," I call out to Michelina who pulls up in front of us, slightly winded, but radiant.

"My hero," she shouts, hurling herself at Gabrielle. Caught in her enthusiastic embrace Gabrielle's eyes dart about in panic, as though he fears Michelin's fierce hug will snap his bones like matchsticks.

Gabrielle's pained expression causes me to laugh and when Michelina steps back, I introduce him to Juan who almost crushes Gabrielle's frail hand in his strong grip.

"No guns," Gabrielle cautions. "I lose my license."

"No guns?" Juan looks questioningly at me.

"No guns," I affirm.

"Okay." Juan agrees. Ripping out the cartridges, he throws them among the rocks, then tosses the weapons in a patch of tall grass. Getting into the front seat with his backpack he tells Gabrielle, "Let's move out."

Gabrielle gets behind the wheel and has to jerk on his badly dented door to get it to close. The screech of metal makes Michelina, beside me in the back seat, wince.

Gabrielle turns the key in the ignition, pushes the starter button and the motor rumbles to life, then stalls. "Flooded, we wait," he says. As we impatiently wait the sky turns light and the ground fog begins to dissipate, lifting like a ghostly veil before it vanishes altogether. Once more Gabrielle pushes the starter and this time the motor catches. A cloud of oily smoke belches from the exhaust as Gabrielle back up, turns the car around; and bouncing across the stony parking lot, he directs the car down the mountain. Suddenly Juan points toward the sky. "Look! Vultures flying in circles." Swiveling his head around he gives me a knowing smile.

"Guess he never made it," I comment.

"Whew, good thing for us," says Juan.

"The Mont Joli?" asks Gabrielle.

"*S'il vous plait,*" says Michelina. "God, I can't wait to have a bath and wash my hair."

"And I can't wait to see Hemingway," I add. "Poor little chap, he must think we've abandoned him."

"How come you brought your dog to Haiti?" asks Juan.

Michelina gets a case of the giggles and interjects, "I didn't want Peter picking up any strays at the beach."

"Low blow," Juan remarks, turning red. "Damn, this road is steep." He has to straight-arm the dash to keep from sliding off the front seat. "You're not about to let me forget this, are you?"

"Not likely," she tells him.

As we pull up in front of the Mont Joli Hotel, I see several soldiers standing by the hotel entrance. They seem to be scanning faces and checking guests' documentation. "Those guys may be looking for you, Juan. Best you stay in the car with Gabrielle."

"That's all I need," he says, sarcastically, and urges Gabrielle to hurry and drive his taxi into the parking lot.

The soldiers stop Michelina and me, but they are only interested in checking our passports.

Gabrielle parks his taxi under the shade of a Samarapa tree, or Jacaranda as it's known elsewhere in the Caribbean. It has a canopy of lacy green leaves and bluish white blossoms that resemble bluebells, enough to protect the taxi's occupants from the heat and glaring sun while we go to our room, pack our bags, retrieve Hemingway and check out. Our plan is to drive to Port au Prince before going on to Jacmel.

When we return to the taxi, Juan is sprawled across the back seat, asleep. Gabrielle, draped across the steering wheel, snores loudly, but he awakes with a start when the teen-age bellboy lifts up the trunk lid to stow the luggage. Blinking rapidly, Gabrielle's expression turns to one of horror when he sees Hemingway in my arms. Uttering a string of Creole expletives, he forces open his battered door, brushes past me and berates the bellboy who quickly removes the luggage from the trunk.

"What's going on?" asks Juan, sitting up in the back seat.

"Out, out," Gabrielle screams at Juan as he jerks the rear door open.

"He told the bellboy he won't drive us," Michelina explains.

"*Le chien*," says the bellboy to Michelina.

"It's because of the dog he won't take us," says Michelina.

In my arms Hemingway squirms to get loose, flattens his ears against his head, and begins barking. Handing him to Michelina, I step up to Gabrielle. "Now listen here, Gabrielle, I —"

"Screw him, he's drunk." interrupts Juan, jumping out of the back seat with his back pack.

Gabrielle turns away from me, slams the back door, and climbs back into his taxi. Jerking the door shut with its usual screech of tortured metal he sticks a skeletal arm out the window and shouts, "Money!"

I hand him a hundred dollar bill and the taxi sputters to life.

"No change," he yells, as his taxi lurches backward, barely missing our luggage.

"Don't worry," says the porter to Michelina, "I'll get you another driver."

Shifting gears, Gabrielle stomps on the accelerator. The taxi spins its wheels, then careens wildly across the parking lot enveloping us in a hail of oily smoke and stinging dirt and gravel.

"*Merde!*" cries Michelina, "I'll have to wash my hair again."

We watch the rapidly disappearing taxi as it bounces onto the highway. From the driver's window a rum bottle sails into the air and shatters on the asphalt highway.

"Another dead soldier!" declares Juan.

While we wait in the shade of the samarapa tree for the bell boy to arrange *for* another driver, we see a silver Mercedes 560 SE sports car driven by a black woman leave the hotel. As it flashes past us Juan says, "My God, it's her . . . Danielle . . . . and she's crying."

"Not your problem, Casanova," snaps Michelina.

CHAPTER 12

The drive through the mountains from Cape Haitian to Port au Prince is a motorist's nightmare, but I know God smiled on us when Gabrielle drove away. With him at the wheel, tanked up on a liter of Babancourt, he would have driven us right off a cliff. Fortunately we have a Mercedes sedan and a skillful but slightly obese driver called Maurice. He wears a red flowered Hawaiian shirt, yellow Bermuda shorts, leather sandals and a grin the size of the Grand Canyon.

The highway, if you can call it that, is a rutted, pot-holed trail strewn with mashed sugar cane cuttings. It is so narrow in places there's barely enough room for a single vehicle. Often we are forced to wait while a relentless parade of gaily decorated Haitian busses (Tap-Taps), lorries, motor cars, donkeys, goats, and pedestrians with various goods balanced on their heads pass by before we're able to continue.

Much of the trip is beside steep mountain precipices so close to the car's wheels that fear takes our breath away, save the driver who is annoyingly cheerful and unquestionably a fatalist. Nevertheless the mountains and valleys along the route are spectacular, though appallingly barren of trees. Instead they bear ugly scars caused by surface erosion of their red clays and sandstone conglomerates. Most pronounced is the erosion of the scarred, starkly denuded Artibonite Valley that once was Haiti's breadbasket. As far as the eye can see the valley appears as though it's been strip-mined; all its timber carted off to manufacture charcoal, Haiti's principal cooking fuel. The once mighty and pristine river that bisects the Artibonite Valley is now a pathetic-looking muddy stream, though during the rainy season it becomes a dangerous raging torrent that sweeps away everything it its path and deposits it as a billowy ocher cloud of sediment into the Caribbean's aquamarine waters.

As we drive down the last mountain toward the picture postcard coastal city of St. Mark with its colorful buildings, tall palms, and azure sea, everyone, except our stoic driver, breathes a sigh of relief. Hemingway, who sensed our anxiousness and remained alert in the mountains curls up and goes to sleep beside Michelina who now frowns at me and pinches her nostrils between thumb and index finger. "What is that ghastly smell?"

"Dead fish!" I reply, as our driver knowingly grins at me in the rear vision mirror and chuckles.

I had hoped we might stay at the Grand Hotel Oloffson in Port Au Prince, but as we drive up to the entrance in the ebbing hours of daylight, Hemingway, with head out the window, barks furiously. Michelina spots his prey, a huge rat that runs across the road and scurries under the hotel's front porch. "I'm not staying here," she says. By her matter of fact tone I know it's no use trying to convince her otherwise. No way she'll even step out of the car.

"Flamboyant," I tell the driver and off we go again, leaving the Grand Hotel Oloffson's gingerbread magnificence to the rodents.

"Now, this is more my style," says Michelina as we pull into a semi-circular drive overlooking a kidney shaped swimming pool and several modern buildings with glass fronts that appear as though just imported from Miami Beach.

"Yeah and check out the view." Juan points to the vast panorama, which in the ebbing light has turned a hue of brilliant green against the Caribbean's indigo backdrop.

"Why is that land so green?" Michelina asks the driver.

"The sugar cane of the Cul de Sac Plain," he replies.

"Did we drive through that on our way here?" she asks.

"Yes, I tell her, but you and Hemingway were snoring."

"Peter, I never snore," she counters indignantly.

Sometimes it's best to just let a denial pass so things don't get out of hand. Claire didn't think she snored either, until I taped her one night and played the tape back to her during breakfast, whereupon, she deposited her plate of scrambled eggs and toast in my lap. I haven't a clue why women are so sensitive about snoring, but they are. I wager tonight Michelina will get even with me . . . no sex!

As the car brakes to a stop Michelina jumps out and makes a mad dash for the swimming pool. Hemingway bounds after her. "Last one in is an old poop," she shouts over her shoulder before diving into the deep end of the pool, clothes and all.

Our driver, amused by Michelina's antics, breaks out in gales of laughter.

Getting out of the Mercedes, Juan collects his backpack and maps from the front seat while I stand with the driver watching Michelina swim underwater across the width of the pool. Hemingway scampers around the deep end to meet her as she surfaces. Crossing the patio from the dining area we see a man in a military uniform walk toward the pool. Tucking a riding crop under one arm, he walks over to the pool's coping and through gold rimmed sun-glasses looks down at Michelina. Laughing, he claps his hands in applause, then reaches down to assist her from the water.

"The general fancies mademoiselle," comments the driver.

"Who is he?" I ask.

"General Augustine, the most powerful man in Haiti." the driver explains. "He and his brother own this hotel."

CHAPTER 13

Seated in the Flamboyant's glass enclosed dining room with its sliding glass doors thrown open to cloudless azure sky and a refreshing onshore breeze, I watch Michelina approach the table. She wears a white tee shirt with "Gianni - Milan" scrawled across the front in cursive letters and pale pink shorts with matching sandals. After I rise to seat her and sit back down, she reaches over and takes my hand.

"Did I snore last night?" she teases.

"You'll have to ask Hemingway, I was chloroformed."

"I was exhausted too. Now, I'm famished. Are you?"

"Not really. I'm only going to have papaya and coffee."

"I'm having a big breakfast," she says as Juan slides into a chair opposite her.

"Nothing beats a good night's sleep," announces Juan, covering a yawn with his hand.

"You ready to order?" I ask Michelina.

She nods.

"Just coffee for me," says Juan. I never eat breakfast."

Michelina squeezes my hand. I look up from my menu to see her gaze fixed on a heavyset black man with curly graying hair and rugged features. He walks by the dining room toward a poolside table occupied by a man wearing a white terry-cloth robe and sunglasses. The black man wears a military uniform and an ugly keloid scar arcs from the corner of his right eye to his jawbone. On his shirt collar polished brass oak leaf clusters denote his rank as a major.

Glancing at him Juan quips, "I'd sure hate to run into *that* dude in a dark alley."

The dining room Maître'd hovering nearby, spots the major and scurries across the pool deck to seat the new arrival.

As the man in the terry-cloth robe and sunglasses stands to greet the major, Michelina remarks, "that's the same man who offered me a hand out of the pool last evening. There's something familiar about him, as if I've met him before."

"You mean General Augustine?"

"What?" exclaims Juan, going ashen faced while Michelina gives me a startled look.

"You know him?"

"No. Our driver told me his name."

"My God! That's Uncle August, my aunt's former boyfriend."

"And Danielle's lover," adds Juan. I've got to get out of here.

"Calm down you two or you'll get their attention. Juan you better go back to your room and wait until I come for you."

"I have to see him," says Michelina, pushing back in her chair.

"Wait a minute. Give Juan time to leave before you march over there; besides I see the major just handed the general a bunch of documents."

"I'm leaving," says Juan. He rises from the table and casually exits the dining room.

"Excuse me, Peter," says Michelina. "I have to do this." Getting up from her chair she drops her napkin on the table and briskly walks out the sliding doors onto the patio toward the general's table.

Seeing her approach, the general suddenly rises from his chair. A smile breaks out on his face. Then his smile turns to open-mouthed surprise as he finds himself locked in Michelina's embrace. Loud enough for me to hear, she squeals, "Uncle August, I've missed you so."

"*Mademoiselle,* You must be mistaken."

"It's Michelina, Uncle August."

"Michelina, I can't believe this," he utters. Holding her by the shoulders, he examines her at arm's length "It's really you?"

"Yes," she says, "Michelina Coidavid . . . all grown up."

Reaching for a chair, he says, "You must join us, my dear."

The major rises. Leaning across the table, he begins to collect the documents the general has been reviewing. Michelina glances at the major. A photograph he holds in his hand momentarily startles her, but just as quickly she smiles and extends her hand as the general appears to introduce each to the other. I'm unable to hear any more of their conversation as it's drowned out by several people taking seats at an adjoining table. Michelina says something to the General, then turns around to point me out. Excusing herself, she reenters the dining room and comes over to the table.

As she approaches, I can see she's trembling slightly. Fighting to maintain self-control, she leans over and kisses me on the cheek while whispering in my ear, "Don't show any surprise, the major just showed the general Juan's photograph."

In a loud voice, she says, "Peter, come meet General Augustine and Major Baguidy."

Taking Michelina's arm, I escort her to the general's table. I can feel my heart pounding inside my chest and I assume Michelina's is doing the same. Giving her arm a reassuring squeeze, I extend my hand to the general.

"General Augustine, Major Baguidy may I present my friend, Peter Grant."

Sliding an American Airlines ticket envelope across the table to the major, the general energetically shakes my hand. "My pleasure," he says with a broad smile and may I present my aide, Major Hector Baguidy."

"Very nice to meet you." I shake both their hands. Releasing my hand, the major reaches for the ticket envelope and as he picks it up, a boarding pass, flutters onto the tabletop. In print I see the name, "D. Fabius."

"*Pardon*," says the Major, adroitly scooping up the boarding pass and dropping it into the Manila envelope he holds in his other hand.

Addressing the major in an offhanded way, the general asks, "You'll look into that matter right away?"

"Certainly, general," the major replies.

"Sorry. Now then," he says to Michelina and me, "we must have a talk. Please, sit down, Mr. Grant."

"Mr. Grant, what brings you to Haiti?" the major inquires.

"I'm accompanying, *Mademoiselle Coidavid,* on a sentimental journey to her birthplace."

"I see," the major says, forcing a smile. "You've visited here before?"

"No, but I find it a fascinating country."

"Besides our abject poverty and our ignorance?"

I sense the major is playing mind games with me, with the general doing nothing to discourage him.

"Actually what has surprised me most is the deplorable deforestation of the Haitian countryside."

"Slash and burn agriculture," comments the general. "I'm afraid it's endemic. Unfortunately we have millions of illiterate peasants."

"Can't something be done to help them?" Michelina asks the general.

"It would take massive amounts of foreign aid," the major responds, staring at me with steely eyes.

I realize he's implying that as I am an American, Haiti's desperate plight is somehow my responsibility, but before I can fashion a reply Michelina says, "Gentlemen, If you're going to engage in political dialog I think I will excuse myself." As she starts to rise from her chair, the general reaches out and takes her hand.

"*Mademoiselle* Coidavid is right, we are being impolite. My apologies."

"Thank you Uncle August," says Michelina, settling back into her chair.

I notice the major nod in agreement as he continues to stare at Michelina. It's as though he's either memorizing her features or attempting to recall something deep in the recesses of his mind. Suddenly his gaze shifts to his wristwatch and he rises from his chair. "Sorry, I must be going."

"Don't forget to phone me from Jacmel?" The general says to his aide.

"As soon as I've taken care of the matter we discussed, general," he replies. "Now, if you'll excuse me." Inclining his head, he bows slightly, "*Mademoiselle Coidavid, e Monsieur Grant,* a pleasure, I assure you."

Half rising from my chair, with the intent of shaking Baguidy's hand, I am forced to sit back down as he ignores my outstretched hand, then turns quickly away and strides rapidly across the grass toward the hotel's main lobby.

"You must excuse the major, Mr. Grant. I'm afraid I burden him with too many matters." Turning to Michelina, the general says, "Now that we're alone, tell me, how is dear Marie Teresa?"

"She's in excellent health Uncle August and thanks to your sage advice her business has flourished."

"I'm glad to hear it. I presume she's happily married?"

"No Uncle August. She never married. I think you were her one true love."

Blushing, the general says, "I had no idea."

"Michelina . . . General," I rise from my chair, "if you'll excuse me, I'll let you talk while I walk Hemingway."

"Hemingway?" says the general.

"Peter's dog," says Michelina, "the one that barked at you when you helped me out of the pool."

"Ah, the fierce little black and tan dog," laughs the general. "What kind is he?"

"A Yorkshire Terrier," I tell him.

"Yes, an assertive English breed, but I must warn you, don't let him wander loose or you risk having him stolen."

"Thank you, general, I'll be careful." Walking away, I try to act casual even though I'm bursting to warn Juan that the army has his photograph and they are looking for him.

Cutting short Hemingway's walk, I stop by Juan's room and tell him about the photograph Major Hector Baguidy showed the general. I also tell him the major is on his way to our destination, Jacmel. Visibly shaken by my news, he inquires about what is taking place between Michelina and the general.

"A long time ago the general was Michelina's surrogate father. He lived in New Orleans with Michelina's aunt."

"They were married?"

"No, no, they never married. Look, I need to tell you some things about Michelina, but it's in the strictest confidence."

"Okay shoot"

To begin with Michelina's real last name is not "Coidavid," it's actually 'Roi' In 1970 Duvalier's Ton-ton Macoutes went to New Orleans, murdered her mother, kidnapped her artist father and she was left abandoned. Michelina's aunt, Teresa Coidavid, took her in and to safeguard Michelina made her use her last name. The reason Michelina and I are in Haiti is to try to find her father. There's evidence he may still be alive, possibly imprisoned somewhere. And the person's name on that rock you took from the cannon may be the only person who knows where to find him. Since Major Hector Baguidy is trying to find you we need to be very wary of him. I don't like the guy and I've been reliably informed he's the general's hatchet man and totally ruthless."

"Jesus, Peter, if anyone finds out what we're doing we're all corpses."

"I hear you, but we've got to get to Claude Fabius before Baquidy can. Baguidy showed the general an American Airlines ticket and a boarding pass with the name 'D. Fabius'. By sheer chance I happened to see it. The boarding pass was unused which means that this Fabius person never left Haiti and is probably in Jacmel because that's where Baguidy is looking for him."

"Wait a second, Peter, you said the initial on the boarding pass was a D?"

"Right, it's probably just a typo."

"Okay, so what's our plan?"

"Pack your stuff, but don't leave this room. I'm going to go over to reception and arrange for a car and driver. We've got to get the hell out of here and get to Jacmel."

On our way back from reception to our room, Hemingway barks and I see Michelina walking toward us from the pool area. She looks upset. "Are you all right?" I ask, giving her a hug.

"No, Peter, I'm scared. Does Juan know yet?"

"I told him to pack up, that I'll arrange for a car and driver to take us all to Jacmel where we need to find Claude Fabius before Baguidy can get to him."

"Oh no, Peter." "What's wrong?"

"The general wants us to dine with him this evening and I felt I had to accept."

"Michelina, it's your call. Either we stay here at Juan's peril and lose the opportunity to find Claude Fabius or we tell Juan he's on his own and we show up for dinner with the general."

Michelina frowns, then breaks into a grin. "We can't abandon Juan and as for dinner, to hell with the general. I'll leave him a message at reception."

The drive to Jacmel takes nearly six hours. Initially we are slowed down outside the slums of Cite Soleil by a gruesome incident. A rioting mob has apparently dragged a man in a military uniform from a red Volvo sedan. They've jammed a gasoline soaked tire over his head and set him afire. Engulfed in flames, he staggers across the road and tumbles into a drainage ditch in a last desperate effort to save himself. The mob surrounds him cheering and dancing as flames and black smoke spiral skyward.

"Oh my God, Peter!" Michelina, who's been keeping Hemingway from barking, presses her face against my chest. Her whole body shudders, repelled by the violence.

Cursing, our driver leans on the horn and defiantly accelerates to get through the mob which remarkably parts and allows us through, but not without a barrage of invectives and fists that rain blows on our car.

"What was all that about?" Juan asks the driver as we break out into the open road.

"*Pierre Lebrun,*" replies the driver.

"Say what?" Juan's eyebrows are arched.

"Pierre Lebrun," the driver answers, was a well-known automobile tire dealer here in Port au Prince. When Duvalier's Ton-Ton Macoutes wanted to execute someone they made a public display of burning the victim alive with one of his tires, soaked with gasoline as you just saw."

"It's barbaric," moans Michelina. "I've never witnessed anything so horrible."

"Who was it do you suppose?" I ask, not really expecting our driver to know.

"His car had military plates," answers the driver. "I didn't see any police or soldiers at the scene so I expect General Augustine probably ordered his assassination."

Michelina covers her mouth with her hands and gives me an incredulous look. "Surely you can't mean that?" she addresses our outspoken driver.

"Sorry, *mademoiselle*, here it's a fact of life." He says with a shrug of his shoulders.

Too stunned to converse, we gaze blankly out the windows at the crush of cars and the sheer mass of half-naked humanity that mills about the roads. Some appear to have a death wish as they step in front of our car without warning and expect us to stop. If we don't stop we are met with angry looks, cursing and an occasional barrage of rocks plucked from the side of the road.

Trapped behind a procession of lorries, Tap-Taps and other vehicles we're forced to creep across the densely populated southern peninsula until we reach Carrefour Fauche. Turning to the southeast we climb brown denuded hills toward Trouin and from there it's a relatively easy sixteen-kilometer drive to Jacmel except for an area where water from a stream flows across part of the road and attracts stray goats, pigs and cattle who come to drink only reluctantly giving way to let us pass.

Approaching the outskirts of Jacmel the weather, already overcast, becomes ominously humid and deathly still. To the southeast, over the ocean, we see dark foreboding clouds. They appear to be a harbinger of heavy rain squalls or perhaps a larger storm.

"I don't like the look of those clouds. This feels like hurricane weather to me," comments Juan.

"You've been in one?" asks Michelina. Hemingway bolts from her lap and pokes his head out the window to bark at a cow eyeing us from the side of the road.

"Down boy!" I instruct Hemingway with negligible results. Turning to Michelina, Juan says, "I was in Florida during Andrew. It was one of the worst ever. Long before it came ashore the air got heavy and oppressive, like it is right now."

"Barometric pressure," I venture.

"I thought it was *my* imagination," says Michelina, but the air does feel moist and heavy."

"Well, I sure hope it's not a hurricane," I say. "We've enough obstacles ahead of us."

"Second that," echoes Juan.

Michelina shudders. "How do you propose we go about finding Claude Fabius?"

"Jacmel," interrupts our stoic driver. Through the front window, we see in the distance a church steeple and several tall buildings.

As everyone stares out the windshield I offer a suggestion. "Let's begin our search at the central market to see if we can find anyone who knows the whereabouts of the Claude Fabius family home."

"Why the market?" asks Michelle.

"Because that's where coffee is sorted and sold. My hunch is the family was probably coffee growers."

Entering Jacmel on the Grand Rue, we pass the Pension Excelsior which, according to our diver, is the oldest hotel in town. We continue on the Grand Rue through the edge of the city to the waterfront. Charming but shabby, the city overlooks a scenic three-kilometer palm fringed horseshoe bay, but its black sand beach is unfortunately quite ugly, littered with boat hulls, mongrel dogs and a few naked children who play in water that, judging from the odor, is polluted by sewage. The narrow grass esplanade that separates us from the beach is also littered with mounds of decaying garbage and the stench is awful.

Noticing my revulsion, Michelina laughs. "Care to go for a swim?"

"Not in this lifetime, thank you very much."

Turning the car around, our driver takes us through the city. Brick mansions with cast iron pillars and balconies resemble charming French Quarter homes of New Orleans. Ascending a hill on the Rue de Marche we come to an imposing cathedral. Opposite stands Jacmel's colorful iron market. Despite the threatening weather it's business as usual inside the red-tile roofed structure, its wistful shuttered cupolas poking skyward at each corner. The building's long galleries form an immense quadrangle of lacework iron that occupies an entire block.

After approaching numerous merchants in individual stalls we find an old woman sorting coffee beans who remembers the Fabius family. Speaking with her in native Creole, our driver gets directions to their old plantation house on the road to Saltrow, a seaside town east of Jacmel. When we're back in the car and heading out of town, the driver relates that the old woman told him a military officer had been canvassing the market shortly before we arrived. The soldier had asked the identical question we had, but the old woman said she and the others had kept silent. None of them, she said, had any desire to cooperate with soldiers, especially such an ugly looking *bocor* with his scarred face."

"What's a *bocor*?" Michelina inquires..

"*Mademoiselle,*" the driver replies, "a *bocor* is a sorcerer who uses supernatural powers to kill his enemies."

"Looks like the natives have the major's number," I remark with a grin, feeling certain we now have a good chance of getting there before Major Baguidy.

The wind begins to pick up as we snake along the shoreline on a rutted dirt road that takes us to Cyvadier, a small white sand beach just outside the eastern edge of Jacmel. As far as the eye can see the Caribbean is windswept and covered by angry-looking white caps. An ominous looking pewter colored sky hovers overhead with an under-layer of fast moving wispy clouds. Along the shoreline slender palm tree trunks flex in the wind gusts like bamboo fly rods, their long fronds rattling noisily.

Seeing the frothy ocean, the wind whipped trees, and the miniature cyclones of dirt and debris that swirl off the road in front of us, our driver becomes edgy. He swivels his head around and glancing at Michelina, then at me, says, "I can't take you much further. I must return to Jacmel before the rain starts else I will become mired in mud here."

"But we're only seven kilometers out of Jacmel," protests Juan. "We have another eleven kilometers to go before we reach the road to the plantation."

"A little further perhaps," mutters the driver.

Approaching Carrefour Raymond, a pristine white sand beach, lined with tall picturesque palm trees, we see wind- driven waves sweep across the beach, break among the trees and send fingers of spume and salt water hissing across the road. Unnerved by the water across the road our driver hits the brakes and lurches to a stop. "I must turn back . . . now," he insists.

"Please, just two more kilometers," pleads Michelina.

"No, I must leave you here and go back to Jacmel." he states emphatically.

"How are we supposed to cope with all our luggage?" Michelina begs for an answer.

Ignoring her plea, the driver shrugs, gets out the car, and opens the trunk. Setting our luggage by the side of the road, he extends his hand for payment.

"Well, I guess that's it," I conclude, opening the door. I pay the driver. Getting back into his Mercedes, he backs up to a place where he can turn around and drives off.

"Bummer," says Juan to Michelina who looks dejected. Holding Hemingway in her arms she averts her head from the wind pelting us with stinging sand.

After a difficult three-kilometer walk carrying heavy luggage in what amounts to a sandstorm, Michelina suddenly stops and points at an object in the distance. "Look!" Her raven hair lashes her face.

Beyond a long rise of rolling hills overgrown with small trees, weeds and grass burned to straw by harsh sunlight and sparse rain, stands a two-story house barely visible on a hilltop among a grove of tall pines.

"Ahead on the left," Juan shouts. "I see it."

"Let's keep moving; we need to get to shelter before the rain overtakes us."

Propelled by strong gusting winds, we are virtually pushed along a rutted dirt road through hectares of what were once healthy coffee bushes, now barely living or simply brittle skeletons. At the final rise, the wind is so powerful it nearly flattens us. About a hundred meters ahead stands a rundown looking two-story wood frame house with brick chimneys. A wide second-story gallery that encompasses the entire structure is reachable by a rusty semi-circular iron staircase with access on either side. The house's front door and windows are boarded up with plywood. Paint has peeled from the siding and there are numerous gaps in the Spanish tile roof where tiles have come loose and lie broken among the weeds and overgrown shrubbery. Tall conifers ring the house and sway and creak as the wind whistles through boughs heavy with clumps of dark green needles. Banana leaves, palmetto fronds and leggy branches of hibiscus and oleander scrape and slap noisily against the house and staircase.

"It looks deserted," Michelina observes.

Hearing a distant roar, I look back over my shoulder. Torrential rain sweeps towards us. "Run for it," I yell over the noise. Releasing Hemingway's leash, I watch him scamper toward shelter underneath the gallery. We follow, our luggage impeding our progress. Hemingway makes it under the gallery, but we are caught in a deluge of icy rain.

The underside of the gallery offers scant protection. Michelina's hair is a dripping snarl of curly black strings, her shirt soaking wet yet erotically transparent. Her teeth chatter.

"Peter, stop gawking at my nipples and get me your windbreaker. I'm freezing."

"We can't stay here." Juan barks, as he stacks our luggage behind some shrubbery. "Are we in a hurricane?" Michelina asks Juan, as she wrings water from her hair while I struggle with my garment bag to get my windbreaker for her.

"I'd say it's the leading edge of one and will most likely intensify within the hour. Wow, look at the wind bend those pine trees."

As I hand Michelina my windbreaker, there's a sharp cracking sound. A large branch from one of the pine sails under the gallery and barely misses us.

"That does it," thunders Juan. "Let's get the hell out of here. Up the stairs everybody." Scooping up Hemingway, my half opened garment bag and one of Michelina's suitcases I dash out into the rain and stagger up the iron staircase to the second floor gallery. Michelina and Juan follow with the rest of our belongings. "This way," I shout. Racing along the gallery, I turn the corner along the western side of the house and find myself in the lee of the storm.

"Look there's a side door!" Michelina whoops. Dropping her suitcase she bangs on the door with both fists, and hollers for someone to open up, but there's no response. As soon as I put Hemingway down he bolts to Michelina's side and with his ears up and his head cocked to one side he scratches at the door.

"Hemingway knows someone's inside," I tell Juan.

"Let's force the door," he says, looking to me for encouragement.

"You bet. Out of the way, Michelina," I shout.

Juan and I back up against the gallery railing. Together we run toward the door and simultaneously hit it with our shoulders. As it bursts open we sprawl face down across a wooden floor while behind us Michelina cries out a warning.

Hovering over us with a shotgun pointed in our faces, is a black woman in leopard pumps, blue jeans and a tiger striped shirt. The frightened look on her face shifts to amazement as she recognizes Juan gazing up at her from the floor. "*Mon Dieu, Juan*" she shrieks, "I nearly shot you!"

Hemingway charges inside to protect me. His barking startles the woman and she drops the shotgun which clatters harmlessly to the floor.

"Danielle, what are you doing here?" Juan demands, as we get up off the floor.

"This is my home," she answers.

"We were told this house belongs to Claude Fabius," says Michelina, scooping up Hemingway and walking over to stand at my side.

"He was my father."

"Was?" Michelina is thoroughly puzzled.

"I haven't seen him since Baby Doc's bodyguards took him away years ago," she explains.

"So you don't know if he's alive or dead?" Michelina inquires.

"No, I don't, but who are you to ask me all these questions?"

Reaching into her pocket, Michelina produces the rock and shows it to Danielle. "I'm Michelina Roi. You see the name on this rock? My father, Robert Roi, carved it. He left it hidden inside the Citadelle and with Juan's help we found it. It says to find Claude Fabius. That why we're here. People in Jacmel told us this was his home."

"I see," Danielle replies. "It was his home. After he was taken away the government expropriated it and later sold it at auction and I secretly acquired it through an agent.

"What happened to *your* father?" Danielle asks Michelina.

"In 1970 Duvalier's Ton-ton Macoutes came to New Orleans, Louisiana murdered my mother and kidnapped my father. He was an artist who was critical of the government. This is my friend, Peter Grant. He and I came to Haiti to try to find him. And didn't we see you with Juan at Cormier Plage?"

"You did. That was General Augustine's doing. He used me to find out who Juan was and why he was interested in the Citadelle. I was the general's mistress, but when his men failed to find Juan and two of them were killed he blamed me. Two days ago he beat me and abandoned me in Cape Haitian.

"That son of a bitch," Juan growls. Taking Danielle by the arm he brings her over into the light from the doorway to examine her. "Jesus, "Your face is badly bruised and swollen. What did he hit you with?"

"A riding crop he always carries with him."

"Listen everyone," I interrupt, "we better repair this door before the storm gets any worse and before Major Baguidy shows up."

"Major Baguidy is coming here? How do you know this?" Danielle's eyes dance with fear.

"Did you have an American Airlines ticket to leave Haiti?"

"Yes, but I faked my departure with Colonel Bertrand in charge of Airport Security. He was always enamored of me and in exchange for sex he agreed to lie and swear that I had flown to Miami. After I left his office I abandoned my car at the airport, took taxis, a bus and a fisherman's boat to get here so no one could follow or trace me."

"Major Baguidy had your ticket in his possession along with an unused boarding pass, Danielle. This morning we witnessed a military man being executed. A mob dragged him from his car and set him aflame with a gasoline-doused tire around his neck."

"Was there a maroon Volvo involved?"

"Yes."

"Oh, *mon Dieux,*" she moans. "Then it was Colonel Bernard. They must have found out he lied to them and now the general has sent Baguidy to kill me."

"That and this storm is reason enough for us to barricade this door and secure the rest of the house," I announce.

"I'll get some nails and tools," offers Danielle.

"And I'll get our flashlight and try to find some candles, since there's apparently no electricity," Michelle pipes in.

When Danielle returns Juan and I hang the broken door and reinforce it with boards nailed into the door frame so it can't be opened. Then we check all the other doors and windows to make certain they're secure. Everything is boarded up, meanwhile the wind has greatly intensified. Wind gusts shake the building and rain that sounds more like sleet lashes the house so hard that water begins to drip from various ceilings.

By candlelight and with Hemingway standing guard I work in the hall to open a hole in the plywood that covers a window overlooking the outside staircase. Michelina comes over to me, speaking in a near whisper. "I must say, I can see why Juan fell for Danielle. She's gorgeous, bruises and all, those huge brown eyes, her exquisite body and nice long legs. And that incredible ebony skin, whew! She may have the morals of a vacuum cleaner but she's a work of art. I'd love to know more about her, especially about how she hooked up with the general."

"Why don't you ask her?"

"I think I will, a little heart to heart girl talk."

"Go for it and let me know."

"Peter, you're a voyeur. I saw you staring at her tits on the beach."

"They're almost as perfect as yours except you have sexier nipples."

"Really?"

"Yes, Juan and I both concur. Now how about letting me finish this work."

"Men, you're all perverts," she complains then turns and stalks off.

Gathering everyone together I outline how we we're going to protect ourselves should Major Baguidy show up. Danielle wants to know if Hemingway will alert us to his arrival. "Don't you worry, if anyone comes near this place he'll start growling."

"Even over the noise from this hurricane? Juan asks.

"Yes, he hears sounds much better than we can, Also we're going to have to take turns watching the staircase. We'll do one hour shifts, one person to watch through the hole I made in the plywood, the other to stand by with the shotgun. We must be careful not have any light in the front hall. If Hemingway starts growling the person with the shotgun will have to poke the gun barrel through the hole and fire at whoever ascends the staircase. And since most of the leaks are on the east and south side of the house I suggest we move furniture from the living room into the dining room. We can seal it off from the hallway with a carpet suspended from the door frame. That way we can illuminate the dining room with candles without fear of someone outside seeing a light in the house. Whoever is not standing watch can remain in the dining room and catch a nap until it's his or her turn. Everyone okay with that?"

"Fine by me," says Juan, adding, "after we move the furniture and hang the rug, Peter, you and I will take the first watch with Hemingway. Let us all say a prayer we can ride out this hurricane because if the wind gets much worse we could lose the house."

As Juan speaks all I can think of is the movie *Key Largo* where everyone inside a small hotel in the Florida Keys is trapped and at the mercy of a powerful hurricane that buffets the house, smashes windows, peels off siding and shingles until the occupants are forced to either decide to ride it out or flee. My musing is interrupted by a blast of wind that makes the house shake like a wet dog. We hear a roof gutter break away and clatter across the tile roof. Some unsecured window shutters slam against the house as sharp snapping sounds accompany them indicating pine branches are now succumbing to the storm's fury. Most unnerving of all is the howling of the wind. We look at one another with apprehension, a tense audience watching and hearing nature's orchestra go berserk. Will the final crescendo bring the house crashing down upon us? Our wait seems interminable, then comes a tremendous crash against the cast iron staircase.

"What's that?" Michelina snaps.

"I think my banana trees just fell across the staircase, Danielle ventures."

Going into the front entry I look through the peep hole and confirm that the trunks of five or six banana trees have indeed toppled over and now block the east staircase. Now the only means of ascent is the west staircase which is in darkness since the storm has turned daylight into dusk. Glancing at my wristwatch, I see it's only five in the afternoon.

Juan and I take up the first watch while the girls rest. I drag up a nearby chair and peer through the plywood opening. Beside my chair is Hemingway, rolled up in a ball. Juan stands behind me with the shotgun. The wind and rain have begun to abate. Fifteen minutes go by, then there is a dead calm and the leaden color of the sky is replaced by diffused sunlight that gives an eerie hue to the landscape. I get up from the chair. "Juan, take a look at this, I think the hurricane has passed over us."

Juan sits and peers outside. "No way," he retorts. "We're in the eye of the storm. In a little while we're going to get hammered again, maybe even worse than before."

"How come?"

"A hurricane rotates counter-clockwise around the eye which could be, say, anywhere between 16 to 80 kilometers wide and the winds on the backside near the eye sometimes are stronger than the ones on the front."

"So we're not out of the woods yet."

"By no means. The sky will soon get dark again with increasing wind gusts and driving rain to follow. Keep your fingers crossed that it's not going to get worse than before or we're sure to lose the house."

I better let the girls know what's happening." I stand the shotgun against the wall before pulling back the rug to enter the dining room where the two women are conversing by candlelight. Just as I finish telling them about the hurricane and what we can expect, Juan calls to me.

Stepping into the hallway I see him in a chair looking through the peephole. Hemingway is on his feet, his left forepaw in the air like a retriever. His ears stand straight up and his head is cocked to one side as though he's trying to discern the direction of the sound he's heard. Then from his throat emerges a low guttural growl.

Stepping up to Juan I bend over him and he edges sideways to make room for me to look through the peephole. The rain is coming down in sheets, but now there's an eerie glow of reflected light shining from beneath the gallery. "Someone's under the gallery with a flashlight," I whisper to Juan.

Standing erect, I walk swiftly across the hall and retrieve the shotgun and hand it to Juan. Then I pick up Hemingway, still growling, to prevent him from barking.

Easing the shotgun barrel through the hole in the plywood Juan slides the safety forward and squints down the barrel.

"A man climbing the stairs," he says, sucking in his breath. As he exhales, his finger tightens against the trigger.

There's a deafening roar. Glass shatters as the shotgun discharges.

Terrified, Hemingway jumps from my arms and bolts toward the dining room. Outside there's a loud thud as Juan shouts– "Got him!"

From the gallery comes a string of curses followed by a volley of gunfire. Bullets rip through the plywood and window framing. Flattening against the wall I watch the shotgun fall from Juan's hands. Clutching at his left arm with his right hand he slowly topples out of his chair onto the floor. "I'm hit," he cries. As I kneel down to help him I can feel the floorboards vibrate. Whoever is outside stumbles down the staircase to the ground.

"Michelina, Danielle, Juan's been shot," I shout.

Shoving the hanging carpet aside the women rush to help. Danielle kneels beside me as Juan rolls over on his back clutching his arm, blood seeping through his clenched fingers. Michelina bends down, snatches up the shotgun and thrusts it through the peephole. Before I can stop her she blindly pulls the trigger and sends another hail of pellets into the darkness.

"What can I do?" implores Danielle.

"I need the flashlight, some clean cloth and antiseptic." I strip off my belt and cinch it above where Juan's hand covers his wound.

"Let go, Juan," I tell him as he moans in pain. "Michelina, I need you to help me. Rip open Juan's shirt sleeve. I need to see the wound."

Kneeling down to assist me, in one quick motion she tears open his sleeve and exposes Juan's bloody arm. Danielle returns with the flashlight which allows me to see the wound. "You're lucky, man. It's only a flesh wound. The bullet passed all the way through."

"Jesus, it hurts like hell."

"I know. Bear with me. I'll patch you up as best I can until we can get you to a doctor.

With a weak smile, Juan struggles up from the floor into a sitting position.

Danielle gives the flashlight to Michelina and goes to get some cloth and something to sterilize Juan's wound. "Keep your arm elevated and stay still until I can bandage the wound."

Danielle returns with strips of cloth and a bottle of rum. Michelina hands Danielle the flashlight then stands up and retrieves the shotgun. "I'll be right back," she says, walking off.

"This is all I could find." Danielle hands me the rum. I look at the label. It's 151 proof.

"Juan," I warn him. "This is really going to hurt."

"Then you better let me have a swig," he says, while Danielle and I laugh, albeit nervously.

As I finish binding up Juan's arm, I hear the sound of wood being pried open. Hemingway barks.

"What's going on?"

"I think Michelina's trying to get out onto the balcony.

"Stop her, Danielle."

Danielle jumps up and chases after Michelina while I assist Juan to his feet. I assist him into the dining room and make him lie down on a couch that we had moved from the living room.

Soon both women return and as Michelina brushes past the carpet and into the dining room I see the shotgun in one hand and in the other a Sauer automatic pistol dangles from her index finger. "This looks like Baguidy's gun," she says, soaked and shivering once again. I noticed it at the hotel. There's blood on the gallery floor so he's somewhere out there in the dark and obviously wounded." Beside her stands Danielle who looks as frightened as a doe caught in the head-lights of an oncoming car.

Getting to my feet I walk over, take the pistol from Michelina and hug her. "You took a big risk going out there alone. Are you all right?"

"Cold and wet is all. I don't know what got into me, adrenaline rush I guess. How's Juan doing?"

"Once we get him to a doctor he'll be fine."

"Peter, what if we find Baguidy dead, how will we ever find out what became of Claude Fabius? He's my only hope of finding Papa." Slumping against my chest, she chokes back a sob.

CHAPTER 14

The following morning at daybreak, I walk out onto the gallery while everyone else is asleep. My little shadow, Hemingway, follows me. The sun is bright and warm and there is little in the cloudless azure sky to indicate that a powerful hurricane has battered us for nearly fourteen hours, except for the fact that the surrounding landscape looks like a desolate battleground. On all sides and as far as I can see there is devastation. Fallen trees, looking like Giacometti's stick figures, lie in jumbled heaps on the sodden earth; broken boughs like limbs in rigor point skyward. Distant hills are scarred where torrential rain has stripped away grasses, earth and clay, leaving underlying reefs of skeletal limestone exposed. In the sky above the denuded hills I spot a lone hawk as it flaps its majestic wings several times, then soars upward on a thermal. Its head swivels as it hunts for prey or perch and then screams its haunting primal cry that echoes an eternal message, life goes on. I become aware of another sound nearby. Rampaging water courses along its newly created path laden with silty debris as it races toward the sea.

Hemingway descends the unblocked side of the staircase to do his duty. The ground is as sodden as a bog and he gingerly picks his way around a vast pool of water that has created a rubble filled moat beneath the staircase and gallery. Juan was indeed perceptive; water did pool around the house's foundation. As Hemingway sniffs at roof tiles and broken branches, I stare into the water below. It's strangely still and my mind envisions, among the colorful flotsam that litters its surface, a bright vermillion carp rising to the surface.

It is only a momentary fiction for my gaze happens upon the carcasses of the fallen banana trees with their wind shredded fronds. Immediately I'm transported back to the harsh reality of nature's power of destruction. Beyond the fallen bananas Hemingway now investigates the torsos of conifers which sprawl haphazardly among their jagged stumps. The once tall and graceful sentinels that whispered odes as viands coursed through their gently swaying boughs are no more. Not a single tree near the house remains standing save a large mango in the lee of the house's southeast corner; it looks like a forlorn sentinel that's been stripped completely of its dark green foliage and luscious fruit.

Examining the blood-stained gallery floor, I wonder what has become of the major. That he's severely wounded is starkly evident, but how gravely is the question. Yet, instinctively I feel somehow he has survived and is not far away. I whistle at Hemingway and beckon him to return. He and I will venture out and look for the major. Juan assured me he only aimed to wound the Major, firing at an arm and hand that appeared to hold a gun.

As I turn to watch Hemingway bound up the stairs, sunlight glints off an object barely visible on a distant hillside. Could it be a reflection of sunlight off the windshield of a car, perhaps the major's vehicle?

Going inside I arm myself. I'm a lousy shot with a pistol so I select the shotgun. If there's trouble there's less chance I'll miss with that as a weapon.

Nearly invisible from Danielle's house, about two kilometers out, sits a military Land Rover. It's parked near the crest of a hill beside the path Michelina, Juan and I took to reach Danielle's house. The vehicle is empty however a key protrudes from the ignition. It's apparent the open terrain and the boggy ground would not have permitted the major to drive unseen to Danielle's house so he left the vehicle and approached the house on foot virtually invisible in the darkness and torrential rain. He, too, must have thought the house empty else why would he have risked shining a torch beneath the gallery? Had he not done so he might have taken us by surprise, Hemingway permitting of course!

My first impulse is to drive the major's Land Rover back to Danielle's house, but Hemingway's agitated barking summons me to a nearby rise. As I walk toward him I hear the loud rush of water that I first became aware of while standing on the gallery. Hemingway stands atop the rim of a hill whose opposite side has partially collapsed into a torrent of dark menacing water that roils with tree trunks, branches and other kinds of debris. A rampaging river newly created by the hurricane follows the path of least resistance as it sweeps toward the ocean in the distance.

Hemingway barks furiously. Something among a tangle of tree trunks, limbs and brush, that diverts the swiftly moving water is fueling his agitation. I hear a hoarse shout and see a man clinging desperately to an uprooted tree that has toppled into the water. Its roots, nearly totally exposed cling to a limestone ledge three meters below us. As Hemingway and I carefully make our way down to the ledge I notice the man in the water is wearing army camouflage.

Grasping the tree's trunk with his left arm and bracing one leg against a thick branch he manages to avoid being swept away. It appears his other arm is useless. Answering his cry for help, I shout, "Major Baquidy, It's Peter Grant. If you want my help you need to tell me something."

"Anything," he shouts back in a voice hoarse with desperation.

"I want to know if Claude Fabius is alive and where I can find him"

"He's alive, Palmiste, Ile de la Tortue."

"Fine, I'll help you, but no funny business. I won't hesitate to shoot you."

Hemingway watches quietly as I straddle the tree trunk. With my feet dangling in the water. I shinny along it until I'm close enough for the major to reach the barrel of the shotgun. "Grab the barrel!"

The major braces himself with his foot, lets go of the tree trunk and arcing his left arm through the air manages to seize the gun barrel. Inching backward along the tree trunk toward the ledge, I tow the major through the water, but the swift moving current suddenly pulls him under. Kicking frantically he rises to the surface but his effort forces me to let go of the shotgun or be pulled into the water with him.

I watch helplessly as the major is swept away. For an instant his eyes register his fate, then he's gone, dragged under. He resurfaces some distance away, flailing the water with his good arm and then vanishes.

Breathless I hug the tree trunk until I can slowly regain my purchase and sit up. Behind me Hemingway barks as he sees the tree trunk begins to shift under me. The combined weight of the major and me has forced the tree trunk deeper into the maelstrom which now begins to tug it from the ledge where its roots hold it. Rapidly I propel myself backward along the trunk where I turn and throw myself atop the ledge just as the tree slowly rolls over and tumbles into the water and is swiftly borne away.

As I crawl up the embankment, two dark brown eyes peer anxiously into mine. An extended paw brushes against my cheek. "Good boy, Hemingway, you have a big treat coming." Reacting to the word, "treat," Hemingway's stumpy little tail goes berserk.

Standing on my lap with his head out the window, Hemingway squints as the wind whips at his fur as I guide the major's Land Rover around debris and pools of water toward Danielle's house. I can see her home looks more a shipwreck than an abode. On the gallery stand Michelina, Danielle and Juan. Warily, they watch me approach in the unfamiliar Land Rover. Juan, taking no chances, sends the women inside while he stands ready with the major's pistol He raises the gun then lowers it as he spies Hemingway's head protruding from the driver's window. I lean on the horn and both of us break into grins.

As the Land Rover slides to a stop and I get out with Hemingway in my arms I'm suddenly enveloped in a whirlwind of embraces and kisses, even a high five.

"Where did you get the wheels?" asks Juan.

"Rover here belonged to a bad ass *bocor* who won't have need for it anymore."

"Baguidy's dead?" asks Michelina's. Her eyes register shock.

"Drowned, but not before I found out that Danielle's father is alive and on the Ile de la Tortue."

"Oh thank God," says Michelina.

"He's alive?" questions Danielle, breaking out in a smile.

"Scout's honor!" I promise, as I extend two fingers above my heart.

Later, while Danielle and Michelina are in the kitchen preparing food, Juan and I talk over the sound of Hemingway's snoring.

"Juan, we need to get you to a doctor."

"I'm trying not to show it but the pain is getting to me and I'm worried about infection. Danielle said there's a good clinic in Jacmel. If you want you can drop me off there on your way to the north coast, but you better haul ass before the military discovers Baguidy and his Land Rover are missing."

"Okay, but what are you planning to do?"

"I guess go back to Port au Prince, check in with the American Embassy and catch a flight back to Miami."

"What about Danielle?"

"Obviously she can't stay here, the house is a total wreck and the general's not going to give up trying to find her. She told me he controls the drug trade and what she knows is ample reason for the general to want her dead. Frankly, I assumed she'd go with you and Michelle to see her father, but maybe she's too frightened to go anywhere but the U.S. Embassy and seek political asylum. If so I'll help her . . . even though she betrayed me."

"You sure that's all there is to it? Those smoldering looks she gives you make me think she'd like to take up where you two left off."

"I've got to admit she's gorgeous and pretty amazing in the sack, but let's face it, Peter, she's a high class hooker out for big bucks and she's way out of my league."

"If you want my take on this, Juan, I don't feel comfortable driving to the north coast with her along. As you say she's better off going with you and seeking asylum at the U.S. Embassy. They'll be very interested to hear from her about the general's activities. Wouldn't you agree it's her best hope of staying alive?"

"Yes, I think you're right."

"And if we find Danielle's father I'll tell him to get in touch with her through the American Embassy."

"Fine, but what are you and Michelle going to do once this quest is over?"

"I'll take Michelina back to New Orleans, then I have to return to New York City."

"Oh, I thought you guys were pretty tight."

"I adore her, Juan, but I've got complications. Although my wife, Claire, and I have separated I'm still legally married. Even if I wanted to I'm not really in a position to offer her a commitment. Besides, as you have undoubtedly noticed there's a substantial age difference between us."

"Well who knows, maybe everything will work out."

"Perhaps. Say, I'm curious about something, Juan. You're a good-looking guy and I've seen the way you attract women. Surely you must be breaking some poor girl's heart in New York City?"

"There is one woman I'd consider marrying, if she'd have me that is. We lived together and stupidly I screwed up our relationship. I thought because she was older than me things might not work out, but now I realize how foolish that was."

"What age difference?"

"Six years. We first met at Tulane University graduate school and lived together for nearly three years. After graduation I accepted a job offer in New York and once I got there I was like a kid in a candy factory, pigging out on all the available skirts in town. Meanwhile the one real relationship I had went into the toilet."

"Too bad!"

"Yeah, but somehow we've still managed to remain friends. She's a blue-eyed blonde in her early forties who doesn't look nearly her age. She's intelligent and fun, with a wicked sense of humor and a charming assertive manner. You would probably enjoy her."

"She's still in New York?"

"Yeah, last time I saw her she told me she was hooked up with a rich older man who wants her to marry him, then they'd live in Europe. Personally, I think he's feeding her a line. She'd be better off with a sophisticated guy like you, Peter. So if things don't work out with Michelina, you might want to look her up."

"I appreciate your suggestion, Juan, but right now I think I have quite a lot on my plate."

"Well, you never know."

"Hey you two." Michelina appears from the kitchen. "Danielle is fixing us some food. I don't know about you guys but I'm starving. So is Hemingway, I'll bet."

"Me too," replies Juan as I stand and help him to his feet.

After a difficult drive, fording washes, detouring around downed trees, avoiding gaping potholes and other debris we arrive in Jacmel and take Juan to the town's medical clinic. The building overflows with the injured and by the time we say goodbye to Juan and Danielle it's nearly mid-afternoon.

From Jacmel it takes us seven hours just to reach the outskirts of Port au Prince. The hurricane damage is unimaginable and we're forced to drive slowly to avoid hitting frightened animals and traumatized people. Dazed natives, some carrying small children, aimlessly shuffle alongside the roads and among fields of flattened sugarcane. People squat by the side of road surrounded by the remnants of their homes, some wailing over their misfortune while others simply stare vacantly into space as though in a trance. Brightly colored pieces of wood, corrugated metal sheets, bundles of thatch, smashed furniture, cooking pots and scraps of clothing lie scattered across a landscape nearly barren save the occasional silkwood tree spared by nature and humans probably because of superstition and mystique surrounding that species. All around us the air is pungent with the stench of death, sewage, and burning charcoal. It makes us queasy and Hemingway gets carsick.

"How can these people possibly cope with all this devastation?" asks Michelina.

"I really don't know, unless they're able to receive humanitarian aid from other nations. It's pretty obvious the Haitian government is virtually helpless in this kind of disaster. There's no semblance of help, everything is total chaos, and the military is nowhere in sight."

"I feel so sorry for these people, they're so dirt poor to begin with, now they're totally overwhelmed," Michelina laments. The sadness in her voice reflects her deep concern. "I just wish there was something we could do."

"Unfortunately, love, as much as I'd like to, there's little we can do. We're already running a big risk if we're caught driving a vehicle belonging to the military."

CHAPTER 15

Gonaives is Haiti's third largest city, where Dessaline declared Haiti's independence from France. Expecting to see a city symbolic of freedom we find only more slums and more abject poverty. By comparison, the city of Jacmel is a jewel.

"It doesn't matter to me if we drive all night," Michelina comments. "I couldn't spend another five minutes in this squalor not even if you offered me the Hope diamond. Anyway, we need to be in Port du Paix by daylight."

"That's one hellish drive. You and I are going to feel like wrung out dish cloths."

"Don't worry, we'll find a hotel and sleep all day. It's not a good idea for us to be seen driving this Land Rover in broad daylight. Is that okay with you, *amor?*"

"Yes, but you'll have to pay the piper when we find a hotel."

"Feeling horny are you? Well, as long as I get a bath and a nap." Leaning over, she kisses my neck, sending chills down my spine. "Consider that a preview of coming distractions."

The road from Gonaives through Gros Morne to Port du Paix is much worse than I can imagine, in fact, it's truly a nightmare of winding up, down and around mountains, a road as treacherous as a rattlesnake. The surface is pitted with potholes and looks as though it's recently been bombed from the air. Navigating the turns and switchbacks in the dark takes extreme concentration and we experience near disaster when a front tire blows on the edge of a steep gorge. Somehow, when she's not at the wheel, Michelina is able to doze off despite the rough ride, but I'm too filled with apprehension to be able to sleep.

In the pale light of dawn we break out of the mountains and enter Port du Paix. Once Haiti's principle port for exporting bananas and coffee, the city is now a haven for illegal immigrants who pay smugglers to sneak them into the United States. Despite that drawback the city has the picturesque charm of a Winslow Homer watercolor with its rustic streets, tidy pastel colored houses, a wide beach promenade and a formidable looking crenellated fortress that once defended the population from marauding foreign fleets and roving bands of pirates. Beyond its battlements stretches a wide channel of sparkling sea which separates the city from a long humpbacked island covered with greenish-brown foliage resembling a sea turtle in shape.

"That must be the Isle Tortue" says Michelina, pointing.

"Elementary, my dear Watson."

"Did anyone ever tell you you're a smart ass?" she quips, eyes flashing.

"You just did."

"Turn left when you reach the sea wall." She ignores my retort. "We should find a hotel along the coast road where we can crash."

"After we get there we better ditch Rover."

"While Hemingway and I get settled in why don't you find a convenient place and run Rover into the sea. Then you can walk back to the hotel and join us," she suggests, giving me an inviting wink.

"Look!"

"Hotel Brise Marina." Michelina reads the sign out loud. "Lovely, now turn right at the sign."

"Back seat driver!"

"Wrong. I'm in the front seat."

"I hardly noticed."

"You will when my clean and irresistibly naked body slithers all over you."

"Promises, promises," I sigh.

"Hurry back from your errand or I may have to find a replacement."

"You wouldn't dare."

Michelina leans over and brushes her lips across my cheek. "Just don't keep me waiting, she coos seductively."

After checking into the pink Art Deco hotel, I return to the Land Rover and drive about two kilometers west where I find shelf of coral rock overhanging the ocean. Putting the vehicle in neutral, I set the handbrake and get out. Making sure I'm not being observed, I reach inside and release the hand brake. Rover slowly rolls forward, gains momentum and as its front wheels tip over the edge, the vehicle flips over on its roof. Quickly filling with water it sinks beneath the sea leaving behind a spasm of air bubbles to mark its passage to the bottom.

By the time I walk back to the hotel, I find Michelina in bed asleep. Hemingway, curled up next to her, yawns and follows me with his eyes, too exhausted to lift his head. After a shower I crawl into bed beside them and pass out.

Late that afternoon, as the aura of a beautiful sunset bathes our room with pink and gold hues, I feel Michelina's warm body snuggle against me. Her hand snakes over my hip, evoking arousal. I roll onto my back and two beautiful soft brown eyes, liquid with passion, stare intently into mine. Climbing astride me, Michelina settles herself and begins to move, slowly at first like a boat rocking in a gentle swell. Raising up, she grips the headboard with her hands, throws her head back, and intensifies her movement. Sliding my hands along her undulating torso I reach up, encircle her swaying breasts and gently squeeze her taut nipples between my fingers. Gasping audibly, she sucks in her breath and with fierce thrusts brings us simultaneously to noisy and exquisite ecstasy. Grumbling his objection, Hemingway leaps off the heaving bed.

The next morning we check out of the hotel and hire a taxi that takes us to St. Louis du Nord where the boat from the village of Cayonne on La Tortue is expected to arrive at nine o'clock for the ten-kilometer return trip across the channel.

"I'm so excited!" Michelin holds Hemingway as he leans out the side window to feel the wind in his face.

"You better face him forward or he may get car sick watching every- thing whizz by."

"Perhaps you should hold him." She lets Hemingway walk across my lap and stick his head out my window. "Peter, do you realize that in a matter of hours we'll meet Claude Fabius and find out about my father?"

"I do, but let's hope Baguidy told me the truth."

"Why do you suppose Claude Fabius would be on this island?"

"I presume he's more or less in exile. The island is isolated from the mainland, with not many inhabitants, and it's not an easy place from which to escape unnoticed."

"What else do you know about Tortue?"

"A fair amount actually. I know the Arawak Indians originally inhab- ited the island. When the Spaniards arrived, along with horses, cattle and pigs in the 1500s they enslaved the Arawaks who gradually died off under Spanish domination. Then in the early 1600s the Spanish abandoned the island."

"Why?"

"Primarily because Central and South America became more important to them."

"For gold, silver, and jewels!"

"Right. Runaway slaves, shipwreck castaways and marooned sailors took over Tortue after the Spaniards left. Over time they became skilled at tracking down and slaughtering the wild cattle and pigs the Spaniards had left behind. They set up a lively trade with passing ships in animal hides and smoked meat, called *bucan,* but the French condemned the trade as illegal because not only was it clandestine but it was untaxed."

"So that's where the term "Buccaneer" comes from," Michelina brightly intones. How long did they remain on Tortuga?"

"The French military took control of northern Haiti around 1640. The buccaneers declined to bow to French authority and pay taxes to the Crown so French troops had to invade the island. They slaugh- tered all the livestock and drove out the buccaneers."

"Where did they go?"

"They sailed away on ships and turned to piracy."

"Making a bad situation even worse," laughs Michelina.

"For sure, those remorseless marauders became the scourge of every seafaring nation."

"What are the interesting sights on the island?"

"There's a few ruined forts, some spectacular caves, and the palace Pauline Bonaparte Leclerc built after her husband, the general, died of yellow fever in 1502 while trying to suppress the slave rebellion."

"Where is this palace?"

"In Palmiste, where we're going. It's mid-way along the mountain range that constitutes the spine of the island."

"Since we're going there, could we see the palace?"

"Sure, but it's almost totally destroyed. I was told French archaeologists had come there and stripped the remains of the palace of all its statuary and columns."

"I'd like to see it anyway."

"Why not?"

"Peter, how do you know all this?"

"Mostly from Selwyn during a trip I made to Haiti many years ago."

"Where did you go?"

"Selwyn and I went most everywhere in Haiti. He was a fantastic guide."

"So," laughs Michelina, "you told the general a big fat lie about never having visited here."

"Yes."

"Why?"

"I felt I'd rather not let him know I knew anything about his country."

"So it was just you and Selwyn." She eyes me suspiciously.

"Not exactly."

"What's that supposed to mean?"

"I had a girl friend along. Does that bother you?"

"A little."

Slipping my arm around her shoulders I pull her to me, kiss her and tell her I adore her.

"Equalmente," she whispers.

We're still locked in an embrace as the taxi pulls to a stop along St. Louis du Nord waterfront. Turning around, the driver catches us kissing. Politely he waits until we separate then points to a small scruffy-looking cabin cruiser that bobbles atop whitecaps as it crosses the channel toward us. "There's your ferry to the Ile," he explains.

Cayonne is a small fishing village on the channel side of La Tortue. A jumble of houses extends along the shoreline and rise halfway up a rugged 330 meter mountain, which is the island's turtle-like spine. In contrast to the village's primitive dirt streets I am amazed to see a paved road ascending the mountain. Before we disembark from the boat I ask the captain where it goes.

"Palmiste," he replies. "It's the only paved road on Tortue. You must take a Tap-Tap. The ride is only about six kilometers from Cayonne. That will be twenty dollars for you and your wife. Your dog is free," he says holding out his hand.

"But you only charged that native woman carrying a stem of plantains on her head a dollar," Michelina grouses.

"I know," he shrugs, "but she's a poor peasant and you are rich Americans, n'est pas?"

"Don't fuss about it," Michelina relents. "Pay him else he might not want to take us back to the mainland."

As we climb up on the wharf with Hemingway and our belongings we hear the unmistakable sound of an approaching helicopter, its rotor blades beating the air. Looking up, I see an olive drab "Huey" helicopter cross the channel, sweep over us and swoop up the side of the mountain. "That's a military chopper!" I exclaim as Hemingway watches it disappear from view over the top of the mountain.

Michelle looks at me. Apprehension fills her eyes. "You don't think —"

"No way, I interrupt. "I saw him drown with my own eyes."

"Do you think the army's looking for us?"

"I hope not."

"Me too."

The Tap-Tap labors the mountain, spewing exhaust, while Hemingway stands in my lap looking out the window. Michelina sits next to me and through gaps in the scrubby underbrush we can see occasional spectacular views of the mainland's corniche with mountains rising behind it. On the opposite side of the bus we see a vast indigo expanse of Caribbean fringed with waves breaking in foamy white patches along the ragged rocky coastline. Pointing out a distant ruin on a promontory Michelina asks me about it.

"It looks to be an old fort. The French probably built it to keep the buccaneers from returning."

"You seem to know a good bit about old forts, how come?"

"When I was a kid, I loved visiting forts. At age eleven I talked my grandfather's chauffeur, Burns, into driving me from Palm Beach to St. Augustine so I could visit Fort San Marco."

Michelina digs an elbow into my ribs. "Sounds to me like you were a very spoiled child."

"No, just bored, there wasn't a lot for a kid my age to do in Palm Beach." I chuckle at the memory.

"It looks like we're stopping," Michelina says.

As the Tap-tap shudders to a stop on the shoulder of the road the driver turns around in his seat and stares at us. Michelina and I grab Hemingway and our belongings, squeeze past some local peasants and get out on the side of the road. The driver mutters something in Creole laced with French which I ignore, as I am looking where his finger points, a crude road between two crumbling stone pillars.

"*Le palais?*" Michelina inquires of the driver.

"*Oui madame.*"

Down the road where the bus is headed I see a number of small houses built on either side of the road. "Palmiste?" I ask the driver.

"*Oui,*" he replies as he leans over, yanks the door closed and drives away enveloping us in a cloud of exhaust and dust. Teary-eyed and coughing we pick up our luggage, walk between the pillars and continue down a rutted road until we reach a vast pile of rubble where Pauline Bonaparte Leclerc and her court had retired to escape the rebellious slaves and the ravages of Yellow Fever that had claimed her husband. The palace is now nothing more than a sad ruin. A few walls and chimneys are all that remain standing, but one can nevertheless sense it's former opulence.

Michelina looks astonished. "It's not at all what I expected."

"Nor I."

"It looks as if it's been bulldozed."

"*Je suis bien certain,*" comes a reply which startles us and causes Hemingway to bark at the intruder.

We both whirl around and come face to face with a black man in filthy coveralls, torn shirt, leather sandals, and a floppy straw hat that shades his gaunt and wrinkled face. "Who are you?" Michelina questions him.

"*Le guardien,*" he answers as I pull Hemingway away from him.

"The caretaker," translates Michelina.

"*Je parle Ingles?*" she asks the man.

"*Oui,*" he replies, looking apprehensively at Hemingway, who flattens his ears and growls. "Will he bite?"

"No," I tell him, and pick the dog up in my arms.

"What happened here?" Michelina asks.

"An earthquake. Afterwards the archaeologists from France came here and took everything of value, pillars, statues, fountains . . . ."

"Archaeologists did this?" Michelina looks puzzled.

"They showed me documents proving they were archaeologists."

"Signed by whom," I ask.

"Magloire," he grins.

"That's over 50 years ago."

"*Oui, Monsieur!*"

"Magloire was president in the early nineteen fifties," I explain to Michelina, who ignores me in her eagerness to ask the man a more important question.

"Does anyone else live here?" she asks. "We are here to find a man by the name of Claude Fabius."

"Ahhh, He was just here, but now he's gone. Soldiers came in a helicopter and took him away."

"Where?" implores Michelina.

"Citadelle, I believe the pilot said."

"Oh no!" Michelina turns her head toward me in obvious distress.

"What's wrong?" asks the perplexed caretaker.

"Just when we thought we'd found Claude Fabius, he's been spirited away," I explain.

"Is there any way I can help you?"

"For whom do you work?" I ask as Michelina puts her head on my shoulder and clings to me like a drowning swimmer.

"The Ministry of Tourism. I've been here for fifty-three years."

"I'm sorry," murmurs Michelina to me. She turns to the caretaker and asks, "Did Claude Fabius live here?"

"*Oui,* for many years. Come, I show you," replies the caretaker.

With Hemingway on his leash, we follow the caretaker through the ruins, ascend a stone staircase, walk through the center of the palace ruins and out the back where we see a small U-shaped building built around a small courtyard. "Most of the building is intact except the west wing which obviously collapsed in the earthquake," he tells us. "In the connecting wing are slave quarters and in the east wing there is a kitchen and a salon. I put a new roof on the building when I came here," he boasts proudly. "Once there were three of us here, but now that *Monsieur* Fabius is gone I am alone."

"Sorry," I say.

"*C'est la vie,*" he replies, with a shrug of his bony shoulders.

"May we go inside?" asks Michelina.

"*Mais oui, madame.*" He leads us through an open doorway in the center of the east wing of the house. To the left we see what was once the kitchen and to the right a meagerly furnished salon. Stepping inside the salon Michelina looks to her left and utters a gasp. I'm also startled at the sight of an entire wall covered with a spectacular, but dampness-ravaged mural that shows soldiers, undoubtedly Spaniards, clad in armor engaged in fierce combat with Indians firing arrows and hurling spears. The outcome of the battle is hardly in doubt for the soldiers armed with harquebuses and long sharp lances have already claimed numerous Indians lives. In the background, at anchor on an indigo sea, lie three caravels and two naos and from some of their cannon issue smoke puffs while several boats loaded with reinforcements row toward the battle on shore.

"Who painted this?" asks Michelina.

"An artist who lived with us for a number of years. His name is Robert Roi," the caretaker explains.

"My father!" she exclaims.

A look of astonishment crosses the caretaker's face. *"Perdone, madame?"*

"Her father," I repeat. "Do you know where he is?"

"I don't. Three years ago Robert became ill. The soldiers came and took him away, probably to the hospital in Cape Haitian."

Michelina looks at me; her eyes begin to tear.

"Lets not jump to any conclusions." I walk over and put my arm around her shoulders. "Would it be all right if we stayed here tonight?" I ask the caretaker.

"Oui, oui, avec plasier," he replies and points to a crude wooden day bed under the mural that doubles as a sofa.

"You're sure?"

"Certainement" monsieur. If you need me I will be in the slave quarter." He points to a doorway to the adjoining wing.

At dawn the following morning rays of bright sunlight stream through open windows and awaken me. I glance over my makeshift pillow, my rolled up trousers, and expect to see Michelina, but only Hemingway stares back at me. Looking up I see Michelina sitting in a lotus position on the floor in the center of the room. Wearing a loosely buttoned shirt she stares at her father's mural, quietly absorbing the inherent beauty of his work.

"Are you all right?" I whisper.

"Yes, but I feel terribly sad. I know we have to leave here to find my father, but I'm torn because I don't want to leave this mural. Even though it's badly damaged, I can't stop looking at it. It's the only original work of his I can remember seeing."

"I'll photograph it for you."

Lowering her gaze, she smiles at me with a sadness that permeates her lovely dark eyes. It's as though she senses there's really not much hope of finding her father alive. "I knew you'd say that. You're so sweet, Peter."

"I promise we'll find him."

"I believe you," she says. Uncrossing her long legs she rises slowly to her feet and walks barefoot to the side of the daybed. Slowly, as if in a trance, she puts Hemingway on the floor and removes her shirt. Her lovely body is lustrous in the glow of sunlight. She sits down beside me and gazes into my eyes. Something melancholy and unspoken passes between us and her eyes begin to fill with tears.

"Peter," she beckons, "make love to me."

Little did I even remotely suspect it would be for the last time.

CHAPTER 16

Michelina carries Hemingway on board a fishing trawler whose salty old captain has agreed to take us to Cape Haitian. We have decided to return to the Citadelle for we're convinced that's where we're most likely to find Claude Fabius.

When I ask our captain the price he wants to take us to Cape Haitian he says, "twelve hundred and fifty gourdes." Michelina looks at the old fellow as if he's taken leave of his senses and I explain to her that he's using an archaic term for Haiti's currency, which is actually equal to about 250 dollars U.S.

"Oh, I thought he was talking about those elongated fruits which the peasants dry and make into utensils."

"No," I laugh, "but that's where the currency's name originates. After Haiti's independence from France the country had very little money. Henri Christophe forced the peasants to deliver to him all their dried gourds which he had made into bowls and pitchers. Then he traded them to British ships for hard currency."

The captain nods his head in agreement while Michelina stares at me with utter skepticism. Shaking her head in disbelief, she picks up Hemingway and says, "We're going below and will take a nap while you and the captain swap trivia."

Well out to sea from Tortue under a cloudless sky, a light breeze and a sparkling sea I suddenly hear a chirping sound. It comes from my garment bag piled atop our luggage in the cockpit. It's my satellite cell phone, whose batteries I had managed to recharge at the hotel where we stayed on the mainland. I quickly retrieve it and answer.

"Peter Grant here."

It's my secretary Catherine on the other end.

"I'm fine, what's going on?"

Not much because it's summer, she tells me but I can hear the hesitation in her voice which indicates a reluctance to tell me why she's really calling.

"Come on Catherine, why are you stammering?"

She responds and it's a torrent of words fired from a Gatling gun, but I'm able to understand that Claire has returned from India, she's back in New York, has taken over my apartment and has hired a nasty divorce lawyer who will make my life hell for he's intending to serve me with ugly divorce papers.

"Do not accept anything from anyone," I instruct her, having a mental image of a neatly folded document inside a sky blue cover. Then she asks where I am and I tell her, "I'm in the Caribbean somewhere off the northern coast of Haiti." She asks me when I'll be back and I say, "I haven't a clue," which of course I haven't. Then she goes on about things piling up and the number of unreturned phone calls and when will she be able to take some time off and what can she do about the pesky process servers? "Now Catherine pull yourself together and hold the fort like the loyal secretary you are and I'll be back to you the minute I know my schedule. Ciao for now."

"Shit," I bellow as loud as Stanley yelled for Stella.

The Captain's head snaps around and momentarily he loses control of the wheel which causes the boat to yaw to starboard, awakening Hemingway who barks and Michelina who now squints at me, her head out the companionway door. "What's the trouble?"

"My wife's taken over my apartment and she's suing me for divorce."

"Is that all? I thought for a moment we were sinking." Shaking her head in disbelief, she turns and disappears below.

I guess a single woman who sleeps with a married man doesn't need to be reminded there's a wife out there somewhere. Going below I sit down on the bunk next to Michelina and try to make amends. She lies on her side facing away from me as she listens to me. I feel her body stiffen where my hand is draped across her hip and she says, "Peter would you please leave me alone?"

"Couldn't we talk?"

"There's nothing I want to talk about."

"How about us?"

"Peter, there is no us, there's you and your other life and there's me who's along for the ride. I don't want to become emotionally involved in your marital problems. Now just let me go to back to sleep?"

"I guess I know when I'm not wanted." Getting up, I snatch Hemingway off the bed.

As I carry him topside I hear, Michelina mutter, "*Pendejo!*"

It's not often I'm called a "sphincter muscle." This is definitely not my day. "Good thing *you're* my buddy," I tell Hemingway who looks at me with bored brown eyes, then gasses me with a dose of dog breath by yawning in my face. *Today must be Friday the 13th.*

That evening as dusk overtakes us, the trawler pulls into the harbor at Cape Haitian. As we cruise past a large freighter named "Martinique," I notice the ship flies the Panamanian flag at its stern and it's tied up under a big gantry crane that lowers heavy cargo into its hull. In front of the freighter's bow we turn sharply to starboard, cross a wide channel and snug up alongside a floating pier with a gangway to the dock suspended on rollers that allows it to adjust automatically to the tide. Michelina, coolly indifferent, stands at the rail facing the dock. Strands of hair blow across her face, which she ignores in an effort to avoid eye contact with me. As she looks up at the dock in the approaching darkness, she suddenly raises her arm and waves frantically. "Juan!"

"Michelina . . . Peter," answers Juan as he trots down the gangway to the pier. Hopping over the gunwale, he lands on the deck and Michelina launches herself into his arms. "What are you doing here?" she squeals, planting a loud kiss on his cheek.

"Looking for you guys," he replies, breaking away from Michelina to embrace me and pound me on the back. "I figured you might take a boat to Cape Haitian from Tortue."

"How did you get here?" I ask him.

"An American doctor flew me here in his plane."

"Where's Danielle?" asks Michelina.

"Apparently she fled when peasants brought Baguidy into the clinic."

"Baguidy! How is that possible?" Michelina wheels around and glares daggers at me. "You told us you saw Baguidy drown," she snaps.

"I —"

Juan interrupts: "Some peasants found him barely alive on the bank of a washed out road. They brought him into the clinic in Jacmel and apparently Danielle spotted him as he was being carried inside the clinic. She sent me a warning through a nurse who notified the doctor who was treating me, the same one who flew me here. I tried to find her, but she just vanished.

"Who's this doctor" asks Michelina. "And how's your arm?"

"My arm's fine, still a bit tender. The doctor is from a famous wealthy American family. He devotes his life to a private clinic for children in the Haitian mountains near the border with the Dominican Republic. Realizing I was in danger, he spirited me out of the clinic, drove me to a nearby airstrip and flew me here in his Cessna. Actually on the way here we spotted your boat with the luggage piled in the cockpit and figured it might be you. We didn't want to buzz you fearing you might think we had hostile intentions. From your boat's heading the good doctor assumed you were on your way to Cape Haitian and here I am."

Tugging at my shirt sleeve, Michelina says, "Peter, I apologize for snapping at you."

"It's okay, forget about it."

Juan hurriedly says, "Listen, we need to get moving before Baguidy hooks up with the general." "They've probably already spoken because a military helicopter took Claude Fabius off the island just as we were arriving. The caretaker at Pauline LeClerc's palace told us he overheard they were bringing him to Cape Haitian."

"We figured they would probably take him to the Citadelle."

"I think you're right," Juan replies. "See that freighter across the channel?"

"The Martinique, what about it?"

"It sails for Nice, France, day after tomorrow. Earlier, I walked down the pier beside her and watched as crates with the name Augustine stenciled on them were lowered into the ship's hold. I sneaked a look at customs declarations on some of the crates. One purported to contain household furnishings and another contained a car."

"Which means the general is planning to leave Haiti," Michele deduces. Her frown expresses her anxiety about finding Claude Fabius and her father before the general departs.

"Not if we can prevent it," glares Juan. "And that son of a bitch Baguidy better not interfere."

"Michelina, will you hold Hemingway while I pay our captain and retrieve our luggage. Do we have transportation Juan?"

"Yes, I've got a rental car and the good doctor gave me some weapons. We can discuss strategy on the way to Milot."

Cumulus clouds cover the moon and plunge the countryside into eerie darkness. The absence of moonlight slows us down. Juan has difficulty navigating the torturous road up the side of the mountain with only the car's parking lights. Arriving at Sans Souci, Juan kills the car lights, drives the length of the parking lot and hides the car behind a grassy mound beside the Christophe Chapel. As Juan shuts off the engine he turns to me, then to Michelina in the back seat and urges us to get some sleep. "I'll keep watch," he promises.

"No need for that," I tell him, "Hemingway will let us know if there's danger."

"I forgot about our watchdog," smiles Juan, reclining his seat backward. I start to say something to Michelina, but she presses her index finger against my lips to silence me.

"We'll talk later," she whispers and then leans over and kisses me softly on the mouth. Her kiss is perfunctory and feels more like "goodbye" than continuing adoration. Nodding an assent, I settle back in my seat to try to go to sleep, while Michelina curls up with Hemingway beside her. Within minutes Juan and Michelina are asleep, but I remain awake, my mind a whirl of troubled thoughts about Michelina's sudden unhappiness with me. Unfortunately, I have no one to blame but myself for the conflicted message I delivered to her about my relationship with Claire.

At ten o'clock in the morning while we await the arrival of tourists, the sky above us turns the color of pewter and the air becomes warm and moist with humidity. Leaving the car we pick our way through San Souci's ruins to a place where we can view the parking lot without being seen. Huddling behind the rear wall of the palace, we sweat profusely while we wait. Suddenly Hemingway growls and strains at his leash. I look over the wall to see two vans rumble into the parking lot. The vehicles crunch to a dusty stop and a hoard of tourists emerge. Immediately they are engaged by flocks of beggars and noisy peddlers who hawk everything from native folk art to cold drinks. Taking advantage of the melee we leave the ruins and blend in with the tourists and soon we are on horseback riding up the mountainside with the tour group. Inconspicuous inside my windbreaker Hemingway is content to ride up the mountain with only his snout poking out of my jacket.

During the ride to the fortress, much to our relief, there are no signs of soldiers along the way. At the summit we rein in our animals and tether them after allowing the tourists to dismount first. Purposely we follow them and as they enter the southwest tower entrance to climb the staircase to the inner courtyard we lag behind. When the last tourist steps into the courtyard, we dash up the stone staircase that takes us to the first gun gallery which we cross, then climb more stairs in the southwest tower and enter a room that overlooks the courtyard. We watch as the tour group descends the stairway from the courtyard into the long cannon gallery that runs the entire length of the eastern wall of the Citadelle.

Sitting on the floor in our observation post, Juan reaches into his backpack and produces two handguns. He hands me an automatic pistol and gives Michelina a revolver. As I contemplate my weapon, I realize it's Baguidy's gun. Reaching back into his duffel bag Juan extracts a sub-machine gun, slides a magazine into its underside, pulls back the slide bolt, and racks a bullet into the chamber.

"Wow, where did you get that?" I ask.

"It's an AK-47, a gift from the good doctor along with the six-shooter I just handed Michelina."

Michelina stares disdainfully at the pistol, now dangling from her index finger. "Juan, what am I supposed to do with this?"

Juan looks at her and chuckles. "Let me show you."

"I hate guns," she protests, looking at me with rapidly blinking eyes that indicate near panic.

"You went after Baguidy, remember."

"That was a shotgun, this is a pistol."

"Well, whether you like it or not you may be forced to use it."

"I don't know how to shoot a pistol."

"Listen to me, it's easy," says Juan, patiently. "Hold it with both hands, like this." Taking it from her, he demonstrates how to grip it. "Hands out in front of you, like this, in a slight crouch, knees bent. Now, aim down the barrel with whichever eye you're most comfortable with, then when you've got whoever it is in your sights gently but firmly pull the trigger with your index finger. Don't jerk the trigger or you'll miss what you're aiming at."

"Each time you squeeze the trigger the gun will fire," I interject. "Just don't shoot me."

"I don't want to shoot anyone," she says trying to hand the gun back to Juan who refuses it.

"All right then, at what area of the body am I supposed to aim?"

"Either at the chest or the stomach. The gun is a Smith and Wesson thirty-eight special. It was popular with police officers before the 9mm Glock automatics displaced them. The bullet's impact will stop a man in his tracks. It will knock him on his back if you hit him in the chest or it will double him over if you hit him in the gut," Juan explains.

Standing up, Michelina aims the pistol out the window, squints down the barrel and pretends to fire at someone.

"Pow!" she exclaims. "Got him."

"Who?" I ask, startled.

"That guy on the opposite tower."

"Get down Michelina," orders Juan. You just aimed at a soldier."

"I thought he was a tourist," gasps Michelina.

"In camouflage? . . . and there's a submachine gun slung over his shoulder."

"Do you think he saw me."

"I don't know, he's now out of sight."

"Mierda!" Michelina shudders.

"Perhaps we better leave here," I say, as Michelina and Juan exchange glances. "You know the fortress, Juan, where shall we go?"

"Let's go down this tower's stairs to the first floor. That way we have multiple options if we need to split."

Taking a defensive position on the first floor of the southeast tower, we crouch behind the wooden carriage of a huge cannon. Our vantage affords us a clear view down a set of stairs that leads into the long cannon gallery where we first encountered Juan. The tourists can be seen milling about at the far end of the gallery talking and gesturing as they snap pictures of bronze and iron cannon lined up in their remarkably intact wooden carriages. After a few moments the guide beckons them to follow him and he leads them toward us. Turning abruptly he directs them up a staircase into the sun splashed courtyard. He seems intent on urging them to hurry and we look silently at one another wondering why. Presently, we hear a distant rumble. Thunder. We realize the tour guide is wary of being caught in a deluge on the way down the mountain. Soon we hear the horses pass by as the tour group heads back down the trail.

The thunder gets louder and Hemingway looks to me for reassurance. He paws at my leg and I pick him up in my arms. The light inside the gun gallery fades rapidly as dark storm clouds close in over the fortress.

"It's spooky enough in here already without a storm," comments Michelina.

"I agree," laughs Juan, "but it may work to our advantage. The thunder will cover up our movements and the rain will prevent anyone else from coming up the trail from San Souci."

"Like soldiers," I offer.

"Exactly. I'll bet only a few soldiers are here. Odds are that most of them will arrive after nightfall."

"To do what?" asks Michelina?

"Remove whatever they have stored here and put it aboard the Martinique," Juan replies as a bolt of lightning crackles across the sky and instantly illuminates our faces like a photographer's flash bulb.

"What do we do about Claude Fabius?" I ask Juan, now barely able to see his silhouette in the dark.

"Assuming he's here we need to get to him before the other troops arrive. I suggest we lure the guards to this end of the cannon gallery and try to eliminate them."

"Kill them you mean?" says Michelina.

"Whatever," Juan shrugs. "Look, if we get them to this end of the gallery we can tilt this gun carriage, send this cannon rolling down the stairs and crush them all."

"I venture this cannon weighs over seventy six hundred pounds. How are we going to tilt the carriage enough to make it roll out?"

"The carriage is full of dry-rot. It's falling apart," replies Juan. "I checked. The wooden wheels on the left side have collapsed and the gun is listing almost thirty degrees. If we can lever up the right side of the carriage, the weight of the gun against the decaying side of the carriage will cause it to give way and send this baby tumbling down the stairs into the gallery. What we need to do is stack up some wooden blocks, shove one end of a sturdy plank under the bottom of the carriage and lever it against the wooden blocks with our combined weight."

"What do we use for a lever?"

"Planks the restorers left here; they're in one of the rooms behind us."

"How did I miss seeing that?" I ask him.

"Easy," responds Michelina, bursting into laughter. "When we filed through the corridor to get here you brought up the rear and I could sense that all you were focused on was my tush."

Had there been any light, Michelina and Juan, who were doubled over laughing, would have seen my face turn scarlet. I readily admit I have always had a fascination with good long legs and a shapely firm derriere.

Torrential rain suddenly interrupts my muse about female anatomy. It lashes the fortress walls amid crescendos of thunder that cause Hemingway to cower in my lap.

Under cover of the noise from the storm and with the occasional use of the flashlight we construct a lever that will tilt the gun carriage enough to topple the cannon out of its carriage and send it down the staircase. Just as we finish the heavy rain turns into a drizzle and the thunder recedes with an occasional boom that reverberates like distant cannon fire. Unexpectedly fog swirls through the open gun ports like strands of spectral vapor. It's as eerie as "Birnam Woods come to Dunsinane."

"Time to summon the troops!" exclaims Juan. Pointing the AK -47 down the long corridor of the gun gallery he fires a quick burst. We hear bullets splatter and ricochet off the floor as they whine down the length of the gun gallery. There's little doubt the sharp staccato sound of the assault rifle has penetrated the Citadelle's deepest recesses.

Michelina holding her hands up to her ears, grimaces at the cacophony of noise, which just as suddenly gives way to the silence of a graveyard.

"Get ready," warns Juan and for the longest time we hear nothing save the sound of our own rapid breathing. Then Hemingway emits a low guttural growl that I quickly suppress. He can detect sound that we cannot and it is only when we see red dots dancing along a nearby wall, that we become aware of the presence of soldiers armed with laser equipped weapons.

"Keep down" whispers Juan. Picking up a small cannon ball, he lobs it a few meters past the bottom of the staircase. The minute it impacts three automatic weapons converge and spit bullets at the impact point. As planned Juan emits a horrible scream, yelling, "I'm hit . . . I'm hit." At the bottom of the staircase we have left a dummy made from Juan's backpack, two burlap sacks and a rain poncho. From a distance it looks human enough to fool the soldiers and they race up the gallery firing at it.

"Now!" whispers Juan. Throwing our bodies across the thick plank we lift up one side of the cannon carriage. It emits an audible groan as its opposite side breaks away and sends the huge gun hurtling down the stone steps into the midst of the startled soldiers. Instantly three are crushed as the cannon rolls over them. The fourth upended by a glancing blow from the cannon's muzzle, struggles to his feet, one arm dangling uselessly at his side. He flees back down the gallery.

"That's Baguidy. Somebody shoot him," Michelina cries. Our weapons lie on the floor and by the time Juan and I retrieve them Baguidy has disappeared into the darkness.

"Why didn't you shoot?" I ask Michelina who holds a revolver in her hand.

"I panicked."

"I'm going after him!" Juan roars, starting down the stairs. Michelina and I follow him. We step around the cannon with the crushed bodies beneath it, then break into a trot down the gloomy expanse of the long gallery.

"Where's Juan?" pants Michelina, grabbing me by the arm.

I stop running. "Quiet! Listen, I hear Hemingway growling."

"We forgot about him. He must have chased after Baguidy."

Suddenly from the end of the gallery comes a horrendous sound like an avalanche caused by something collapsing.

"Juan!" I shout.

"I'm okay," he yells back, "you got the flashlight?"

"Yes," I flick it on. In the distance I see Juan, weapon raised, walking carefully toward Hemingway who stands at the doorway to a large cylindrical room. He lunges forward, then just as quickly backs away, balking at entering.

As I reach Juan I shine the flashlight through the doorway. Choking dust fills the room. A wooden floor which once supported tons of corroding iron cannon balls has collapsed. I look at Juan.

"He ran inside, then everything came crashing down," Juan says.

"The proverbial straw . . . ."

"Got that right." Juan backs away from the dust that billows through the doorway from the room. "No way he could possibly survive that."

"I agree, but that dust won't settle for hours so we best keep moving," and with that I bend over to pick up Hemingway.

CHAPTER 17

As we descend the stairs to the base of the ship's prow I reflect on the strange reverberation I heard as the cannon balls cascaded down upon each other. The noise had escaped through tall narrow windows in the circular chamber and echoed like muted thunder off the surrounding mountains. I now realize that as the temperature drops at night, cooling the corroding cannon balls, pieces of iron flake off and become unstable spheres which tumble down upon one another. Their impact creates the spectral sound that local superstition has fashioned into Christophe's ghostly footsteps atop the Citadelle's battlements.

In front of me Michelina goes down the staircase beside Juan and suddenly I am overcome with a feeling of melancholy as my gut tells me she is gradually slipping out of my life and there's not much I can do about it.

"Heads up," warns Juan as we descend the last few steps to the ground floor. The only sound we hear is the steady hum of a motor, probably a generator that provides current for the low wattage bulbs that illuminate the lobby. On our left is the semi-circular wall of a huge cistern which at one time must have held most of the water for the Citadelle's garrison. Opposite the cistern is a steel door which is partly ajar. Faint light emanates from within. I pull the door open while Juan covers me with his submachine gun. Putting Hemingway down I urge him to go on in to make sure there is nobody inside to ambush us. "Go on," I say and he trots forward. I see nothing in his behavior to indicate trouble so we step inside and discover an immense mound of brick-like objects all wrapped in plastic.

Juan issues an exclamatory whistle then remarks, "Man, there's a mountain of cocaine in here. The general's got himself one hell of a stash."

"That's cocaine?" Michelina is incredulous. "How do you know?"

"Because those are five kilo waterproof bricks," Juan replies, handing me his weapon and picking up one. Reaching into his pocket he takes out a pen knife and stabs the parcel which begins to leak a stream of white powder. "This is pure smack," he says. "Out on the street and once this stuff is cut it'll bring more than a hundred grand retail."

"What do you mean . . . cut?" asks Michelina.

"Degraded, mixed with stuff like sugar to reduce its potency."

Hemingway, wanders around the drug mound to explore and starts barking. We hear a scraping noise and a muffled sound like someone struggling to speak. Juan grabs the AK-47 from me and edges around the pile of cocaine while Michelina and I remain behind.

"Jesus," exclaims Juan, give me a hand here."

Michelina and I race around the pile of drugs and see a silver-haired man gagged and bound to a chair with rope. Struggling vainly to free himself, his frightened eyes stare at us and he grunts for help. Furiously fighting against his restraints, he nearly causes the chair to tip over.

Michelina rushes by me and hovering over the man she works at undoing his gag. As it comes free Juan asks, "Who are you?"

"Claude Fabius," the man gasps. "Where are the soldiers?"

"Dead, all four of them, Juan answers.

"Thank God, that Major planned to kill me."

"We know about Baguidy," Michelina says, loosening his ropes. "We recently rode out a hurricane with your daughter in Jacmel." Claude Fabius looks up at Michelina, his eyes flashing anger. "I have no daughter."

I confront him. "Danielle told us she was your daughter."

"No," he states emphatically, "she's no daughter of mine, she's nothing but a whore. My wife couldn't have children so we adopted Danielle. By age fifteen she was an uncontrollable child in a woman's body. One afternoon when she was swimming with her friends at

Cydavier Beach she ran away with a young man on a motorcycle. He gave her drugs and seduced her. We were powerless to do anything. The young man was the President's son."

"Baby Doc?"

"Yes." He bows his head. "She was with Baby Doc in Petionville until he got married, then his new wife, Michelle, had Danielle thrown out of the apartment he had paid for her to live in. Then along came a Ton-ton Macoute by the name of Hector Baguidy. He was one of Duvalier's bodyguards and he took Danielle in and turned her into a prostitute."

"He was her pimp?" Juan inquires.

"Yes, she was amazingly beautiful. Baguidy made his living from her liaisons with rich Haitians and tourists who frequented places like Ibo Lele, El Rancho, and Habitation Le Clerc. Later Baguidy introduced her to General Augustine and she became his mistress."

"No wonder she didn't want to see her father," Juan remarks.

"I don't ever wish to lay eyes on her," says Claude Fabius. "That miserable child destroyed my life."

"I'm sorry," says Michelina kneeling down and rubbing Claude Fabius' wrists where the ropes cut into his flesh and left angry red welts. "I must ask you something." She reaches into her pocket, produces a rock and shows it to him. Have you ever seen this before?"

"No, but I'm not surprised to see it because we trusted one another implicitly. Where did you find it?"

"Here in this fortress, hidden inside the barrel of a cannon."

A smile crosses Claude Fabius' face. "That clever devil, I salute him."

"What can you tell me about my father?"

"Your father?"

"Yes, my father I implore you." Michelina's, eyes fill with tears.

"You must be the little girl he talked about?"

"Not so little anymore," she responds then hastens to plead, "Can you tell me if he's alive? Her eyes beseech an answer, but the stricken look on Claude Fabius' face says everything. Leaning her forehead on Claude Fabius's knee Michelina breaks into heart rendering sobs.

Hemingway and I go to her side as Claude Fabius reaches out and tenderly puts his hand on her head. "I'm so sorry," he repeats over and over.

Taking Michelina by the shoulders I lift her to her feet. She turns and burying her face against my neck breaks into racking sobs that convulse her entire body. "All this for nothing," she blurts out. Pushing back, her face contorted in agony she begins to beat her fists against my chest.

"Calm down, Michelina," I say forcefully. Mister Fabius has something more to tell you."

Claude Fabius rises from his chair, unsteady on his feet yet determined to speak to the grief stricken woman before him.

Taking her by the hand, he gently tugs her toward him. "Come, there's something I must show you, something your father found. It belongs to you now."

"What is it?" she manages to ask through her grief.

"Come," he escorts her toward the steel door, across the foyer where he stops at the curve of the cistern where it joins the abutting wall. Reaching up along a seam in the cistern he removes a loose piece of mortar and carefully extricates an object which he places in the palm of her hand.

Michelina and Juan and I stare blankly at a gold coin. "I don't understand," she murmurs, wiping away tears with her other hand.

My God," Juan says, "that's an English gold rose "guinea . . . . George the Third, if I'm not mistaken. Is that part of . . . ?"

"Exactly," interjects Claude Fabius, "Christophe's treasure. Robert Roi found this coin when it was somehow washed out through a crack in the cistern. Don't you see? This cistern is full of gold and silver coins. Apparently after his riding accident Christophe was in such pain and misery that he went quite mad. Paranoid about being overthrown he must have secretly emptied his treasure chests by dumping their contents into the cistern." Patting the cistern's wall he continues. "There's a fortune inside and you are the only ones, besides me, who knows about it."

"My father found this?" Michelina gapes in amazement.

"Yes. He entrusted me to give you the coin and also to tell you that he left you a legacy of his work."

"What do you mean?"

"All he said was to tell you that you must thoroughly search his studio."

"Thank you, I'll do that, but can you please tell me how he died."

"Peacefully, I'm happy to say. His heart gave out in his sleep. It happened about two years ago. I always knew someone would come looking for Robert and I asked the old caretaker not to divulge any information, which is why he didn't tell you himself. I assume you saw the lovely mural he painted."

"Yes, but unfortunately it's in dreadful condition."

"Nevertheless, he had such an amazing God given talent."

Suddenly, without warning I break into a sweat and I feel dizzy. I sense the walls of the fortress are closing in on me. My breath feels constricted and I'm in the throes of panic. It's a familiar sensation. Claustrophobia. I had first experienced it inside a squash court which is why I never dared play the sport. From experience I know I have to get out in the open. Calling Hemingway, I bolt for the passageway, race through it and emerge outside. Gasping for air, I lean back against the fortress wall, swallow deep breaths of fresh air and begin to calm down. Hemingway, stands on his hind legs, his forepaws against my leg, as he peers up anxiously at me. "It's okay," I tell him, "I just needed some air." Then as my eyes adjust to the darkness I hear a rustling noise. Barking, Hemingway darts toward a clump of bushes beside the fortress wall. Pulling out Baguidy's pistol that I had wedged between my shirt and the back of my jeans I take aim at the bush.

"Blimey, don't shoot pleads a woman's voice. . . I'm on *your* side."

"Hands in the air. Step forward into the light where I can see you," I command as my heart tries to escape my chest. Realizing I'm silhouetted by the passageway light I step aside and fade into the shadows.

"Jolly good," comes a reply. "Would you mind calling off your dog."

"Hemingway!"

"Fancy that! The name is bigger than the dog," she wise-cracks emerging from thick foliage onto a dirt path beside the fortress wall. A curvaceous blonde in jeans, a leather jacket and running shoes walks forward into the dim arc of light from the passageway. A crooked smirk erupts from an oval face that features dancing blue eyes set between a pert aquiline nose.

"Tis only Lady Jane . . . seeking Rochester," she jokes.

"Can the theatrics," I reply as recognition suddenly kicks in. "What the hell are you doing here, Ms. Bridges?"

"London, if you don't mind. And be a nice chap, Peter Grant. Point that weapon elsewhere and I shall divulge all."

Lowering the pistol, I complain, "You gave me quite an ugly start."

"Thank you, loaded guns make me nervous. Sorry to interrupt your muse or whatever all that heavy breathing was about."

"Claustrophobia."

"Oh come now, Haiti's not that crowded. By the way where's that randy lad Juanito?"

"Inside with an elderly captive, a grief stricken woman and a small mountain of smack."

"You don't say. Well I've come to help you blokes clear out of here before General Augustine arrives with his entourage of lorries and soldiers to reclaim his cocaine."

"How do you know about the drugs?"

"Crikey, I'm his bloody fiancée, leastwise that's what I hope he assumes I am."

"Hold it. I'm confused. You're engaged to be married to General Augustine? That's preposterous."

"On the contrary, it's quite simple really." Stepping closer to me, she tosses her blonde locks and looks searchingly into my eyes. "I'm officially on loan to the general from the Drug Enforcement Agency. UNESCO is my cover. We've had our eye on General Augustine for years, but until recently we haven't been able to prove his involvement in drug smuggling. Three weeks ago U.S. Customs in the Port of New Orleans intercepted a cocaine shipment hidden inside sugar sacks destined for a bakery owned by one Teresa Coidavid, a former Haitian national and also a former mistress of the general."

"Well, I'll be damned."

"Does that come as a surprise?"

"Not totally, I've had my reservations about the woman. London, I'd consider it a personal favor if you don't mention this to her niece, Michelina, who is presently inside the fortress. Her aunt, Teresa Coidavid, raised her and she's just learned of her long missing father's death."

"Fine for now, but I must warn you this will soon become public after I've lured the general onto the high seas where the U. S. Coast Guard is standing by in the Straits of Florida to intercept the Martinique and take him into custody."

"Including the drugs, I assume?"

"Yes and his collection of antiques and fine art. I can assure you that where valuables are concerned the general is a clone of Hitler's Herman Goering. He's cleaned out Haitian homes of their finest antiques and works of art by painters like Hippolyte, Bazile, Obin, Roi, Bigaud, Benoit and Joseph to name a few."

"London, how on earth did you find out the general was using this fortress for storing stolen goods and drugs?"

"The eye in the sky."

"Of course, satellite surveillance, I should have guessed."

"So tell me, Peter, how did you manage to avoid the guards when you arrived here?"

"We had no choice but to kill them."

"Major Baguidy, too?"

"Yes."

"Drat, I had hoped we might take him alive. What happened?"

"Baguidy and his men came after us. We overturned a cannon which crushed all but the Major. While escaping from us he ran inside a room full of cannon shot. The floor collapsed and he was buried under an avalanche of cannon balls."

"So their deaths might appear to be accidental?"

"One could reasonably infer that."

"Good. I don't want the general to think otherwise."

"What do you think his reaction will be when he discovers Baguidy is missing?"

"My dear chap, the general doesn't give a fig about anyone but the general, that I can assure you. His only concern is being aboard the Martinique when it weighs anchor tomorrow morning and having all his treasures aboard which includes me. If Major Baguidy doesn't appear, well, that's just one less bloke to divvy up the spoils with. Now, listen Peter, I've a vehicle in the car park at the foot of the mountain and I'll be driving all of you to a *safe house* in Cape Haitian. You'll spend the night there and tomorrow you'll be whisked out of Haiti."

"Okay, but what about our car?"

"Just leave it."

"Our luggage is in it."

"Then you'll transfer it to mine."

"Right. By the way, where does General Augustine think *you* are?"

"Aboard the Martinique, having my beauty rest in preparation for being ravished on the high seas."

"How on earth did you find out we were here?"

"Gabrielle, your former taxi driver. He's a snitch. Amazing what twenty dollars U.S. and a liter of Babancourt will buy. He spotted you on your way up here and tipped us off."

"Who's us?"

"That I can't tell you and if I did I'd have to kill you. My, what a pity that would be." Giving me a languid look she reaches out, caresses my rough unshaven face with her fingers. "I rather like scruffy intellectuals," she remarks, and leans in to affix her lovely soft lips to my mouth."

"Are we interrupting something?" asks Michelina, silhouetted in the passageway entry. Juan stands behind her, slack jawed. Clearly London is the last person in the world he expects to see.

"Surprise," London sings out, walking over to embrace Juan and give him a kiss. Michelina appears addled by London's show of affection and asks, "Who are you?"

"London Bridges."

Michelina puts her hand to her mouth trying to suppress a laugh.

"That's really my name," London asserts, rather haughtily.

Michelina glares at Juan. One of those looks that promises a full interrogation of his past, an investigation of his closet for any skeletons and judging by the number of women attracted to Juan's devastating good looks she's likely uncover an ossuary.

After introductions wane London returns to my side and stakes a claim to my left arm. I feel a soft ample breast nestle against me as she tugs on her shirt-sleeve to reveal an ostentatious Rolex watch with a diamond studded face. "Engagement present," she mutters, as she catches me ogling it. "I think we best get cracking if we're to avoid a confrontation with the military."

"From the general?" I mutter nudging her with my elbow.

"Believe me I fucking well earned it," she replies, towing me down the path beside the fortress.

"And what about that story you told me about Juan just being a casual lunch date?"

"So I lied," she shrugs, her words barely audible.

"Just a second." I stoop down to pick up Hemingway and turning to Juan I ask him to assist Claude Fabius down the steep trail until we reach San Souci.

During the drive to the *safe house* in Cape Haitian, Michelina sits in the back seat between Juan and Claude Fabius while I sit next to London who's at the wheel. Claude regales Michelina with stories about her father and what a handsome and dignified gentleman he was. When he says that it's patently obvious where Michelina has inherited her height and beauty, I can't resist a wisecrack.

"Designer genes," I remark, smiling at my own remarks.

"Say what?" challenges London, giving me a sideways glance.

"You don't miss much," I laugh.

"Not if I can help it."

"I was just trying to be clever concerning genes."

"Levi Straus or Mendel's Laws of Inheritance?"

"Both."

Glancing down at my filthy blue jeans, she remarks, "I venture yours could use a good scrubbing else they'll soon be standing up by themselves."

In the back seat Michelina and Juan break out laughing, but their amusement ends abruptly when London slams on the brakes with a cry of "Bloody hell!"

In the distance a conga line of headlights rounds a sweeping curve and heads directly towards us. "Oh-oh, looks like the general's convoy," I say.

"Affirmative," says London as the car comes to a screeching halt. Snapping off the headlights she throws the vehicle into reverse, leans over the back seat and steers the car past a small native hut surrounded by banana trees. Braking hard, she throws the gearshift into drive and pulls smartly off the road among the thick green trunks. As she kills the engine, she warns, "Not a peep out of anyone."

London gives my thigh a friendly pat and whispers, "Keep Hemingway quiet. Juan, hand me that AK-47." "You know how to use that?" I ask.

"Certainly." Taking it from Juan, she flips off the safety and points the barrel out the window. "Okay boys, come and have at it."

Chuckling, I put Hemingway in my lap and glance into the back seat. Michelina gives me a weak smile as she and Claude Fabius hunker down and Juan pokes Michelina's pistol out the side window.

The wait for the convoy seems interminable. I find myself holding my breath. It seems like the best way to remain quiet. Everyone seems to be doing the same, waiting perhaps for the noise of the approaching convoy to drown out their exhalations. Happily there is no sign of life from the hut beside us. As I reflect on this bit of good fortune a pair of single headlights sweeps past, two motorcycles, side by side, followed by a Humvee, then one lorry after another roars by. I count twenty trucks followed by another pair of motorcycles, one of which suddenly decelerates and pulls off onto the shoulder on our side of the road. A soldier gets off the idling bike and walks toward the banana trees. A pit stop, I surmise, when abruptly he stops, does a double take then reaches for his pistol.

London knocks him down with a quick burst of fire.

"Jesus!" exclaims Juan.

"He looked like he was about to do more than relieve himself," she says and calmly hands me the smoking weapon. Starting the car's engine, she surges forward, knocks down several banana trees, than careens wildly through tall grass until the wheels lurch back onto asphalt.

Shortly after ten o'clock, we pull into an alley beside a charming three story wooden Victorian house painted yellow with mango green colored gingerbread trim, shutters and doors.

"Where are we?" I ask London.

"On the northern edge of Cape Haitian's commercial district," she answers.

As we enter the house I see the ground floor is an art gallery with living quarters on the second and third floors. This used to be 'Jasmin Joseph's studio,' explains London.

"I've been in this house before," Claude Fabius offers. "I was here with my wife and we met the artist. We both loved his work, but back then I couldn't afford to buy even the smallest painting."

"All right," says London, "everyone upstairs and get some sleep. Tomorrow morning at 5:45 a.m. a driver in a black SUV with tinted windows will be here to take you to Caracol where you'll board a fishing boat that will take you to the Dominican Republic. I need all of you out of here before news of the general's capture reaches Haiti."

"Why?" I ask.

"Because there's likely to be civil strife and anarchy when the people realize their de-facto leader has abandoned them and fled the country."

"What about Jean-Claude Baptiste?"

"He's the general's pawn. The people will depose him as president, assuming they don't kill him first. And Michelina, I think it's time you knew the real reason General Augustine kept your father a virtual prisoner."

"Because of his seditious art?"

"No, because your father's captivity guaranteed Baptiste's cooperation to do the General's bidding, explains London."

"How?" Michelina looks startled by London's comment.

"Jean-Claude Baptiste was your grandfather's bastard child with a black mistress named, Claudia Baptiste who died in childbirth. Your grandmother took pity on the infant and raised him as one of her own. He and your father were close in age and inseparable until Jean-Claude, fearful of being executed by Duvalier, fled to America, reclaimed his mother's surname and became a powerful spokesman for Haitian democracy."

"I had no idea my father had a half-brother," says Michelina. "Much less one who is the President of Haiti."

"London, I assume your story is verifiable?" I ask.

"Absolutely," she replies. "Michelina's entitled to see the documents whenever she wants."

"On another matter, London, what do we do about documents for Claude?" I ask.

"Your driver will have an American passport for Claude. He'll have a Polaroid camera and an official stamp to affix Claude's photo to his passport."

"How come we're traveling by boat?" Juan asks. "Couldn't your man just run us across the border?"

"You're likely to run into trouble that way. Most border guards expect bribes from foreigners to gain entry to the Dominican Republic. We can't risk having you detained. Now, I have to get back aboard the ship before anyone discovers I'm not there."

"When will we see you again?" Juan inquires.

"Soon. In Miami, I expect, bye for now."

After London leaves, Michelina goes upstairs by herself. It's the first time I've slept without her beside me and I suspect it won't be the last. Our adventure together has apparently ended. The failure to find her father alive coupled with my personal problems with Claire has apparently doomed our relationship. Bidding good night to Claude, Fabius and Juan, I drag my weary body upstairs and flop down on the first empty bed I find.

CHAPTER 18

Puerto Plata! Its name conjures up images of "The Admiral," the Spanish Main, treasure galleons, gold doubloons and silver pieces of eight. The place sounds inviting, romantic, and adventurous but the mirage abruptly ends past the headland where the imposing crenellated walls of the fortress of San Filipe guard Puerto Plata's harbor. The Atlantic port city, founded by Christopher Columbus in 1502, is situated on what is called the amber coast of the Dominican Republic. It is a charming-looking city from a distance, but close up it's a dismal disappointment. Besides Fort San Filipe, the only other redemptive feature is the 780 meter Loma Isabel de Torres with its statue of Christ atop its summit. His visage and outstretched arms embrace all of Puerto Plata. Good thing! The weathered, run down city can use all the divine intervention it can handle.

As we sail into the harbor I note the forlorn-looking storm battered retaining wall that keeps the tide from inundating the Malecon, the city's beachfront promenade and roadway. Across the boulevard a few seedy bars stand among scores of poor quality wooden two and three-story houses badly in need of repair and paint.

Seawater, reflecting the sheen of a hummingbird's feathers, rushes up the sand and as it recedes, it leaves behind its oily iridescence among balls of tar, piles of tiny coquina shells and tangles of kelp and Sargasso weed wallowing in the surge like gobs of spinach fettuccini. The sand is a dirty gray, littered with trash and pungent with the odor of dead fish and rotting refuse. Hemingway alertly watches stray mongrels who seek overlooked morsels, as they roam the water's edge until an occasional breaking wave sends them scurrying to higher ground.

As our self-appointed skipper eases the fishing boat alongside a battered quay and ties up, a five man welcoming committee walks down the pier to greet us. One wears a suit, another has on a white guayabera, and the other three are dressed in impressive-looking dark blue uniforms covered with copious amounts of gold braid. The suit and the guayabera are bareheaded while the uniforms all wear matching gold rimmed Ray Bans that glint in the shadows of their long billed military caps like carriage lamps under gabled porches. From their belts hang black leather holsters containing big ugly-looking automatic pistols, undoubtedly 9 millimeter Llamas. Their demeanor is businesslike and to a man they seem genuinely unenthusiastic about our arrival on Dominican soil. Admittedly, we are a motley-looking lot, windblown and soaked to the skin by ocean spray. In all there are eight of us, three Haitian fishermen, black as bituminous coal, an elderly Haitian mulatto who holds the hand of an olive skinned siren, two disheveled Caucasians and a small black and tan dog.

As the suit leans over the rail to introduce himself, Hemingway flattens his ears against his head, goes into an attack stance and barks. It's evident he doesn't care for the American who identifies himself as Wilfred Neilson, Charge d' Affair of the American Embassy. Expressionless, the guayabera stands behind the diplomat while alongside him the three uniforms ogle the stunning long-legged *chica* wearing the nearly transparent tee shirt and the incredibly tight shorts. Neilson's accent, his haughty demeanor and perfunctory greeting label him a New England establishment snob whose dossier likely reads Groton, Harvard, and Georgetown prior to State Department. I speculate if he speaks Spanish and my hunch that he doesn't proves correct. Undoubtedly he considers the native tongue beneath his Brahman dignity.

"These uniformed gentlemen are from immigration, "says Neilson. "They will need to inspect your passports and your luggage. If you are carrying any firearms I suggest you surrender them immediately. Drugs and contraband are strictly forbidden. I assume you have the necessary documentation for *that* animal," Neilson adds, rolling his eyes.

"I have papers for my Yorkie. "I give him an icy glare.

Winking at Juan and me, Michelina steps forward to the bow and strikes up a conversation with the immigration officials. "Hola, que tal?"

They break into smiles and chorus, "*Bien, bien gracias, y ustedes?*"

"*Mas o menos, bien, pero calarse hasta los huesos,*" she says, nonchalantly holding her arms akimbo to call attention to her drenched torso.

The guayabera and the uniforms dissolve into laughter, as she refers to the obvious fact that she's soaked to the bone. Her self-deprecating smile indicates her lack of concern that the four of them appear fascinated by her anatomy. "*Quiere nuestras passaportes?*" she asks.

"*Si, por favor,*" replies the senior inspector.

Neilson, seething over Michelina's effrontery, watches silently as she takes charge, removes our passports from her shoulder bag and hands them to the chief inspector.

"*Gracias.*"

"*De nada,*" she replies. "You're welcome." Reaching once more into the bag, she produces a wad of folded papers and hands them to the chief inspector while the other inspectors pass around the passports and visually match photographs to their owners. "*Por el perrito, se llama, Hemingway,*" explains Michelina, referring to Hemingway's documents'

"*Hemingway?*"

"*Si.*"

"*Como el escritorio famoso?*"

"*Por cierto si.*" Michelina acknowledges that Hemingway had of course been named after the famous writer.

"Este documento, vaccination *para* rabies, *si?*"

"Si."

"Y este, certificado de salud."

"Si."

"Y que es esto?" asks the inspector, waving a long sheet of paper covered with typewritten names.

"Certificado de pedigree. Esta es como un arbol de la familia."

"*Claro,*" replies the chief inspector, examining Hemingway's family tree.

"*Hay cinco championes aqui,*" he says, clearly impressed that Hemingway is the descendant of five champion show dogs. "*A sus ordenes, Senor Hemingway,* "the chief inspector, tips his hat to Hemingway. "At your service!"

With his forepaws on the gunwale Hemingway looks up at the Inspector and happily wags his tail.

The inspectors come aboard and while they search our luggage, Juan silently hands them the AK-47 and the pistols. Neilson, who remains on the dock, stares at the guns and shakes his head in disgust. No doubt he assumes we've created some kind of international incident for which he'll be taken to account. "Gentlemen, we must hurry," he says glancing impatiently at his watch.

"Why?" I ask.

"Your flight to Miami leaves in two hours."

"I thought we were checking into a hotel."

"I think not." He gives a dismissive wave of his hand. Turning to the guayabera, he suggests, "Help them with their luggage, Javier." Then turning his attention to the Haitian crew, he says, "You three will not be allowed ashore and you will put out to sea when we're done here."

In unison the three black men in the stern of the boat flash toothy smiles. They are merely being polite. They haven't a clue what the American diplomat has said.

"*Que idiota,*" Michelina remarks as she gives Neilson a reproachful glance.

"Un otro Pendejo," whispers the Chief Inspector, grinning at Michelina.

"*Claro, Jefe,* "she laughs. Taking a dry shirt out of her suitcase she strips the wet tee shirt over her head and hands it to the Chief Inspector, who nearly falls overboard staring at Michelina's bare breasts. "Su propina," your tip, she declares, putting on the dry shirt which she gathers up by the shirttail and knots under her bosom.

"Mas que suficiente, senorita," replies the chief inspector, his face bright pink as he stumbles from the boat onto the pier.

Michelina smirks at Juan and me. "I hope you realize that tee shirt just saved you guys a bundle of cash."

"Hereafter you shall be known as Flash Gordon!" quips Juan.

While Neilson continues to impatiently scowl at us we burst out laughing.

"Do you get the feeling the Charge d' Affair doesn't approve of us?" Juan offers.

"Who cares," shrugs Michelina, "he'll soon be history."

"Sooner than you think," I remark. "He's taking us directly to the airport."

"The old dump and run," Juan frowns.

"Exactly, he wants us gone, but the best news is we'll all be in Miami by this evening."

"Except me," interjects Claude Fabius. "I'm staying here until the Haitian Government changes hands, then I'm going home."

CHAPTER 19

After clearing Miami immigration and customs, Michelina insists we go to South Beach, an area that throbs with the beat of salsa and teems with sensual *senoritas,* each one lovelier than the next as they vie for attention with provocative dress and dark flirtatious eyes. South Beach is uniformly art deco and the predominant hot color is flamingo pink. There are endless ribbons of glowing neon and music undulates out of glitzy shops, restaurants and dance bars. *Toda la gente bailar a la musica!* – Everybody dance to the music.

As expected Michelina's feelings toward me have cooled and can best be described as tepid. So being distracted by the glamour of South Beach is probably good medicine for an injured heart. I can have some fun and table my sorrows.

Following a late dinner, Michelina excuses herself and returns to the hotel. Juan and I make the rounds of some of the hot spots, dance bars like Opium, Crobar, Krave, and Tantra. We boogie a bunch with the local senoritas, drink too much and reel back to the Tides as dawn peeks over the eastern horizon.

By the time I awake it is already afternoon and the opposite side of my king-sized bed is glaringly vacant, despite offers of companionship from a number of willing *Latinas* who had ground some amazing looking anatomy against me on various dance floors. Wisely, I had demurred. I'm already in the doghouse with Michelina, not to mention an estranged wife.

The worst part of having a hangover is that all sorts of stuff that needs doing trickles through one's mind like water through a colander. The knack is to grab some before it gets away, then act on it. Now that I'm back in the United States, I remember my first priority is to phone my secretary and find out if she's still in my employ. If I'm lucky she'll answer, then I'll find out if I still have a business left and if anyone's clamoring for my services, of course, taking into account summertime when things are usually slow anyway. Then I'll need an update on Claire's activities. And after all that's out of the way I'll check the television news and the newspapers for word about the seizure of the Martinigue and General Augustine's capture. But first I need to scrounge up a cure for my hangover, preferably a quiet one as I don't think I can handle tablets that spew out fizzy bubbles like a scuba diver with a faulty regulator.

After two Excedrin, a spicy Spanish omelet with rye toast and an iced coffee, I feel well enough to phone my office in New York. Praise God, Catherine answers.

"Catherine, Peter here."

"Where are you?" she shouts.

"Ouch Catherine, that hurts."

"Ah-ha, nursing a hangover, are we?"

"Got that right."

"Sooooooooo, where are you?" She now sounds more like a wife than a secretary. "I've been frantic with worry."

"Miami."

"South Beach, right?"

"Un-huh. How'd you know?"

"It figures. I've always wanted to visit South Beach, but you consistently get everywhere before I do –."

"I spoil it for you; is that what you were about to say?"

"Well . . . yes. You always carry on about all the glamorous places you've been that I haven't. And by the time you're finished talking about it I feel as though I've been there and done that, except that I would have liked to have actually been there myself."

"Sorry. I didn't realize I was such a bore."

"You're not a bore, Peter. It's just that you treat me like I'm your mother and I know that's cruel to say since you grew up without one.

What I mean is, you tell me everything, absolutely everything down to the last detail, and I'm not sure my poor addled little brain can absorb all that data."

"Catherine, that's because I trust you and rely on your judgment."

"Yes, I know Peter and I appreciate that, but it's just, how shall I put it, too, too much for one sad little me to cope with."

"I'll try to be more sensitive, Catherine, I promise." Catherine is a gem, but she's her own worst enemy. Low esteem I think it's called. She's actually a very attractive woman, highly intelligent, hardworking, totally trustworthy, and extremely caring. I couldn't ask for more. But she hides her good looks behind granny glasses perched half-way down her nose, wears frumpy clothing, and puts her lovely chestnut hair up in a tangled bun like a pioneer woman driving a Conestoga across windswept prairies.

"I'd appreciate that. Thank you! Now, where did you say you were staying, Peter?"

"I didn't but it's The Tides."

"I think you should move to The Shore Club. *According to Vanity Fair* that's the . . . *in place.*"

"Next trip, perhaps." Catherine is single, in her early forties. She indulges herself in romance novels and travel magazines though she rarely ever goes anywhere. She can provide a travel monologue on almost any destination you name, no matter how remote. You want to fly-fish in Patagonia? Ask Catherine. Though she's never been there she's an expert. She'll tell you how to get to Baraloche, what hotel to stay in, and what leaders and flies you'll need on the Lamar River, though to my knowledge she's never seen a trout except in a fish market. I suspect she memorizes *The New York Time's* travel section, *Travel and Leisure,* the *Travel Channel* and E-Entertainment's *Wild On Series,* which I occasionally watch too as I'm smitten with Brook Burke's lovely body. Catherine may be a walking *Fodor's, but* just once I'd love to shove her inside Elizabeth Arden's front door and see what emerges after a serious makeover. I'd be delighted to write the check and I know both of us would be pleasantly surprised. Maybe not exactly Aphrodite, but close enough. Now that's a great present for Secretaries Week.

"I have scads of messages for you, Peter."

"Only the most urgent, please."

"The Gilcrease wants you to examine a Remington they wish to bid on at Doyle's fall art auction."

"Call them back and tell them I'll see to it week after next."

"Douglas Christie rang up. He needs to speak to you, says it's urgent."

"I have his phone numbers, I'll ring him as soon as we're done."

"You received good news from the attorney representing author Melrose's estate. They're going to publish Selwyn Podmore's book."

"Wonderful."

"Oh yes, and Claire called. She's in your apartment as you know but she insists you move into a hotel when you return. She muttered something about infidelity and said for you to have your attorney contact her attorney to arrange for service."

"I don't have a divorce lawyer. Who's she using?"

"You won't like this, Peter, but it's Gregorio Basilico, the Sardinian shark."

"Jesus, that's all I need." Basilico is one of those egomaniac divorce lawyers who thinks an Armani suits turns him into Casanova. He's notorious for wining, dining and bedding his lady clients and using the tabloids as his judge and jury. He gets more press than the "Teflon Don" and "The Donald" all put together and he can smell blood in the water faster than a great white. "So when exactly did this man-eating pelagic surface, Catherine?"

"Yesterday in *The Post,* page three, a food-frenzy photo of Claire with Basilico lunching at the Four Seasons ... the usual dribble. Shall I read it to you?"

"What, and ruin what's left of my day?"

Next, I ring up Douglas Christie. He's at home and from his sympathetic tone of voice I detect he's obviously read *The Post.* Doesn't *everyone?*

"Hey," I say right off the bat, "don't sweat it Doug. Like coffee, this divorce has been brewing for a long time. Actually, I'm relieved she's decided to file."

"You're okay with leaks to the press about being a *control freak, an espousal abuser* and a *womanizer?*"

"I wasn't aware of the first two, but they're both fabrications. As to the latter, I plead the Fifth. That crap is just Basilico's way of garnering sympathy for his client and trying to embarrass me in the tabloids so he can get a big settlement for Claire and carve another notch in his bedpost. Don't worry, Doug, I'm not planning on swimming in those shark infested waters."

"Atta' boy, Peter," replies Douglas, "keep a low profile and maintain your dignity. As my father used to say, cream always rises to the top."

"Yeah, if it doesn't sour on the way up. What is it that's so urgent?"

"The Coast Guard was unable to apprehend the Martinique."

"What?" I shout, startling Hemingway who leaps to his feet and begins barking. "Easy Boy!"

"Apparently the general smelled a rat and diverted the freighter to Havana, where he's now holding London Bridges hostage. He's willing to exchange her for your girl-friend's aunt who is in Federal custody on warrants for drug smuggling, possession and dealing."

"What about your man in Havana, can't he handle this?"

"Our man in Havana is in deep cover, assigned to protect London who hardly qualifies as *our man.*"

Ignoring his astute anatomical observation, I reply, "She told me she works for the DEA."

"That's what she's supposed to say."

"I see. Well, now that you spooks have made a mess of things what do we do now?"

"What do you mean *we?* You don't work for the 'company', but I told the director about you and he and I agreed that you'd be the perfect person to go to Havana and make the swap."

"Damn it all, Douglas, why me?"

"Because you have links to Teresa Coidavid and London too. You're the perfect intermediary."

"Scapegoat, you mean. You're agency is willing to let the general and Michelina's aunt get away Scot free after what they've done."

"I didn't say that, but first and foremost we need London back unharmed. Then we intend to intern the freighter and its crew in Miami and recover the drugs and all the valuables the general stole from Haitian citizens."

"And he's willing to give up all that?"

"For his freedom, you bet. I hate to think how many millions the general has got stashed in Swiss Banks. The deal is the general and Teresa Coidavid get free a pass to France, however, should they ever try crossing a French border, they'll be arrested."

"Okay," I sigh, "what's the program?"

"You're to be at All American Aviation at Miami International tomorrow morning at eight o'clock, no girlfriends, no dogs, just you. You'll be flying aboard a twin Cessna with Ms. Coidavid and the necessary documents to clear you through Cuban Immigration and Customs."

"What did you guys do, bribe *El Comandante?*"

"Nope, we got word to Fidel through back channels that he's got a rotten apple in his barrel. We offered to remove it and save him another international black eye, for harboring a drug lord. He agreed."

"So what's the drill when we arrive in Havana?"

"A car will be waiting at the airport to take you and auntie into the Old City. You'll exchange auntie for London with the general at a restaurant called Bodeguita del Medio in Old Havana exactly at noon."

"If my memory serves me, that place was one of Ernest Hemingway's hangouts." At the mention of the writer's name, Hemingway's ears stand up and he eyes me expectantly."

"Sorry, old buddy," I tell him. "You're not allowed to go."

Looking crestfallen, he lies down and stares up at me, in an obvious attempt to make me feel guilty.

"Peter, to whom are you speaking?" asks Douglas.

"My dog! Sorry about that."

"Listen carefully, Peter. Should you have a problem of any kind at the Bodeguita complain to the bartender that you ordered a daiquiri instead of a mojita. He'll know what to do. Assuming all goes as planned, you'll leave the restaurant, get in the car with London and proceed to the Hemingway Marina where at three p.m. sharp you'll board 'El Cohiba,' a 55-foot Hatteras cruiser. Kick back and enjoy the ride back to Miami."

"Is it okay if I troll for marlin?"

"If you think you can catch one at 21 knots."

"What about letting me smuggle in a box of Montecristos?"

"Don't push me, Peter, you know Cuban cigars are illegal."

Later that afternoon I inform Juan of my plans and arrange to have him look after Hemingway while I'm away. I also make him swear not to tell Michelina anything about my plans. I don't want her to find out about the general's escape; nor, more importantly, do I want her to know that I'll be swapping her Aunt Teresa for London Bridges.

That evening I beg off joining everyone for dinner. Instead, I pick at room service food and watch some absurd TV sitcom. It features a lithesome leather clad Latin teenager with slick black hair, huge dark eyes and an angry pout, her one expression, as she roars around aboard 250 cc's of a futuristic motorcycle nuking aliens with her ray-gun as she attempts to save the planet. My only mental challenge is wondering how much Botox it must have taken to get her lips to look pouty enough for the role. Her sheer energy and agility wears me out and I nod off to sleep during a hair commercial where a sexy model gives me an alluring smile and an enticing, *"Because I'm worth it."*

Aren't they all?

CHAPTER 20

The flight to Havana is only fifty minutes and except for a rain squall it's uneventful. The best kind! Marie-Teresa Coidavid stares daggers at me while maintaining her silence. It suits me just fine. She seems to have no trace of remorse over selling out her sister and brother-in-law to Hector Baguidy, Papa Doc Duvalier's hit man. When I tell her of his demise her first reaction is surprise, then she glowers at me through contemptuous eyes, compressing her lips to narrow slits and clenching her handcuffed fists until they turn white. Her furious body language is as telling as any confession and it's good she's restrained; otherwise she'd surely try to attack me and the pilots and send us all plummeting into the ocean.

As we make our approach into the airport, the pilots see a fast moving tropical rain squall blanket the area. It causes us to abort our landing and make a wide circle over Havana. Looking out the starboard window, I recognize Morro Castle. Then as the plane banks and flies diagonally across the inner harbor past the stately buildings of Old Havana clustered along the waterfront, I'm looking at vacant piers save where an oil tanker and two large dark-hulled freighters are docked. "Can you make out if one of those freighters is the Martinique?" I call out to the cockpit.

Picking up binoculars, the co-pilot scans the two ships. "What flag is she flying?"

"Panamanian," I reply.

"She's the first one. The other is flying Liberian colors."

As we bank to port, away from the city, I watch the rain-squall move out over the ocean leaving behind wet airport runways shimmering in the sunlight. Moments later our wheels impact the runway and as we coast to the end of the landing strip two jeeps carrying armed militia meet us. They escort our Cessna to a parking area where a Cuban military officer boards the plane, checks our credentials, then orders Teresa Coidavid and me to disembark. As I go down the boarding ladder the pilot hands me the key to Teresa's handcuffs. Once we're settled inside the waiting car, I unlock them. She rubs her wrists as I watch our plane taxi back onto a runway and take off as quickly as it had landed. Before it disappears from view, I do a double take realizing the plane bears no identifying markings of any kind. Very spooky.

After following the military jeeps through a checkpoint where they park, we proceed onto the highway toward Havana. During the ride I glance at Teresa Coidavid, wondering what her reaction will be when she comes face-to-face with the former lover she hasn't seen in over twenty years.

La Bodeguita del Medio, is a relic of the 1940s. The restaurant is situated in the oldest section of Havana near the harbor on a narrow street that teems with cars, trucks, people, stray dogs, feral cats, goats, an occasional rooster or chicken and the ever-ubiquitous pigeons and sparrows. The restaurant's exterior, like most of Havana, is dingy and desperately in need of paint; but inside it is rustic and charming with a small wood paneled bar and a maze of intimate wood paneled passageways and dining rooms. I can tell from the aromas and the posted menu that the food is robust but simple; soup, salad, roast pork, fried chicken, fried plantains, beans and rice. One dish in particular evokes a smile, Moros y Cristianos, the Cuban designation for black beans and white rice. Moors and Christians! There seems to be plenty of food for the tourists, foreign businessmen, and Castro's military, but as usual, little for the natives who are forced to eke out a meager existence on government rations. Keeping an eye on Michelina's aunt, I sidle up to the bar and order the house special, a mojito. Good choice! The first sip is infectious. No wonder Hemingway liked this joint. As I turn to scan the entrance, London enters followed by the general. She looks apprehensive until she spots me leaning up against the bar, then her eyes sparkle like diamonds and she breaks into a broad smile.

"Hello, love," she says casually as if she'd been frequenting this joint for ages. "I say, what's that you're having?"

"A mojito." I nod to the general who looks all business and responds silently in kind as he takes Marie-Teresa Coidavid's gnarled hand, bows gallantly, and bestows a feigned kiss on it.

"May I join you," asks London, eyeing the unctuous greeting the general has bestowed on his former paramour. "I'd say you got the best of this deal," she whispers.

I flash London a knowing smile then signal the bartender for another mojito. Keeping an eye on the general's every move, I hand London her drink.

"Cheers, love," she says, taking a swallow.

The general stares at me and without offering his hand says, "We meet again Mr. Grant. How is the lovely *mademoiselle Michelina*?"

"Very well, thanks. I'll tell her you asked about her. Will you join us for a drink?"

"I think not. Marie-Teresa and I should be leaving. Time for us to be going, wouldn't you agree my dear?"

"Yes, but may I first have a glass of water?"

"Certainly," he replies, but makes no effort to get it for her. As she steps up to the bar the general says to London with a haughty smirk, "Do give my compliments to your superiors for their wise decision to accede to my demands."

"I'll not run any more errands for the likes of you, general." Her eyes blaze with anger as she adds, "tell them yourself."

As a dismissive smile breaks across the general's face, a comely black woman wearing dark glasses walks into the bar.

The general seeing the surprise on my face starts to turn around, but all he sees is the flash from the muzzle of the gun that explodes in his face.

"Danielle!" I shout as the general reels to one side, emits a half-strangled groan, then sprawls across the bar room floor. For an instant he flops and shudders like a gaffed tuna, then expires in an ever-widening pool of blood. Everyone is frozen, stunned into silence by the deafening report of the gun and the ghastly sight of the now faceless general. Screaming an angry epithet, Danielle drops the murder weapon and flees from the scene.

"Crikey, you know that woman?" asks London. She seizes my arm and together we bolt after her.

"It's his former mistress!" I respond. Racing for the restaurant's entrance we hear the screech of brakes and a sickening thud followed by a cacophony of shouts, cries and screams. Outside we push through a quickly gathering crowd of horrified onlookers gathered at the curb where Danielle's crushed body lies under the rear wheels of a large Mercedes lorry.

Shaking me, London says, "We have to—"

"It's her alright," I interrupt. "I'd recognize those leopard shoes anywhere."

"Peter, we've got out of here before the police arrive." Calmly, London escorts me to our waiting car, shoves me into the back seat and climbs in after me. "Carry on," she tells the driver.

Aware of the curious who converge on the accident scene the driver leans on his horn and clears a path as he pulls away from the curb. Slowly negotiating the narrow street we descend toward the harbor and just as we're turning onto the Old Havana waterfront the wail of sirens pierces the air. Reflected in the driver's mirror, blue lights flash behind us.

"Whew, narrow escape," I say, turning to London. "He who hesitates . . ." she grins, nudging me with an elbow.

"I know . . . but how about . . . *'Looks like we made it, one more time,'* I sing.

"Blimey, you've no voice at all. Is that supposed to be a Paul McCartney song?"

"Nope, Barry Manilow, and unfortunately you're right; I can't carry a tune in a wheelbarrow."

"Peter, you're a ripper."

"Is that supposed to be a compliment?"

"Certainly, I adore your quick wit. Now, why do you suppose that leggy black lass offed the general?"

"Hell hath no fury —."

"Dumped?"

"Very recently and then the general sent his hatchet man to finish her off."

"Hector Baquidy?"

"Yes. Juan, Michelina and I were holed up in Danielle's house in Jacmel during the recent hurricane when the major showed up."

"I don't think I want to know how you all got there, undoubtedly it was Juanito. He beds comely birds of all colors and walks of life."

"You've got his number. Anyway, Juan wounded Baguidy with a shotgun and got shot in the arm by the major. The following day I was certain I witnessed the major drown in a rampaging river but by some miracle he managed to survive and ended up in the same hospital in Jacmel where we took Juan to have his wound treated. Danielle stayed with him and saw the major being brought into the same hospital and she vanished."

"Then she must have known the general's plans, made it to Cape Haitian and stowed aboard the Martinique to get her revenge. Gads, Peter, do you realize in all that chaos we forgot all about Teresa Coidavid?"

"Actually I'm more concerned about our unpaid bar bill."

"Not to fret, Enrique will see to it."

"Enrique?"

"The bartender."

"Ah, I remember now, he's one of your chaps . . . and speaking of bars do you mind if we stop by The Floridita and put this ugliness behind us with the best daiquiri in town?"

"Jolly good idea. Isn't that one of Papa Hemingway's favorite watering holes?"

"Sure is and his bronze bust overlooks the bar."

"Then we must pay homage."

"He'll be pleased. *Por favor, chofer, La Floridita.*"

Two hours later and happily inebriated after four delicious daiquiris each, we depart Papa Hemingway's bronze visage and its art-deco surroundings. It's now early afternoon as we sweep through residential Miramar on the way to the Hemingway Marina where our boat awaits us. The grand houses of the rich, built before the Revolution, are a mellow blur behind tall palms, peeling stucco walls and iron fences festooned with cascading riots of crimson, vermilion and magenta Bouganvillea. A powerful scent, sweet as perfume, permeates the air.

"What's that smell?" I ask London.

"Jasmine," she replies staring at me with lustful blue eyes. "I think it only fair to warn you, Peter, I left my inhibitions at the Floridita."

"Did you?"

Grinning impishly, London slides onto my lap, presses her breasts against my chest and smothers me with lovely warm kisses.

"What are you doing?" I ask.

"I'm employing a persuasive psychological technique I learned at Langley designed to soften up captives. We call it *foreploy!*"

"I think my resistance is stiffening."

"Yes, I think so which means I'll have to force myself upon you until you capitulate."

"If you must, then have at it."

London leans over and her lovely full lips lock against mine as her inquisitive tongue explores my mouth.

Drawing back, London gazes languidly into my eyes and says, "You are a super kisser Peter."

"Thank you my dear, at my age I take all the compliments I can get. Oh, and also . . . I surrender."

"You can't. I'm not through yet."

"Can you reserve this exquisite torture for the trip to Miami?"

"Where there's better motion on the ocean?"

CHAPTER 21

As we plough through an indigo sea on our way to Miami, any previous notion I had trolling for billfish quickly vanishes along with visions of Cuban cigars. London, who professes she's as randy as a Barzigan sable in estrus, drags me below, shoves me into the master state room and strips off our clothing. Then she playfully wrestles me onto the bed. Her curvaceous torso, ample breasts and shapely legs entice me like an orchid lures a hummingbird to its sweet viscous nectar. Our teasing and probing of each other's bodies becomes exquisite torture until, unable to resist any longer, we suddenly couple and gradually succumb to the rhythmic roll and pitch of the boat sending London into a frenzy of passionate yelps and loud moans of ecstasy. Fortunately the throbbing cadence of the vessel's powerful marine diesels mutes her jubilation, or so it seems.

Later as the crew ties up the yacht at the Macarthur Causeway Marina, London reluctantly frees me from her edacious embrace and allows me to shower, though not without a certain amount of frisky intervention. After shaving and dressing I go topside where the crew patiently awaits. Wise to the ways of the sea, they watch me haul my enervated body up the stairs and onto the deck. Their stares remind me of expectant moviegoers searching the faces of departing patrons for their reaction to the film. My cheerful demeanor suggests a performance deserving of an Oscar and they acknowledge me with friendly nods and discreet smiles tinged ever so slightly with envy.

Generally, I find sailors to be decent judges of the beauty of the fairer sex, perhaps it's because those long days at sea give rise to an imagination fertile with dreams of voluptuous mermaids, sirens and

Nereid. Or maybe it's simply the aphrodisiac effect of motion, sun and salt spray. Whatever! As I give London a hand up on deck I sense their collective anticipation. And as she emerges into the golden rays of sunset, I am not disappointed to see admiration illuminate every face as they gaze upon London as though she were a Botticelli Venus rising from her seashell. Lucky me!

CHAPTER 22

I t is early evening under a warm and cloudless sky beginning to turn the same deep indigo as the ocean. Soon the twilight will fade to dusk followed by stars that will salt the sky, but they will best be observed from the beach lying just the other side of Ocean Avenue's gaudy glare.

London and I sit at a round table on the terrace of The Tides sipping frozen daiquiris, again out of deference to Ernest, of course, as we gaze at the multi-ethnic river of humanity that ebbs and flows past our table. It is the hour of the *paseo,* the five-thirty to seven nightly procession so familiar to all Spaniards and Latinos. People watching is the chief attraction at this hour of the evening as we await the return of Michelina, Juan and Hemingway. There is something languid and sensual about this human stream, its current rife with laughter, conversation, admiration, and flirtation. London garners her share of stares from the strollers mainly due to her blonde hair and an eye-catching outfit, a daringly transparent gold lame blouse that plunges into tight black jeans above black stiletto-heeled sling-backs. Sitting beside this visual feast, I suddenly become aware of my own anxiety that Michelina will intuitively sense that London and I have been intimate. Despite the fact my relationship with Michelina has waned, I still can't help feeling a sense of betrayal.

"Rather silly, don't you think?"

"What?" London startles me from my musing.

"Fretting about what Michelina will think."

"How did you know I was thinking that?"

"You are so transparent, Peter, it's all over your face like a sunburn." Laughing, she leans over and plants a kiss on my cheek. Then like an artist admiring a canvas, she studies the glossy lip print on my cheek. "You're branded now so there's no doubting to whom you belong."

"That's cruel."

"Hardly. I know Michelina feels bad about inflicting grief on you over your wife, but the truth is she's not only preoccupied with her father's loss but she's also attracted to Juan."

"I guessed as much."

"Well, you should know that in Cape Haitian just before I left she came right out and asked me if I was interested in you. I thought it a bit cheeky, but I told her I certainly wouldn't kick you out of bed. Usually I'm not that forthcoming with another woman, but I happen to like Michelina. We're both independent and very much on the same wave length. I know she thinks you're a very special man. She told me she loved you but she needed to end the relationship."

"Why?"

"Because even though you're separated, in her eyes you're still married."

"My wife's suing me for divorce, London."

"I know, but what I'm about to say is confidential girl talk and if you compromise me for telling you this, you're toast, understand?"

"Perfectly."

"As you know Michelina is Catholic. She's been feeling guilty about being in an intimate relationship with a married man and never once have you ever told her she was the most important person in your life and that you needed her. Now, that's something we gals jolly well want to hear from a man; it's called emotional security. So the bad news, I'm afraid, is that your romance with Michelina is finished, but the good news is she still cares deeply for you. Frankly, I suspect it will come as a relief to her to learn you're interested in me."

"You think so?"

"Yes. Now stop going on about her or you're going to make *me* feel like a *puta*."

"London, back already," says Michelina, taking us by surprise as she leans over to air kiss London on both cheeks.

Bounding out of my chair I shake Juan's hand and take Hemingway from him. "Hi, little guy," I say as Hemingway squirms in my arms and licks my face.

Michelina turns to me, gives me a hug and a peck on the cheek. "Feeling better?" she asks. Juan looks sheepish and he's covered up my absence by telling Michelina I was sick.

"I'm fine now. Thanks for asking."

"What were you saying about a whore?" Michelina asks London.

"Oh, I was reminiscing with Peter about the prostitutes in Havana, how they roam the marinas after dark in glitzy, spandex outfits while looking for foreign yachts where they trade their bodies for a place to sleep. The boat captains call them *Jineteras.*"

"Jockeys," says Juan, processing the word. "Oh, I get it," he laughs.

"Wait a minute," Michelina barges in, her eyes wide with surprise. "Are you implying that you and Peter were in Cuba together?"

"Michelina," I plead, "please sit down, I need to tell you what's been going on."

"Then you weren't sick after all," she concludes, giving Juan and me a look of incredulity.

"I think it's time for a martini?" Juan waves his hand to attract a waiter.

Sitting down beside London, Michelina crosses her legs and turns to me. Spotting London's lipstick smudge on my cheek she tells Juan, "Make mine a double."

London takes Hemingway from me, puts him in her lap and feeds him a shelled pistachio nut which he crunches up and swallows.

After Juan gives the waiter a drink order, I explain. "Yesterday afternoon I spoke with my C.I.A. friend, Douglas Christy, who's been working with London to break up the Haitian drug cartel."

"You're a spy!" exclaims Michelina, whirling and looking aghast at London.

"Sorry, I couldn't tell you earlier, Michelina. It's a question of secrecy and need-to=know regulations."

"Christy told me that when General Augustine left Haiti he apparently became suspicious of London when a member of the crew spotted her returning to the ship and informed on her. As a result he took her hostage after they left port and ordered the captain to divert the Martinique to Havana. Once in Cuba, he advised the Mexican Embassy that he was willing to trade London, the vessel and all its cargo in exchange for your Aunt Teresa, who was in Federal custody on drug smuggling charges."

"My Aunt Teresa!" Michelina gasps. "You can't be serious."

"It's true," says London. "Federal authorities arrested her after a huge shipment of cocaine was found in sugar sacks consigned to her New Orleans Bakery."

"Oh my God." Michelina turns ashen.

I continue, "Because I had an involvement with you and your aunt, Douglas asked me to act as the intermediary to make the exchange. So early this morning I boarded a private jet at Miami International Airport with your aunt already aboard. During the flight I mentioned to her about Baquidy's death and her reaction assured me she knew him well. I can only surmise from her refusal to answer any of my questions that she had a hand in your father's kidnapping."

"And my mother's murder, but why?"

"Probably jealousy and unquestionably greed, but for some unknown reason she never mentioned your existence to Baguidy or his men which is why you're even alive."

"This is incredible," declares Michelina, as the waiter arrives with our drinks. *"Permisso,"* she says, removes her glass from his tray and takes a big swallow then gasps, "Whew, I needed that."

After the waiter leaves, I resume. "After we landed at Havana airport we were driven to a restaurant in Old Havana where the exchange took place. However, during the exchange Danielle suddenly appeared out of nowhere, shot and killed the general in front of us."

"Then what happened?"

"Danielle bolted out of the restaurant before any of us could stop her. She ran headlong into the street and was run over by a truck."

"She's dead?"

"Apparently she died instantly," says London. "Peter confirmed it was Danielle by the leopard pumps that were lying in the street by her body."

"I can't believe all this," says Michelina, covering her face with her hands. "Auntie Teresa was like a mother to me and to think all this time I loved and trusted her."

"Michelina, now you know why your aunt was so secretive. She had a lot to hide. Also, though I can't prove it, I suspect in her own warped way she wanted the general to think perhaps you were his daughter."

"Why? I don't understand."

"The only reason I can think of why she didn't tell Baguidy that her sister and her husband had a daughter was so she could claim you as her daughter and try to get the general to marry her."

"So giving me the Coidavid name had nothing to do with protecting me from my mother's killers," she says, her voice now filled with indignation.

"Right, they never even knew you existed."

Trance-like Michelina gazes off into space. Picking up her glass, she takes another swallow of her martini. Tears well up in her eyes. "How could she do such a thing, have her own sister murdered?" she mutters, as a tear rolls down her cheek.

"I think you'll find it's all about the money from the sale of the property to Habitation Le Clerc's developers. Duvalier allowed her to keep the money because she promised herself to the regime and she became a willing pawn in their drug trafficking network."

London puts an arm around Michelina. "You'll feel better if you just let it out," she says softly. "I hope you'll forgive us for deceiving you."

"Of course, I will, but what happens now?"

"Tomorrow I have to fly to New York," I tell Michelina, but then I need to get together with you in New Orleans and help you uncover that mysterious legacy."

"And I'll be staying put here until the Martinigue docks," says London.

"Then what?" I ask her.

"I don't know actually."

"And you, Juan?" I ask.

"I'll hang with Michelina, as long as she'll put up with me," he responds with a sheepish grin.

"On that note let's all go have dinner somewhere."

"I'm dying to have Joe's Stone Crab," says London.

The next morning, in the Latin tradition, we all troop out to the hotel limousine and ride out to Miami International Airport. Hemingway and I are the only ones leaving and just before we board the flight Michelina takes me aside.

"Peter, I want to apologize for what you must surely feel is my indifference. I don't want you flying off to New York with hurt feelings and lingering questions about us so I thought I would speak frankly with you."

"Okay."

"Your conversation with Claire triggered my own feelings of guilt, sleeping with a married man, something I vowed never to do. But I did it anyway because I fell in love with you, but when you never let me know how you felt about me I felt betrayed."

"I'm sorry, because in my own peculiar way I do love you. Sometimes I'm just not very good at expressing myself."

"I accept that and I understand the difficult situation you're in, I truly do. Had you asked I would have stuck it out with you, but I thought you had rejected me. And there's something else, Peter. And it's difficult for me to say this to you, but I do want to spend time with Juan. I want to see if we're at all compatible."

"It's kind of you to tell me that."

"Peter, I can't possibly tell you how wonderful and kind you've been. You didn't deserve my bad behavior on the boat to Cape Haitian, but suddenly I felt terribly alone and vulnerable."

"That was my fault, I only thought about myself. Anyway for what it's worth, Claire has filed for divorce. Frankly, it's a relief. Now I can get *my* life in order."

"I don't ever want to be without you in my life, Peter. I will always be there for you if you need me. You're my guardian angel. You risked your life for me and without you I wouldn't be standing here."

"Michelina, the real guardian angel was Juan. It was his knowledge of the Citadelle and his quick thinking that saved both of us."

Putting a finger to my lips, Michelina silences me. "Listen to me, from day one you were my protector. Had you not looked after me in New Orleans who knows what my aunt might have done to me after she tried to scare us, having me followed and hanging a disemboweled goat in your doorway."

"That's not what I'll remember."

"Oh, you mean making love?"

"Yes."

"No wonder I adore you," she laughs, "You're a hopeless romantic."

"Perhaps we ought to leave our parting at that else if you say more I'll just get terribly sad. I just want to tell you, Michelina, how much I regret not telling you how much I needed you."

"Thank you, Peter, but better late than never. I'm happy to see that you and London get along, though I must confess, it makes me a bit envious."

"She said you'd say that."

"Keep her happy, Peter. She's a terrific woman. I know she likes you and fortunately for you she's not as judgmental as me."

"Would my not being married have made a difference?"

"Honestly, Peter, I don't think so. It became apparent you and I have different priorities."

"I expect you're right, I am a bit selfish."

"Peter, you stay the way you are. You're a lovely Renaissance man and I will always cherish our time together. Now, before I start crying, kiss me."

"With pleasure."

"That's fifty dollars extra," she giggles then flings herself into my arms and gives me a memorable farewell.

CHAPTER 23

It's difficult saying goodbye to Michelina and Juan after all that we've been through, but having to leave London behind really disturbs me. Suddenly, I feel adrift, a rudderless ship. I will now have to face Claire alone and London won't be along to back me up.

On the plane ride home I have a bad case of the blues. Hemingway mirrors my feeling and looks almost as forlorn as I feel as he peers through the grillwork of his dog carrier, under the seat in front of me. Air regulations prevent me from taking him out of his carrier. Drowning my sorrows with alcohol isn't an option because if I drink on airplanes all I end up with is a wicked headache. And God knows, with Claire's divorce papers, all the ugly notoriety, and my apartment held hostage, I already have an Excedrin one.

Something London said as I was leaving her embrace in Miami makes me laugh aloud, which causes a few passengers to glare nervously at me until they satisfy themselves I'm not a fiendish terrorist about to destroy the plane. She told me that in lieu of the real thing we can always have fun engaging in "phone sex." "At least you won't have to pay a 900 number three dollars a minute just to get off with a stranger," she said jabbing an index finger into my ribs.

Upon landing, I realize for the first time in my life I have no place to go, nor do I have a clue where Hemingway and I will stay in New York. Naturally, I will consult on the phone with my all-knowing tour guide secretary, Catherine. If anyone can advise me of a hotel to stay in, she can. She's a Cancer, a nester and has the instincts of a homing pigeon.

"My goodness, Peter, where are you?"

"JFK, Catherine. Hemingway and I are homeless."

"I've good news, Peter, you're not homeless anymore. Claire's come to her senses. I don't know exactly what happened, but according to *The Post* things didn't go well with that shark, Basilico."

"I don't even want to hazard a guess," I reply sarcastically.

"Well, anyway, she fired him . . . and she's withdrawn the divorce papers . . . and now all she wants is a reconciliation. She told me to tell you she can't wait for you to come home so she can make amends. She claims all along her problem has been insecurity and she's never felt that Two Beekman was *her* home. She said moving into *your* bachelor's pad as a bride left her without her identity. She said she was so swallowed up among your possessions that she never was able to put down a tap root."

"A tap root? Claire's not a house plant."

"My sentiments entirely. Why if it had been me, I would have been perfectly content living with your antiques and paintings and such, that is to say if I . . . well you know what I mean."

"What *do* you mean, Catherine?"

"That if *I* was your wife . . . pure supposition you understand, I would have been ecstatic to be there, what with your exquisite taste and all. So I don't understand why Claire plans to have Naomi Dhurandhar turn your gorgeous living room into a zenana."

"What! Claire's redecorating my living room? That Dhurandhar woman is the most outrageous and expensive interior decorator in New York. I'd sooner live in a brothel than inhabit one of her abortions."

"I told Claire you'd be upset, but she says the apartment will be so beautiful with all its colorful pillows and light and airy fabrics that it will make you feel as though you're in the Taj Mahal."

"Jesus!"

"There's more. She says the apartment will be featured in all the chic decorators' magazines, *Architectural Digest, House and Garden, Town and Country* and so on."

"Shit! Catherine, ring up the Beekman Towers and book me a room for the night. Oh, and be sure to tell them to expect Hemingway."

"Oh my! Are you sure, *The Beekman Towers*?"

"It won't tarnish my image for heaven's sake, it's only for one night until I get sorted out."

"Oh dear! Whatever shall I tell Claire?"

"Whatever you want just don't tell her where I am. On second thought tell her I'm in deep mourning over my living room, I'm knocking myself out with sleeping pills, and I'll ring her in the morning."

Hemingway is delighted with my hotel choice as it's on Mitchell Place, barely a block from my apartment. When we get out of the taxi, he immediately recognizes his favorite fire hydrant and tows me to it while he sniffs at it like a *Vogue* reader sampling the perfume scent from a fold over advertising tab. After satisfying his curiosity, he lifts a hind leg and leaves his own cologne behind.

It feels weird, staying so close to my apartment, but I can't face the prospect of contesting the apartment's fate or take the chance on the very real possibility Claire might try to seduce me. Really! She's practically a stranger and there's my affair with Michelina and a new relationship with London to consider. I don't need another replay of regret and recrimination. I guess the only civilized way to handle this situation is to invite Claire to lunch, someplace quiet, but public where we can talk.

I awake, feeling strangely empty and alone, until Hemingway reminds me I'm not. Leaving the foot of the bed, he scrunches up against me, rolls over on his back and waits for me to rub his tummy. Some habits never die and clearly this is one that won't. As I scratch his tummy and his ears, I feel a compelling urge to hear London's voice. Perhaps her clipped British accent will rejuvenate me and clear the cobwebs from my mind, the result of the sleeping pill I took.

Reaching over to the night stand, I pull my satellite cell phone out of its battery charger, scroll to her number in my directory and press "Talk."

"Bridges here."

"Hi London, 'tis I, Peter."

"Hello, love. Where are you?"

"In a hotel right around the bend from my apartment and I'm lazing about in the feathers."

"Starkers?"

"Of course, are you?"

"Naturally. Peter have you an—?"

"Like Gibraltar!" I interrupt.

"Mmmmm, I guess that means you miss me?"

"If you were here, you'd find out how much."

"My, what a randy lad you are this morning."

"And what are *you* up to?"

"I was about to pop into the shower, but now that you've phoned I think I'll just dilly-dally a bit."

"What're you thinking?"

"About how lovely it would be to have a piece of the . . . *The Rock!*"

"Need a hand?"

"I'd love one, but unfortunately you can't reach me. Talk dirty to me, love. Tell me what you'd do to me with that big, hard . . . drat, hold on a second, my cell phone is ringing."

While I wait for London, Hemingway stands up, reaches out with a paw and gently swipes my chin, a signal indicating he needs to go for his morning walk.

"Peter, sorry, love, that was Customs calling. I have to meet with them at the Port of Miami.

"You can't even—?"

"There's no time," she interrupts. "I'd adore having an orgasm with you, but *tempus fugit*. The Martinique arrives from Cuba this evening and offloading begins at daybreak."

"Then what?"

"Well, we need to talk about that, something quite lucrative just surfaced, but I haven't time to talk about it now."

I feel a wave of uncertainty inundate me like a Bay of Fundy tide. "Are you telling me you're not coming to New York?"

"Peter, please, I can't discuss this right now. I have to get dressed and get over to Customs."

"It all sounds quite mysterious." My mind is awhirl. Hemingway impatiently paws at me to go out. "I know you're in a rush, London, and I've got to take Hemingway for his walk, can we talk later?"

"Sure, love, and please try not to get upset. You know I adore you, you lovely man. Hemingway as well . . . *Ciao* for now."

"Yeah, you too."

After my disconcerting conversation with London, I don't remember much about walking Hemingway. I can't imagine what London's intentions are, all I know is that I'm feeling isolated and upset. As I worry my doorman at Two Beekman spots us, gasps as if he's seen an apparition and flees into the building's lobby. His strange behavior compels me to forget my conundrum and focus instead on his questionable loyalty and the generous amount of cash I usually proffer him at Christmas. This year he may be in for a shock, assuming I'm able to repossess my digs.

Claire readily agrees to meet me for lunch at L'Absinthe, a favorite French Bistro on East 67th Street. She arrives late as usual and enters wearing a slinky apple green sheath daringly supported by two gold straps thin as linguini that precariously avert complete nudity. She takes leggy strides toward me, a perfect smile etched on her lovely face, as her long straight blonde hair, defying the humidity, swishes like the tail of a race horse.

Returning her smile with genuine admiration, I rise to greet her.

"Hello darling," she says, air kissing me European style.

"Claire!" I reply as she glides into the banquette beside me. Immediately she takes my left hand in hers, squeezes it and coos, "I'd adore a glass of Chardonnay . . . among other things," she adds suggestively.

I signal the waiter and order a bottle of Trefethen.

"I was terribly disappointed you didn't come home last night," her lower lip extends in a mock pout as her gem-like pale green eyes bore into mine. "I really wanted to be with you."

"I'm sorry, it's just that I feel like a perfect stranger."

"I know we've been apart a while, but I'll make it up to you, I promise, especially now that I know who I am and what it is I need. You have no idea how much I learned about myself in India."

"More than in Venice I trust."

"Please don't bring up Venice; I've purged that from my mind."

"Like one of those broccoli enemas you—?"

"Darling, don't be vulgar, you'll spoil lunch."

The waiter brings the wine, opens it and pours me a splash. I pick up the glass, look at the color then hold the glass to my ear and pretend to listen. "That's definitely a still wine," I say to the waiter who stares back stoically, completely oblivious to my attempt at humor.

Claire bursts out laughing. "Peter that is *sooooo* hysterical!" She gives my fingers another squeeze.

Smiling awkwardly, the waiter fills our glasses, places the bottle in an ice bucket and hands us menus. After several glasses of wine the tension between us dissipates and we enjoy a long and very liquid lunch.

It's after five o'clock when we reel out of the restaurant and slip into a taxi. We first recover Hemingway and my luggage from the Beekman Towers then we resolutely plod up Mitchell Place and around the corner to Two Beekman.

In the living room of my apartment, which now has the gossamer look of a Rudolph Valentino film, I am transported into temporary shock. Tugging me into a corner, Claire distracts me from the decor by opening up the backgammon table. "Darling, we'll play when you get back from walking Hemingway, meanwhile I'll open another bottle of *vino.*"

She knows I'm a sucker for backgammon, especially since she's such a jolly good competitor. So I hurry around the block with Hemingway and return to the apartment where I drown my disapproval over the new decor in a bottle of Caymas Conundrum, which seems an appropriate libation. "Conundrum" aptly sums up my state of mind and my relationship with Claire. As we indulge in our wine and "the cruelest game," Claire urges me to make our game of backgammon more interesting by gambling, not for money, but for our clothing, loser take something off. With the dice in hand I roll a series of four straight doubles and in no time Claire, stark naked and giggling, drags me into the bedroom.

Around nine-thirty that night I am awakened by a dreadful beeping sound from the portable phone on the bedside table. Snoring softly, Claire lies next to me wearing only her diamond and emerald wedding band. Much to my amazement I lift up the sheet and discover I'm still wearing my boxer shorts. I'm now certain that I had never engaged in the act of cohabitation which Claire so eagerly anticipated. Obviously we had tumbled into bed with lascivious intent, but soused to the eyebrows we had merely passed out in one another's embrace.

My head feels as though it's been compacted and my mouth tastes like I imagine used kitty litter might be like. Picking up the phone, I gurgle, "Hello!"

"Peter, is that you?"

"It was . . . about nine hours ago."

"Jesus, man, you sound like hell."

"More like death warmed over. Who is this?"

"Get a grip man, it's Douglas."

"Douglas! How the hell are you?" A warm body rolls against me and I know it's not Hemingway because I feel two mounds of soft flesh press against my back. A smooth leg snakes over mine and I feel something downy against my right buttock. On my neck there's a wave of hot breath as a hand traverses my stomach, exploring inside the waistband of my boxer shorts.

"Whoa . . . stop!"

"Un-uh!" she replies, probing deeper into my shorts.

"Stop what?" Douglas wants to know.

"Not you Doug," I reply, rolling over on my stomach.

"Hey, no fair," she complains.

"Claire, I'm on the phone."

"Hang up, I want you."

Abruptly, I swing my legs over the side of the bed, twist around and sit up. Big mistake! My head throbs like a pneumatic drill and I nearly faint. Bending over with my head between my knees, I ask Douglas, "Why are you calling me?"

"I've got alarming news out of Cuba. Enrique, the bartender at Bodeguita del Medio, just reported that the woman run over by the truck apparently had by a male accomplice who right after the General's assassination stabbed and killed Teresa Coidavid as she fled from the restaurant. We have an eyewitness who said the man had a close-shaved head and a crippled right arm. He ran away toward the docks and escaped."

"My God," I sputter as Claire's hand snakes around my waist and reaches for my crotch.

"Damn it, Peter, hang up, I want to fuck."

"Hemingway!" I call out.

"Hemingway! . . . oh shit! I forgot about him," she shrieks as he leaps onto the bed. "Peter! For God's sake stop him. He's licking my tush."

"Something wrong there?" asks Douglas.

"My dog's on the bed."

"Peter, I don't want him watching us."

Covering the phone with the palm of my hand I turn to Claire who avoids Hemingway by cowering behind a pillow. "That's what watch dogs are supposed to do, Claire. . . . WATCH!"

"What the hell's going on there?" asks Douglas, his voice partially muffled by my hand.

"Hang on, Doug." Standing up, I turn and back away from the bed while Claire tries to shoo Hemingway, but he only thinks she wants to play. Crouching down amid the rumpled bed sheets, he lunges at her and barks.

Doug chortles. "Sounds like a yapper. Listen, Peter, this is important. I can't raise London Bridges on her cell phone and she's already checked out of the Tides Hotel. She may be in danger; Enrique thinks the Coidavid woman's murderer may be a stowaway aboard the Martinique."

"Jesus, Douglas, that woman's niece is with Bridges and they're both at risk. What are you going to do?"

"I've sent some of our chaps out to look for Bridges, but we need you to fly to Miami A.S.A.P. We've booked you on American's red eye, at twelve-ten a.m. There's a ticket at the counter in your name. Two of our agents will meet your flight at Miami International. You need to get to Bridges and this other woman before that other chap does."

"I know where they'll be at dawn," I reply, watching Claire swing a pillow at Hemingway. He dodges and dives off the bed. She chases after him and he bounds past me and scoots out the bedroom door, which Claire slams behind him. Striding up to me with raw lust in her eyes, she tears the phone from my hand and pitches it across the room. "Now, it's my turn," she pants. Seizing my boxers by the fly, she rips them off me.

"No way, Claire," I protest, backing away from her with my hands covering my manhood, "I'm flying to Miami."

"What?" she screams. "It's that mystery woman again, isn't it?" She doesn't wait for an answer, but gets red in the face and explodes, "If you leave me unfulfilled like this, don't expect me to be here when you get back . . . and another thing, don't even think about leaving that nasty little mutt with me."

Hmmmmm, this may work out better than I had hoped.

CHAPTER 24

Hemingway and I sleep all the way to Miami, but I'm still hung over as I carry him off the plane. Douglas's men meet us at the gate and escort us to a souped-up black Ford Crown Victoria. Driving east, we race along nearly deserted boulevards, across empty causeways and bridges toward the Miami marine terminal. The sun, a shimmering vermilion ball, climbs into the morning sky as we reach the docks and pull up in the shadow of a freighter with "Martinique," written in bold block letters on its stern under the now familiar Panamanian flag. Not fifty yards away, beside a forklift, stands London, Michelina and Juan talking with several customs inspectors while a gang of longshoremen, wearing hard hats and carrying lunch pails, approach from a parking area beside an immense dockside warehouse.

Juan looks up and sees me. "Hey, look who's here!" I get out of the agent's car with Hemingway in my arms.

London and Michelina break into smiles and run to greet me as the two agents begin laughing. "Is this who we're supposed to protect you from?" queries agent Daniels.

Agent Monzon exclaims, "*hola*, awesome chicas, man, you gone need our help for sure."

Laughing only makes my head hurt more. Throwing themselves at me, Michelina and London smother me and Hemingway with hugs and kisses.

"Okay ladies, enough. Stand aside and give our man some air," says Daniels, grinning at his partner Monzon.

"Peter, what are you doing here, and who are these men?" asks Michelina.

"Ladies, meet Agents Daniels and Monzon. They work for London's employer and I'm here because Douglas has been desperately trying to reach her without success."

"Former employer," corrects London. "I sent Douglas my resignation and I accidentally drowned my cell phone in the toilet while I was packing which is why he couldn't reach me."

At first her announcement startles me, but then I realize it's undoubtedly what she wanted to talk to me about. Then seeing a mental image of her dropping her cell phone in the toilet and I get tickled.

"It's not funny, Peter. That bloody phone cost me a hundred and fifty quid," she replies.

"You flew down here just to find us?" asks Michelina as Juan joins us.

"I sure did. Juan, say hello to Agents Daniels and Monzon."

While they exchange greetings, I put Hemingway on his lead and set him on the dock. "I've got disturbing news, Michelina."

"What is it?"

"Your Aunt is dead, she was stabbed to death by a man who fits the description of Hector Baguidy."

"How's that possible?" Juan asks, "we witnessed his death inside the Citadelle."

"We assumed we had, but if you'll remember there was a virtually impenetrable cloud of dust and debris and we didn't wait around until after the dust settled."

"Are you suggesting Baguidy may be hiding aboard the Martinique," Michelina asks, turning ashen.

"We're not certain that he is, but he poses a serious threat to our safety if he is aboard which is why Agents Daniels and Monzon are here to protect us."

Monzon pats his jacket where his gun hangs suspended from a shoulder holster, as Daniels announces, "I'm senior agent in charge and I'll need all of you to keep out of harm's way while agent Monzon and I coordinate the offloading of cargo with the longshoremen's foreman and our Customs agents. Any questions?"

"Okay, then where would you like us?" asks Juan.

"Out of the way, but close by where we can keep an eye on you if there's trouble. Agent Monzon will move our car parallel to the warehouse and I suggest you stay behind it with the warehouse at your back. If there's trouble you can duck down behind the car and stay put until we come for you. Am I clear? Agent Bridges, I haven't any confirmation about any resignation on your part so I'm placing you in charge of your group."

"I don't have a weapon," London declares.

"Agent Monzon, give her the riot gun from the trunk of the car."

Behind the agent's Ford Crown Victoria we watch as two giant gantry cranes lift crates and boxes from the ship's hold and deposit them gently upon the pier. As the cargo comes to rest on the concrete, crews of longshoremen proceed to open the crates; then Customs officers enter to inspect their contents. Once they are finished they direct the dock workers to reseal them, then forklift operators move them into warehouse bays. The workers move quickly and efficiently, but the roar of machinery is so intense we can barely communicate with one another.

"Look at the size of that!" Juan points to a huge wooden crate rising from the aft hold of the Martinique. "What do you suppose is inside that?"

"I haven't a clue," I shout. As the large box swings away from the ship and begins a slow ascent to the pier, Suddenly Hemingway jerks his leash from my grasp and dashes toward the crate.

"Hemingway, down," I shout, but his furious barking drowns out my command.

"What's he doing?" asks Michelina.

"I don't know." I shout at him again to no avail, then take off running after him.

Seeing Hemingway dash across the dock toward the huge crate with me in pursuit Agents Daniels and Monzon instinctively react. Warning the Customs men and workers to take cover they draw their guns and advance toward the crate. As it touches down on the concrete the end of the crate facing the agents bursts open. Amid a hail of splintering wood a black Mercedes sedan with dark tinted windows emerges and speeds toward them. Momentarily startled, they freeze then raise their handguns and open fire at the accelerating vehicle. Bullets ricochet off the car and whine through the air as the agents separate and scatter from the car's path.

I abandon chasing Hemingway, turn and sprint back toward the protection of the Crown Victoria.

"Bloody hell, that car's armored," shouts London. Placing the riot gun on the Crown Victoria's hood, she reaches out and pulls me to safety as the Mercedes spins out in a cloud of burning rubber, rolls backward to a stop then quickly accelerates forward.

"It's heading for us," yells Juan as Hemingway suddenly appears at my feet. "Run!" Juan screams.

Ignoring him, London strides from behind the Crown Victoria. Completely exposed she stands directly in the path of the onrushing vehicle and raises the riot gun to her shoulder.

Frozen, in abject horror, Juan, Michelins and I watch the car bear down upon her like a huge Muria bull charging a torero. Calmly and deliberately she sights down the gun barrel and pulls the trigger. The right front tire of the Mercedes explodes and the car veers hard right missing London by mere centimeters. Wildly, it careens across the dock, climbs the side of the partially collapsed crate from which it had emerged and vaults into the air. Twisting over onto its left side, it arcs out over the pier's edge and slams the freighter's bow in a thundering crescendo of metal impacting metal.

London slowly turns her head and smiles at us, then tossing her hair, she strides quickly toward the spot where the crushed Mercedes has sunk beneath the hull of the Martinigue.

"Ole," screams Juan in jubilant approval.

"Dios Mio!" a wide-eyed Michelina exclaims, "that was either the dumbest or the most courageous act I've ever witnessed."

CHAPTER 25

When the Miami Police finally pull General Augustine's Mercedes out of the harbor we all breathe a collective sigh of relief. The mangled remains of Hector Baguidy lie in the driver's seat. Beside him is an eerie souvenir, the general's cherished riding crop.

London had played a dangerous game of chicken with Hector Baguidy and fortunately she emerged unscathed. Perhaps, like Michelina said, "she may have taken a foolhardy gamble," but I suspect she had confidence in her own ability with the weapon she used to disable the oncoming vehicle. Putting herself in danger in order to protect us was an extraordinarily act of heroism and that night in our South Beach hotel room I convincingly demonstrate into the wee hours of the morning how grateful I am. Then she proceeds to tell me she has resigned from the CIA because a lucrative opportunity has suddenly surfaced and she wants to take advantage of it. "Peter you know how I feel about waking up one day an aging Mata Hari with nothing better to do than putter among the roses."

"I can't argue with that logic," I tell her.

"I knew you'd understand," she replies.

The following Morning as Michelina and Hemingway and I prepare to fly off to New Orleans, London gives me a languid goodbye kiss that reduces me to a smoldering ruin. "I'll be in New York before you know it," she assures me, chucks Hemingway under his chin, then hugs Michelina with a barely audible whispered admonition about looking after me, but not too intimately.

That very same afternoon Michelina and I arrive at her Aunt's home, which, from a notice on the front door, advises us the house has been seized by the Federal Government.

"What do we do now?" asks Michelina.

"Go around to the back of the house and check out the studio. If there's no notice on the door we'll try to get inside."

"No problem," she says, "Auntie hid a key out back."

The path to the studio is overgrown with oleander, banana and palmetto fronds which we push aside. Hemingway scoots underneath the foliage and is already eagerly pawing at the door when we get there.

"No notice," says Michelina, grinning broadly, as her fingers root around in an urn with ivy spilling out of it. Soon she produces a rusty key and hands it to me.

Inserting the key in the lock I turn it and hear a click. I push on the door, but it is wedged against the frame. "When's the last time anybody tried opening this door?"

Michelina answers, "Too many years ago."

Hemingway whines, his tail wagging furiously as he scratches at the door.

"Why is he doing that?" asks Michelina.

"I presume we'll soon find out," I reply. Throwing my shoulder into the door, it flies open and Hemingway charges inside, barking furiously as he tears through what was once an old kitchen and then disappears into another room.

"There's something in here," says Michelina, grabbing me by the arm. "I can hear it scrambling around."

"It's probably a rat," I tell her.

"I hate rats," she says, clutching me harder.

It's okay, I assure her and escort her into the studio where we find Hemingway standing beside some stacked boxes alternately barking and charging at a hole in the wall just above the baseboard. On the floor by the hole lie scattered pods from Cypress trees and other debris.

"Squirrels," I observe.

Michelina lets go of my sleeve and emits a sigh of relief.

Bending over Hemingway I examine the hole. Grey hairs are stuck to part of the plaster. As I look closer, I see a glint of gold which appears to be wood covered with gilt. "Michelina, look here, I think there's a painting hidden inside this wall."

Turning I see Michelina holding her hands to her face, so overcome with joy that her hands shake like palmetto fronds in a windstorm.

Leaving her to look after Hemingway I return to our rental car, remove the tool kit and jack handle and take them back to the studio.

Two hours later we are staring in awe of an exquisite portrait of a young girl with her beautiful mother among a brilliant display of flora and fauna. The young girl is perhaps three to four years old: clearly it is Michelina. Suddenly the painting's subject is in my arms covering my face and neck with tender kisses and a flood of tears as Hemingway stares up at us. "Thank you, God, Thank you, Father, Thank you, Peter," she repeats over and over.

CHAPTER 26

Claire's threat to leave which she uttered as her final outburst has become reality. When Hemingway and I finally arrive at Two Beekman we find her gone, along with all her personal possessions. There's not even a note. But just to be certain she's really not there Hemingway investigates every inch of the apartment before he reclaims his accustomed place on the bed. Frankly I'm relieved to be alone, but I feel edgy not knowing where Claire may be. Knowing her capricious ways, I feel certain she'll surface soon enough, but in the meantime, I have a living room that desperately needs a makeover, a business that needs to be resurrected and . . . who knows what new adventures may lie ahead.

Musing about my parting with Michelina, I reach into my pocket for the British gold rose guinea from the Citadelle that she insisted I take as a present from her and suddenly it dawns on me what London meant by her lucrative opportunity. "I'll be damned," I say out loud, startling Hemingway who lounges on the sofa. Obviously she was referring to Christophe's treasure. Undoubtedly she convinced the Captain of the Martinigue to deep six the loot off the north coast of Cuba on the trip back to Miami and together they'll go back and recover it. She never had any intention of returning to New York and I'll bet if I call her apartment I'll find her phone's already been disconnected.

I pick up my cell phone and call her apartment. An operator advises me the number is no longer in service. I then start to call her cell phone, but remember that she drowned it in the toilet. There's one last ray of hope, I phone Douglas.

"Peter Grant here, Douglas."

"Sorry I haven't gotten back to you old boy, but you did a splendid job in Miami. We're very grateful."

"Thanks. Any word from London?"

"Her resignation is all."

"You're looking for her I take it?"

"I am."

"Smashing girl, I'm sure you must have found out." Awfully clever, highly talented, but as capricious as a summer breeze. I trust you're not one of her many discards?"

"Hardly," I lie with a chuckle so as not to sound upset. "She said she would be coming to New York to pack up her belongings and we'd get together, but it seems I've lost her cell phone number." "As you know we routinely check up on our alumni and you happen to be in luck."

"I was just informed she went on holiday to Cuba through Mexico."

"I suspected as much. Well . . . good chatting with you Douglas. I'll be in touch."

"Excellent, Peter. Bye now."

When I hang up, I feel sick.

Flipping the gold coin in the air with my thumb, I manage a smile in honor of London Bridges and ask Hemingway to call out heads we go for a walk or tails we have a cocktail. Uncomprehending, Hemingway stares at me while George III's image stares up at me from the carpet. A walk it is, I announce and Hemingway bolts for the front door where he awaits his leash.

As we stroll Beekman Place toward Fifty-third Street I feel a gentle tap on my shoulder. Turning around, a sparkling pair of emerald eyes framed by gorgeous auburn hair inspects my face.

"Remember me?"

"Dawn . . . Dawn Harriman," I stammer, as Hemingway stares up at her and wags his tail.

"Right you are," she smiles, taking my free arm. "I'd love that cup of coffee if your offer still stands."

"Of course, but the sun's over the yardarm. Wouldn't you prefer a cocktail? Besides, Hemingway isn't allowed in the coffee shop. Would you care to join me for a drink at my apartment?"

"Cartainly, I'd love to see where you live."

"Ahh . . . what about your boyfriend? Is that a problem for you?"

"We broke up."

"I'm sorry."

"Don't be, he was a cad. I left for a casting call one afternoon, forgot my script and had to return. I caught the bastard in our bed with a tall married blonde."

"Really, but how did you know she was married?"

"Because the only thing she was wearing was a diamond and emerald wedding band."

"*Claire!*" I suddenly tense from surprise and Dawn, whose arm is entwined in mine, feels my reaction.

"Something wrong?" she asks.

"No," it's just something I needed to do that slipped my mind."

"Gosh, I do that all the time," she laughs, happily hugging my arm. "May I pick up Hemingway? He's so adorable."

"Neither one of us mind," I grin as she stoops down to pick him up.

Cuddling Hemingway in her arms, she turns to me and says, "I need your advice on a family matter."

"What's that?"

"I understand you're an art expert. My mom and dad live in California and they have this enormous art collection, over 320 Hudson River paintings. He's been collecting for fifty years and he and my mother are afraid to go out anywhere for fear of a fire or a burglary. Insuring the collection is prohibitive because it's too costly. They're captives in their own home, baby sitters to an amazing art collection worth millions. They need to get a life."

"You've come to the right man, my dear." Escorting this lovely woman past my open-mouthed doorman, the one who's going to get his comeuppance at Christmas, I walk her through our building's art-deco lobby and into the elevator. The rising sensation reminds me of another happy occasion, an ascent up a steep mountain with a beautiful young woman with enchanting dimples and beauty marks on her chin and ankle in the desperately poor nation of Haiti where "*there are no more mountains beyond the mountains nor any hope beyond despair.*"

THE AUTHOR

Donald G. Geddes III is a former native New York Investment Advisor. His clients included a long list of high net worth individuals, sports figures, Hollywood celebrities and European elite. An artful *bon vivant* and widely known undersea explorer Geddes is a Choate School and George Washington University graduate who is at home most anywhere in the world. He was a decade long resident of New Orleans Historic French Quarter before moving to the Fauberg-Marigny with his native New Orleans artist wife, Marilyn, and their Yorkshire terrier, "Hemingway." Post Katrina they now reside in Northern Virginia. Geddes is a distinguished author of published documents about historic shipwrecks and he writes autobiographical short stories. *Citadelle* is his second novel of the *Peter Grant Chronicles.* His first book, *Ruins of Grandeur,* set in Venice, Italy was the recipient of the silver medal for Mystery/Suspense/Thriller at the 13th annual Independent Publisher Book Awards in 2009.

32141924R00139

Made in the USA
Lexington, KY
08 May 2014